DROWN IN YOU

HARMONY WEST

Copyright © 2024 by Harmony West

Cover Design © 2024 by Beholden Book Covers

Mask art © 2024 by Zoe Maxwell

Published by Westword Press

All rights reserved. No part of this book may be reproduced in any form or by any electronic or mechanical means, including information storage and retrieval systems, without written permission from the author.

This is a work of fiction. Names, characters, places, and incidents are the product of the author's imagination or are used fictitiously. Any resemblance to actual events, locales, or persons living or dead is purely coincidental and not intended by the author.

ISBN (paperback): 979-8-9881181-6-9

Also by Harmony West

Diamond Devils Series

If You Dare

Drown in You

Devil You Know

Die for You

Saint and Sinner Duet

Her Saint

His Sinner

Standalones

Always with You

Captivate Me

For the readers who finished If You Dare in a sitting and asked for more masked hockey men, this one is for you

Chapter 1

Sienna

D<small>EATH IS</small> the three men lurking in the shadows.

They've trailed me around town before, but this is the first time they've found me alone.

I text Juliet.

> SIENNA
> They're following me.

Stephen, Kade, and of course, Marcus.

The injury to his back may have abruptly ended his football career, but it doesn't stop him from chasing me.

My phone buzzes.

> JULIET
> Where are you??

> SIENNA
> Nearly home. Passing the park soon.

My apartment is in sight. Mom is probably still waiting up for me despite her early shift.

I should know better than to be out past dark. Especially alone. Especially in this town. There are no safe corners for me here. Not anymore.

Not after what I did.

They're getting closer, the cruel laughter and taunts drawing nearer. But I can't make a run for it. They're football players at the local university. Other than Marcus, they're all in the best shape of their lives.

If I run, they'll give chase. And I don't want to find out what they'll do to me when they catch me.

Another text from Juliet.

> **JULIET**
> I'm coming.

> **SIENNA**
> Don't

But I don't get a chance to hit Send before a meaty hand wrenches the phone from my grasp and another slips over my mouth.

My heart stops.

Beside me, Stephen leers, holding up my phone with a sickening grin, his rich-boy veneers on full display. Kade yanks me back against his hard, solid body, jolting my heart to life again.

I scream against his hand, the heat of dread burning my cheeks and the back of my neck.

No one will hear what they do to me. No one will care.

The putrid odor of sweat and alcohol seeping from their pores is one I won't ever forget.

From the shadows, Marcus ambles in front of me. His hazel eyes cold and vacant, jaw square and hard. Solid muscles still bulge beneath his clothes despite the months he's been trading the gym for physical therapy. The poster boy for fraternities across the nation.

Before it happened, we barely knew each other. Students at the same university whose paths never crossed until Juliet introduced us. I meant little to him then, and I mean nothing to him now.

Panic makes my frantically pounding heart climb to my throat. After a targeted campaign to turn me into the town pariah and torment me from a distance since that night, they're finally doing more than scaring me.

Tonight, they'll make me pay for what I did.

"Where you going, Sienna?" Marcus's voice grows fangs and drags down my spine.

"Home." The word is muffled by Kade's hand still covering my mouth.

They all laugh. They're not letting me go home.

Maybe Juliet will call the cops. Maybe she'll call Mom, who's much closer and the only other person in this town on my side. No one other than my mother and my best friend will care what Marcus, Stephen, and Kade are about to do to me.

When everyone else hears the news, they'll think I deserved it.

Marcus nods at his henchmen. "Take her to the park."

Stephen tucks my phone into his pocket and latches onto my arm, his grip unyielding and tight enough to bring burning tears to my eyes. Marcus's lackeys drag me toward the trees. I wriggle and kick and scream, heart thumping harder with every failed escape attempt and every inch closer to my demise.

I fucked up. Maybe I deserve what's coming to me, but I can't go down without a fight.

Once we get close to a tree past the nearest park bench, Kade hurls me forward, my back slamming against the bark and knocking the wind out of me.

I don't get a chance to catch my breath before Marcus lands the first blow to my stomach.

My head swims with the pain, and I gasp out the little remaining air in my lungs.

Stephen aims a kick at my leg and my shin splinters. Tears spring to my eyes.

Kade's cruel laugh precedes his fist striking against my skull.

My vision darkens, the stabbing pain in my temple drowning out the agony radiating through the rest of my body.

Mom. Juliet. Ten. What will happen to them if I'm gone? Will Juliet think to tell Ten what happened to me? I'll die before he and I ever get a chance to meet. Before I ever get to see the face beneath the mask.

And Mom . . . Mom will be lost without me. I'm all she has left.

"Stop!" I cry out, bending at the waist and covering my head with my arms. The protection they offer is flimsy. I might as well not try to shield myself at all for the little good they'll do against my assailants' fists.

Marcus shoves me to the ground, straddling me and pinning me against the cold, unyielding earth. His body is a boulder on top of me. Anything he wants to do to me, he can. I am powerless to stop him.

"Don't, Marcus!" Tears from the horrifying mix of pain and terror spill down my face.

He leans closer, beer breath flooding my nose as he growls in my ear, "You think you can accuse me of some sick shit I didn't do? You think you can get away with ruining my life?" He pulls back slightly so I get a clear view of the malicious smile distorting his face. "If you're going to accuse me, I might as well be guilty."

Raw terror threatens to make my heart burst. "No, Marcus!

Please, don't. Please don't do this. Everyone knows it wasn't true—"

"Maybe you should've realized that before you nearly fucking killed me." With one hand, he pins my shoulder down while the other finds the button on my jeans.

I wriggle desperately beneath him, heart pounding impossibly hard while his teammates egg him on. "Should we take turns?" Kade runs a hand through his greasy hair, his snaggle-toothed grin enough to turn my stomach. "Or should we all fuck her at once?"

Marcus gets my jeans unbuttoned and my zipper down.

No, no, no. This can't be happening—

"Hey!" A husky, feminine voice cuts through the silent darkness surrounding us. "I'm calling the cops!"

"Fuck," Stephen hisses.

But Marcus doesn't budge from his position on top of me. "Stay out of this, Juliet."

She glowers at him. Half his size but completely unafraid. Nothing scares Juliet. "Get the fuck off her, Marcus. Now."

"How the fuck are you still taking her side?" His lip curls into a snarl. "You were there that night. You know exactly what happened."

Juliet steps closer, emerging from the darkness beyond Stephen and Kade. While most adults still confuse me for a high school student, no one expects Juliet to be any younger than twenty-five. If not for the youthful tautness of her skin, most would note her regal posture and the lift to her chin and expect her to be the CEO of a multimillion-dollar company, not a college student. A goth queen in a short black skirt, inky thigh-high socks, and an unzipped jacket. In her hurry to get to me, she didn't have time to slip on her usual array of white gold jewelry.

People respect her. Fear her, even. She's the only reason I'm not already dead.

"Sienna was just trying to be a good friend. It was a mistake."

I squeeze my eyes shut. *A mistake.* A mistake I didn't know I was making until it was too late.

"What were you going to do?" Juliet demands. "Rape her?"

"Of course not," Marcus spits. "I wanted to scare the shit out of her."

He finally slides off me and fresh tears spill down my cheeks. This time in relief.

The flashlight from Juliet's phone lands on my face. "It looks like you did a lot more than that."

Pain from the strike against my temple radiates down to my eye now. When my fingertips graze delicately over the skin, it's already swollen.

"She deserved it," Kade hisses. "She ruined our boy's life."

"Really?" Juliet's glare burns a hole in Kade's skull. "Because it seems like he's trying to ruin it himself by getting thrown in prison."

Stephen laughs, tossing my phone onto the ground beside me. But every part of me aches too much to reach for it. "Like the cops will ever lock him up for something he does to *her*."

"Want to find out?" Juliet's threat almost convinces me she believes the cops would actually give a shit. That anyone in this town would choose me over the golden boys.

Maybe if Marcus wasn't here, Stephen and Kade wouldn't let her stop them. But Marcus won't let anything happen to Juliet. She didn't cause this mess.

I did.

Not to mention, it's Juliet's parents paying for Marcus's medical bills and physical therapy.

"Juliet—" he starts to protest.

"Get out of here, Marcus."

His jaw clenches, but he hobbles past her. He'll never move as fast as he used to. Never again be the star quarterback. Never play in the NFL.

Because of me.

I ruined his life. I stole his future.

When the football players finally retreat into the darkness, I spit up blood. Every part of me aches, stomach and legs and head crying out in agony. Now that the terror is subsiding, the pain grows unbearable.

This won't be the last time. Next time will be worse. Next time, I might not survive what they do to me.

Juliet crouches, her dark boots inches from my nose. Her long, black hair streaked with shocks of red is tamed into a side braid, freshly wet from the shower. Her blue eyes roam over me, examining my injuries while her hand rubs soothing strokes over my shoulder.

She bites her lip. For perhaps the first time in her life, Juliet is scared. "You can't stay here, Sienna."

"I know," I whisper.

I knew the second they got their hands on me. The second Stephen snatched my phone from my grasp. Whatever they had in store for me, they couldn't let me call for help.

They're not going to stop. They'll never stop until they decide I've paid for what I've done. That I've paid my debt.

And I have an impossibly huge debt to pay.

Juliet reaches for my fingers and squeezes. "If they get their hands on you again, they'll kill you."

Chapter 2

Luke

My dream girl is dead.

She's in a casket, skin almost translucent, hands folded together on her stomach. Her blonde hair has been drained of color, and she's in an ankle-length white dress. She wouldn't be caught dead wearing that if she was alive.

I rip off my jersey, pushing through the crowd to get to her as they lower her into her awaiting grave, casket still open.

"Stop!" I shout. "I need to put this on her!"

She should be buried in my jersey. The name *Valentine* stitched across her back until we're both nothing but dust.

But they don't stop. They don't hear me, even as I scream my throat raw, the desperation clenching my heart as her coffin hits the bottom of the grave and they pour the dirt over her body.

I scream for them to close the lid. But no sound comes out.

My hands are see-through. I'm a ghost too.

I lurch awake, a cold sweat coating the back of my neck, my chest, my pits. Hop out of bed to toss water on my face and brace against the sink, bags beneath my eyes to mark all the sleepless nights that have come before this one.

I sneak back down the hallway to my room, careful not to alert Bud, who will wake the whole house. Coming home on break is always an adjustment. I miss sharing a house with the Devils who would all shrug it off if they saw me wandering around like a zombie at three in the morning.

Not getting away with that shit around my mother. Since I've been home, she's plied me with chicken soup, grilled ham and cheese, saltine crackers, peanut butter sandwiches. Every comfort food she can think of.

I grab my phone off my nightstand to fire off a text to the one person I know is lying awake with me. A smile pulls at my lips when I spot the message already waiting.

> SIENNA
>
> I want one of those old cameras where you can't even see the photo you just took. You use it once and those are all the photos you get.

Sienna and I met on social media when we were angsty fifteen-year-olds. Our parents had just started dating, and when I found out Mike had an estranged daughter he hadn't seen since she was nine, I snapped a photo in a mask, made a new account under the nickname Ten for my jersey number freshman year, and reached out to her.

I knew what it was like to lose a parent. Even if I'd never met her, I knew her pain. But I couldn't reach out to her as Luke, son of her dad's new girlfriend. She wouldn't open up to me if she knew who I really was.

Not sure what I expected to come of it. Nothing, really. Figured she'd probably ignore me when I messaged her. But she didn't.

Hi. I like your mask.

Right away, she was the sweetest girl I'd ever met. The kind of girl who didn't deserve a shitty dad but definitely deserved a good friend.

That's what we've been for each other since, even after our parents' brief relationship ended. She might not know my real name or face, she might believe the lie I fed her about living in California, she might not suspect the California number I acquired to text her is from an app, but everything else is real.

TEN

> You know they actually put a camera on that phone in your hand. You can take as many pictures as you want.

As expected, her response comes seconds later.

SIENNA

Ass.

TEN

> Why do you want a disposable camera?

SIENNA

Because it's not about perfection or curating an aesthetic social media feed. It's about capturing the moment, with all its beautiful imperfections.

TEN

> You sure you want to be a nurse? Pretty sure poetry is your calling.

SIENNA

I can have hobbies.

TEN

> I thought your only hobby was reading smut.

SIENNA

That's just the main one.

TEN

How dirty is your book tonight?

SIENNA

Absolutely filthy.

I grin. Sienna somehow manages to bring a smile to my face whenever I forget how to use the muscles that curl my lips up.

My phone chimes with another message.

SIENNA

Why are you awake?

No one knows about the nightmares that have been plaguing me since Chloe died, not even Sienna—the memories twisted by my sleeping brain into funerals that are even more disturbing than the real one was.

Everyone around me knows what happened to Chloe, but nobody knows what happened to me after Chloe died. My brain isn't wired right anymore. Not since I saw her body in that casket, looking like she wasn't even dead. A sleeping beauty who merely needed a kiss to awaken.

But I'm no prince, and my kiss would never bring her back to life.

No one would understand why I still can't shake Chloe's death months later. She wasn't even officially my girlfriend yet. We hadn't gone any further than kissing. It's the guilt that haunts me. The guilt that I could've done something to save her.

I tell Sienna everything, but I couldn't bring myself to tell her about that night. Couldn't stomach her thinking less of me because I didn't protect my friend. Because I failed her.

TEN

Couldn't sleep. You?

SIENNA

Same. Normally you only text me at three in the morning when you're drunk to tell me how much you love me.

TEN

Gotta lay off the booze. My buddies are getting sick of me telling them how much I love them every week.

SIENNA

Is everyone in your phone subjected to this torment?

TEN

My professor is filing for a restraining order as we speak.

SIENNA

You know what helps me sleep?

TEN

What?

SIENNA

Smutty books.

In my sweats, my cock twitches. The only books I read are nonfiction, but part of me can't help but want to open up whatever smutty books keep her company at night. I miss her selfies now that she's deleted all her social media and wiped her existence from the internet. The photos snapped in pretty little summer dresses and shorts that cut off just below her ass.

She still hasn't told me why she expunged her existence from the internet. What happened that drove her into hiding.

Just felt like I wanted to start living my life unplugged.

That's the first time I ever suspected she was lying to me. I haven't been able to shake off the gnawing feeling since.

Drown in You

TEN

I would've thought only boring books would help you sleep.

SIENNA

Smutty books solve all problems. Seriously, though. Need me to sing you to sleep?

My heart skips, even though I know this is just another one of Sienna's jokes. We've never talked on the phone, and we never will.

TEN

Would you do it if I said yes?

SIENNA

Absolutely not. I have a terrible singing voice.

TEN

That's my favorite kind to fall asleep to.

SIENNA

You're funny. Put on one of those boring nonfiction audiobooks you like to listen to and I'm sure you'll be out in no time.

TEN

They're not boring. You're just not interested in reading anything other than smut.

SIENNA

Obviously. Why read anything else? Goodnight.

TEN

Sweet dreams.

I ditch my phone on my bedside table, stripping off my shirt before dropping down to the floor and pumping out fifty push-ups. Only the sweat and pain quiet the thoughts in my head anymore. Luckily, killing myself in the gym and on the ice increases my chances of getting drafted and getting the hell out of this town.

Away from the memories and the dream girl who now haunts my nightmares.

OVER AN ELABORATE BREAKFAST OF EGGS, bacon, pancakes, waffles, and toast, Ma pouts. "I've hardly seen you your entire break."

"That's because Coach only gave us ten days, Ma." The first two weeks of break, we stayed on campus, living and breathing hockey. Coach said he won't murder us over one or two cheat meals and a couple of spiked eggnogs, but he will if we go on a junk food bender for ten days.

For me, it's easier to abstain entirely than try to moderate, so I've steered clear of the Christmas cookies, much to Ma's dismay. But I'll indulge her now that the days before spring semester are counting down and eat a couple of pancakes slathered in butter.

"Where's Mike?" I mumble around a mouthful of fluffy, buttery goodness. Simple carbs are reserved for practices and game days for extra boosts of energy but fuck it.

Bud lays at my feet and I slip him a strip of bacon. He's been glued to my side since I got home. Maybe it's just because he missed me, but a part of me is convinced he knows something's up. Normally, he's a rambunctious, high-energy golden retriever, but lately, all he wants to do is lay at my feet.

A message from Sienna pops up from my texting app. A screenshot of a cheap, disposable camera.

Under the table, I text her back.

Drown in You

TEN
Dork.

"He's still sleeping." Ma gives me a thin smile. She's up at the crack of dawn every morning like clockwork. Her boyfriend prefers to stay up until two a.m. and roll out of bed at nine. Ma reaches from her seat at the dining room table next to me and squeezes my hand. "How are you feeling?"

Ever since Chloe died—more specifically, ever since my meltdown after her funeral—Ma has been watching me with wary eyes. A ticking bomb, a glass antique teetering on the edge. If she takes her eyes off me for a second, that's when I'll shatter.

"Never been better."

"I heard you working out in your room again this morning. It's not healthy, honey. You're pushing yourself too hard. Is this about Chloe?" When I don't answer, she squeezes my hand. Of course it's about Chloe. And Pop and Violet. How I failed all of them. "There's nothing you could've done for her, Luke. You need to stop punishing yourself."

I shake her off and clutch my fork, shoveling in a flavorless bite. "Drop it, Ma."

How can I stop punishing myself over Chloe's death when I could have stopped it? I shouldn't have been drinking that night. I should've noticed Trey spiking drinks. I should've been with her instead of getting drunk with my buddies. I could've kept her alive.

I may not be the reason Chloe is dead, but I should've been there for her. I wasn't.

I didn't protect her. Didn't protect any of them. Didn't save them when they needed me.

"Good morning." Mike yawns when he finally enters the

dining room with messy hair and pajama pants. "Breakfast smells amazing."

Ma brightens and claps her hands together. "Oh good, you're up! Now we can share the good news!"

"What good news?" I'm already wary but grateful for the change in subject.

Ma and Mike reunited at the therapist's office a few months ago. Mike confided in her about how he'd been unsuccessfully trying to reconnect with Sienna. I knew she was getting his texts but couldn't bring herself to respond to him. Couldn't figure out how to talk to the father who abandoned her after his divorce. Ma decided to give him a second chance, but I'm still not convinced their relationship is much more than friendship. That's why she was in therapy in the first place—she was lonely.

At least Mike isn't the empty husk I met all those years ago. The man with a vacant look in his eyes, like nothing in the whole world mattered to him. But even if he's done a one-eighty and Ma wants to give him a second chance, that doesn't mean he deserves one with Sienna.

Mike grins, squeezing Ma's shoulders while she delivers the news with a megawatt smile. "We're getting married! This Friday!"

A dull buzz drones in my ears while I replay her words, trying to make sense of them.

Married. Friday.

Married.

What the *fuck*.

Ma's radiant smile and Mike's bright eyes tell me they expect me to be happy for them, but they just got back together a few months ago and they already have one failed relationship under their belt.

Her face starts to fall when I don't match her excitement.

I drop my fork. "Who gets married in the winter?"

"A winter ceremony will be lovely! Winter is a magical time of year. It'll be a small ceremony, just you and Sienna and our close families. You remember Sienna—Mike's daughter. She's right around your age. I'm sure you two will get along great!" She bounces in her seat with sheer joy and the news has me grinding my teeth. "You'll have a sister, Luke! Isn't this so exciting?"

Sienna. Sister.

No. No fucking way. Am I supposed to pretend like I'm not the masked man who's been catfishing her for years at every family reunion? Suppress a laugh during the holidays when she texts Ten a funny meme under the table?

I won't be able to keep up the lie anymore if we're fucking related. I'll lose her.

Mike hasn't been a father to Sienna in years, and he'll never be one to me. We won't be a family, even if Ma decides to marry him. And I'll never think of Sienna as my fucking *sister*.

"We hope she'll be there," Mike adds.

If Sienna refuses to respond to his texts, she's sure as hell not showing up to his wedding. "You two have only been together for a few months."

Ma's bright smile wanes. "When you know, you know."

Like that isn't the most generic, recycled Hallmark line. My chair screeches when I stand, Bud jumping to his feet and skittering out of the room before I can follow him. "You want to marry a guy you barely know, who moved in two weeks ago and has a daughter you've never met, go ahead. Just don't ask me to be at the wedding."

I ignore Ma's protests at my back and Mike's murmured reassurances. This wedding is a really fucking bad idea, and I'm not going to sit there and watch as she strikes the match and sends her whole life up in flames. Mine with it.

Chapter 3

Sienna

IN MY BEDROOM, Juliet attempts to conceal the purple bruise blooming around my eye. Her own makeup is dark and thick, lashes long and devastating. Even without makeup, Juliet has the kind of beauty that's hard to look away from.

She huffs, dropping her ring-adorned hands hopelessly into her lap. Her bracelets clatter with the movement. "I have a feeling it's going to get worse before it gets better."

I flash a bright smile. "Hey, at least they didn't kill me, right?"

My best friend scowls. "What did your mom say?"

"Oh, she's planning on shipping me off to a university in another country."

Mom absolutely lost it when Juliet brought me home, and she drove me straight to the ER. I listened while the nurses and doctor examined me, taking mental notes like I will when I finally complete my Gen Ed courses and start clinicals.

My prognosis is good. Lots of visible contusions and bruised ribs, but no breaks, fractures, or concussion. A miracle.

But you only get one miracle, and if Marcus and his

henchmen get their hands on me a second time, I'm not sure I'll walk away again.

"Honestly, that might not be a bad idea. At least until the drama cools down." Juliet returns my makeup to the top of my dresser.

I snort. "If those are the conditions, I might as well plan on never coming back. This town is going to hate me forever." I reach for her hand and squeeze. "I'm sorry I screwed things up between you and Marcus."

Juliet yanks her hand from my grasp and punches me in the arm. "For the last time, stop apologizing. He was a fling, and you did what you had to do. You were being a good friend. So if your mom ships you off to a university in London, I'll come with you."

"What if she sends me to Australia?"

Her lips purse. "With the giant spiders and killer kangaroos? Hell no, you're on your own."

On my bed beside me, my phone chimes. Dread washes over me. My father has been texting me for months now, lengthy apologies about how he should've been a better father to me and a better husband to my mom. How he should've made more of an effort with me in the decade since their divorce instead of relegating our relationship to birthday phone calls and holiday cards.

Apparently, Mom told him what happened with Marcus. Now he wants to be a dad again. Protect his little girl even though he hasn't been around to do that for years.

Part of me wants to find a way to forgive him—the people-pleaser part that wants to make everyone happy and avoid conflict. Another part of me doesn't want to have a relationship with him again. But I also can't bring myself to tell him no. So instead, I don't say anything at all, letting all his texts go unanswered. Even months later, he hasn't given up.

"Is it the sperm donor?" Juliet's lips purse at my phone like the device repulses her.

She's been adamant from the beginning that I should block him. Even Ten, who lost his dad years ago, hasn't pushed me to mend my relationship with my father. No guilt-tripping, *if-my-dad-was-still-alive* nonsense. Even when I asked him what I should do, he wouldn't give me a straight answer.

Whatever relationship you do or don't have with him should be on your terms.

When I check my phone screen, my shoulders relax. It's not my father—it's Ten.

I chew on my lip when I read his message so Juliet doesn't catch me grinning at my phone like an idiot.

> **TEN**
> Guess who bought a disposable camera today? You're a bad influence.

I haven't told him about what happened in the park. He doesn't even know about the incident with Marcus that started this whole mess. I typed up and deleted so many messages explaining the situation, but ultimately, I couldn't bring myself to send any of them. Ten is an athlete, a hockey player with NHL aspirations. What would he think if he knew what I did? I couldn't bear it if his opinion of me changed. Other than Mom and Juliet, he's the only person I have left.

Juliet's pierced nose nearly collides with my phone. "Ooh, Ten. Your masked man!"

Before I can stop her, she snatches my phone. I swat at her, but she's already off the bed. "Asshole! Give it back!"

Juliet's grin is downright wicked. "Tell him to send you a photo in a Purge mask. That's my favorite."

My ringtone blares over my protest. Juliet's mouth falls open like she actually expects it to be Ten calling me. But we've never actually talked on the phone or video chatted. We stick to DMs and texts like normal twenty-somethings, although sometimes I hope that he'll call me out of the blue because he finally wants to hear my voice and wants me to hear his. That he'll call with a proposal: *Let's meet.*

But when Juliet's eyes narrow at the screen, I know it's not Ten. "Who is it?"

She turns the screen toward me. "The sperm donor."

"Oh my god." My father's *calling* me now? He should've taken the hint—dozens of ignored texts later—that I don't want to talk to him. My stomach is already twisted up in knots. "Ignore it."

Instead, Juliet swipes her finger across the screen.

"Juliet, *no!*" I snatch for the phone, but she holds it out of reach. I'm going to *kill* her.

"Mr. Carter. How can I help you?" She ignores the double middle fingers I hold up.

Over the speaker, Dad's uncertain voice is somehow foreign and familiar at the same time. "Um, hello. Who am I speaking with?"

She thrusts the phone toward me. I mute it and hiss, "What the hell are you doing?"

"You need to tell him to fuck off. Tell him to stop harassing you and leave you the hell alone."

She might be able to do that, but she knows damn well that I can't. I take a long, deep breath, trying to calm my pounding heart. I hit the Mute button again and plaster a smile on my face. "Hi, Dad."

"Sienna!" The cheer in his voice surprises me. The father I remember was quiet, reserved, stressed. Maybe he's just that relieved not to be dealing with Juliet. I love her, but I can't blame him. Aside from Marcus and his cronies, she's the scariest person I know. "How are you feeling?"

"Um. I'm okay." *Every part of my body aches from where I was kicked and punched and my brain is wracked with horrifying memories about being pinned down in the dirt by a former football player twice my size, but other than that, totally fine.*

"I'm so sorry about the circumstances, but I wanted to let you know that we're really excited you're coming to stay with us. Deb already has a room ready for you."

My heart stops in my chest. What the hell is he talking about? Who's Deb? "What?"

"I'm sure your mom already told you all the details about the wedding, but I can text you the address so you have it. Don't worry about a dress—it'll be very casual. Just a few guests."

"What wedding?"

Juliet plops down onto my bed and mouths, *what the fuck?*

The enthusiasm dips in his tone. "Your mom didn't tell you?"

My bedroom door creaks open, and Mom shuffles in with a basket full of clean laundry. Something's going on. Mom never does my laundry unless she has bad news.

Her brown hair, the same shade as mine, is unbrushed and wavy from where she slept on it while it was damp. Her shirt has a mysterious stain on the shoulder, and she's in the stretched-out, faded jeans that she only wears around the apartment. She's been just as stressed as me since the incident with Marcus, and it shows in every line on her face.

She takes one look at Juliet's best but failed attempt to cover the bruise on my face and sighs, setting the basket on my bed. "I was just about to tell her, Mike."

"Right." He clears his throat. "I'll let you two catch up. Give me a call back."

I hang up, hand trembling.

Wedding. Coming to stay with us. Mom can't seriously be

shipping me off to visit the estranged father I haven't seen in a decade. She wouldn't accept an invitation to his wedding on my behalf, let alone behind my back.

"The sperm donor's getting married?" Juliet blurts.

"This Friday," Mom confirms, her voice just as exhausted as the rest of her.

My heart breaks for her. Since the divorce, Mom has bounced from guy to guy. Though she's never said it, I think she's been searching for my father's replacement, and she's never found him. She must be gutted knowing he's moving on with someone else.

"I don't get why I have to be there. He wasn't at my prom or my high school graduation. Why should I be at his wedding?"

"Preach," Juliet calls.

Mom bites her lip. "I told him you need somewhere to stay."

My heart drops to my feet. "Like to *live*?"

She can't seriously expect me to move in with the father I haven't seen since I was a kid and his new wife I've never met.

"Yes. For now." The lines around her eyes and between her brows have deepened in the months since the incident. "You need a safe place to stay, and Wakefield isn't it. Your father said you're welcome to come live with them and transfer to Diamond University. They'll help you move into your dorm after the wedding. He'll be on his honeymoon, but he won't be gone long and you'll be on campus surrounded by security guards. And his fiancé has a son at Diamond, so there will be someone there if you need anything."

In silence, Juliet and I exchange a wide-eyed glance. I can't believe Mom just dropped a major bombshell on me in a voice that someone would use to report bad weather. Like we won't be living hours apart for the first time in my life. Like I'll somehow be safer and happier living with total strangers.

"You can't be serious."

She sighs, knowing this is exactly how I would take the news. That's why she arranged everything behind my back. "Your safety is my number one concern. You aren't safe here anymore, Sienna."

"She's not wrong." Juliet squeezes my hand, a rare display of physical affection. She's worried about me too.

I want to keep fighting Mom on it, but she's right. I'm not safe here. Even though the prospect of leaving makes my stomach twist, part of me desperately wants to get the hell out of Wakefield and away from the football team that's put a target on my back.

My father has been trying to mend our relationship, and even if it's awkward as hell, I'll be spending most of my time on campus. Maybe it won't be so bad.

"So . . . when am I going? It'll take at least a few weeks to transfer to a different college." Who knows what will happen to me in that time.

"I sent in your application over a month ago." Mom's grip drops from the laundry basket, brushing her hair behind her ears with both hands. Her nervous habit. "I just . . . couldn't bring myself to tell you. I still wasn't sure I could bear letting you go. But I shouldn't have let this continue as long as it has. Last night could've ended so much worse."

Her hands are shaking now, lip quivering with them, and Juliet's blue eyes are wide when she nudges me to hug her.

I wrap my arms around my mom and she sniffles into my shoulder. We've been the same height since I turned fifteen, and since then, she's felt more like a sister than a mom. She's so busy trying to keep a roof over our heads that she forgets things like grocery shopping and turning off the oven and locking the door before bed. If I'm living with my father, who will take care of my mom?

For the first time since the incident, rage boils in my veins at Marcus for putting us in this position.

"I can't go, Mom." I squeeze her tighter. "You need me."

She shakes her head. "What I need is for my daughter to be safe, and you aren't here."

"But who will wake you up when you forget to set your alarm? Who will make sure the electric bill gets paid? Who—"

"Me." She pulls back, brown eyes resolute. "It's not your job to take care of me—it's my job to take care of you. I'll be fine." She swipes at the tear on my cheek before nodding at my phone. "Let your father know you're coming."

Chapter 4

Luke

My breath clouds in front of me when I hit the ice, dawn barely cracking over the horizon.

Coach would be pissed if he knew I was out here. *There's a time for training and a time for recovery.* That's what this break is supposed to be. Rest and recovery. But the only time I can clear the thoughts and memories from my mind is when I'm pushing my body to the brink.

My skates cut through the ice, the lone pair until the ghost of another soars across.

The ghost of the girl I once thought of as a dream. Now my nightmare.

Chloe deserved to be more than a dream. She deserved to be a whole person. A girl with flaws and quirks and annoying habits. A girl who chewed too loud or talked too much or never got anywhere on time. If she was still here, I could've learned those things about her. Maybe we would've discovered we weren't a good fit at all. Maybe we would've realized we were better as friends.

"Luke!"

My head whips to the other side of the ice, convinced I heard Chloe calling out to me.

But when the shout comes again, it's from the opposite direction. No ghosts in sight.

A mother shouts at her son racing for the frozen pond until she wrangles him into submission.

My heart pounds in my ears, from chasing the puck for the past hour and my mind convincing me for the briefest moment that Chloe had been resurrected from the dead.

Or that I was truly losing my fucking mind.

With the sun reflecting off the ice and families bringing their kids to skate, I pack up and head home, limbs drained and heart struggling to pump the blood in my veins.

But at least I didn't think about Chloe until the end, my mind too consumed by the burn and strain. Too bad the peace never lasts. She always comes back to me with a vengeance—long, blonde hair, bright blue eyes, and a huge smile to match her bigger-than-life personality. Now the corpse in the casket.

By the time I trudge through the front door, I want to claw my brain out of my head. My hand itches to reach for my phone and text Sienna. My favorite distraction.

Bud barks and races up to me, tail wagging.

"Luke?" Ma calls. "Can you join us in the family room?"

I ditch my bag on the floor, scratch Bud's head, and sigh. The family room is where Ma delivers bad news. When our last dog died, when the Novaks announced the date for Chloe's funeral, when she told me Mike would be moving in. All the shit guaranteed to upset me, she reserves for this room.

Ma and Mike are seated together on one couch, and I take the other across from them, Bud flopping at my feet. The family room is stiff and formal, decorated and organized like a staged room in a house up for sale.

I clasp my hands between my knees, foot bouncing.

Already eager to get the hell out of this room and soak in the shower for an hour. "What's up?"

Ma glances at Mike. This has to be some shit about the wedding. Ma's going to insist on my attendance and Mike's about to ask me to be his best man, which was obviously her idea.

He grins. "Sienna is coming to stay with us!"

To stay.

Sienna is going to be fucking *living* here.

It's bad enough that we're about to be step-siblings in the eyes of the law. Bad enough that she might show up at the wedding and somehow put all the pieces together. But to be under the same roof?

There's no fucking way she won't figure out Ten's real identity. Every time she messages Ten, my phone will chime. She's smart—she'll catch on fast.

And then I'll lose her forever.

"Why the hell is she staying here?"

Ma flinches but forces a smile. "I was thinking you could show her around campus. We'll be on our honeymoon, but I was hoping you and your teammates could help her move into the dorm."

Jesus. Living in my house, attending the same university. I always thought if I ever met Sienna in person someday, the friendship between us would grow into something more. But I never did come up with a solution about how I'd get away with catfishing her from day one.

If she moves in, that friendship has to end. I won't be able to keep up the ruse anymore. Not when I plan on taking this secret to the grave.

My hands curl into fists. "Why is she moving here?"

Mike shifts uncomfortably. "We think it's in her best interest."

Does this have something to do with why she disappeared from social media? Why she suddenly wanted to live her life "unplugged"? Something's going on that she's not telling me.

So I guess we've both got our secrets now.

I stand. Because Ma wants to marry a guy she's already dumped once, now I have to give up Sienna. The one person I've been able to count on, the one person I've trusted with almost everything. The universe is fucked. "She can find somebody else to move her shit in. Maybe, I don't know, her dad."

Ma glances at Mike as if she expects him to defend her like my father would. *Don't talk to your mother like that.* But he doesn't. He's smarter than that—he knows it wouldn't end well for him.

"I don't know what's gotten into you lately, Luke," Ma calls at my back. "But you're a part of this family, and you'll be at the wedding."

She's using her courtroom voice now. She's not fucking around. I turn to face her and lean against the wall, arms folded because I'm not either.

If she wants me at that wedding, she'll have to knock me out and drag me. I'm not showing up in a suit and pretending like I approve of this shit. I don't care if Mike is a decent guy—they haven't been together that long.

But even if they'd been together the past five years, I wouldn't want her to marry him. I can't stand by and let her make Sienna my stepsister with a smile on my face.

"We're adults and we make our own decisions, with or without your approval." Ma perches with her hands on her hips in front of me now. "I don't care how old you are—you live under my roof and I'm still your mother. If I say you'll be at the wedding, you'll be at the wedding. Or you can pay for your tuition and housing on your own."

So she's playing that card. It's too late before next semester to apply for loans, and there's no way in hell I'm giving up my spot on the Diamond Devils hockey team.

Other than talking to Sienna, hockey is the only thing that clears my mind. Getting drafted to the NHL was Pop's dream for me. I won't let him down. Not again.

I shrug, teeth clenched. "Fine."

When I turn to leave the room, Ma calls after me. "You'll help Sienna move into her dorm too. Maybe you can ask Wes and Knox and some of your other friends to help."

"Whatever. I'm going to shower."

This isn't how meeting her was supposed to go. We weren't supposed to meet at all. We'd keep up this online friendship forever, and I'd never have to reveal the disappointing man beneath the mask.

Upstairs, I check my phone, the steam rising from the shower.

My heart sinks when I spot the messages from Sienna.

> SIENNA
>
> So apparently I'm moving in with my father.
>
> I'm kind of nervous.

Before, I would've responded the second I read her texts. Would've reassured her that I'd help her get through anything. Would've told her she's the bravest girl I know.

Instead, I turn the sound off on my app notifications and lock the screen.

I'm ghosting her when she needs me the most. Ghosting my best friend.

Drown in You

Sienna is a no-show at our parents' wedding. The tight knot in my chest loosens. Maybe she changed her mind. She's staying with her mom and I won't expose my secret after all. I won't lose her.

At the reception in the hotel, my family bombards me with questions about hockey and classes and girlfriends. Doesn't help that a lot of hockey players marry young, so everyone expects me to find a college sweetheart who will become my wife.

By the time I escape to the hotel bar, I want to rip off the stiff, starchy suit and down a bottle of their hardest liquor.

I grab a stool and nearly mutter a prayer when the bartender doesn't ask for my ID. He must read the need for a drink all over my face.

Sienna texted me a bunch of times since the reception started, explaining the car troubles she had before she could leave for her father's wedding and how she showed up late to the reception and now can't gather up the courage to go in there.

I wish I could be the support she needs. Hold out my arm and help her face her father and all those strangers, but I can't. I slip my phone back into my pocket.

When I glimpse the only other person at the bar adjacent to me, my breath catches. Somebody who's having a worse night than I am.

A few empty glasses sit in front of her that she must have downed before the bartender could clear them away. The glass in her hand is half empty, the liquid inside dark and promising a blackout.

She's heartbreakingly gorgeous. Long, soft brown hair drifting in waves down her back, delicate nose, and a round face that'll keep her looking twenty for the next ten years. Her lips and nails are painted a vibrant red like she's planning on meeting someone here. A girl who keeps glancing at her phone like she got stood up.

Or like she's on the run from whatever asshole gave her that nasty bruise on her temple.

Her piercing green eyes land on me.

The moment I've been anticipating since Ma announced the wedding. I'm not the mystery man behind the mask anymore, and she's not just a pretty face online. She's real.

Sienna Carter.

Except she wasn't supposed to show up battered and bruised. My teeth grind together, fists clenching. Who the fuck did that to her? I'll kill him.

Her lips purse and she stands, heels clicking with every step.

She flops onto the stool beside me, her dress rising dangerously high on her thighs clad in dark tights. My mouth goes dry. Never in a million years would I have imagined meeting her looking like *this*.

"It's rude to stare." She sighs, taking another swig from her glass. Her voice is this delicate soprano, soft and breathy and I want to hear it again. Need to.

"So I've heard." I snatch the whiskey in front of me and take a sip.

Up close, she's even more beautiful. Natural beauty hidden under a thick layer of makeup—a failed attempt to conceal the nasty bruise.

Now is my chance to come clean. Tell her who I am, reveal Ten's true identity. *I'm not actually from California. I used an app to text you from a number with a California area code. I wear a mask so you never find out who I really am. Now I'm your stepbrother.*

I pull out the disposable camera and set it in front of her.

She picks it up tentatively, a confused but delighted smile crawling across her lips. "What's this for?"

Heart pounding in my ears, I try to force my tongue to form the words. But all that comes out is: "They're passing them out at the reception. I swiped one." I gesture to her dress. "That's why you're here, isn't it?"

"If I was here for the reception, why would I be out here with you?" She snaps a photo of me, and despite that bruise and whatever hell she's been through, she's still managing to smile at someone she believes to be a stranger.

"That's what I'm wondering."

When she catches me staring at that bruise, she sighs. "Before you ask, I fell."

God, she's a terrible liar. No way in hell she got that bruise from a fall. No way in hell that bruise isn't related to exactly why she's here in the first place. But I play along. "Yeah? Where at?"

"On ice." She smiles sweetly, and those red lips make my cock twitch. *Fuck.*

Don't imagine them wrapped around your dick, don't imagine them wrapped around your dick—I'm one hundred percent imagining them wrapped around my dick. Wouldn't be the first time. "You skate?"

"No. Hence the falling." She tucks the camera in her purse and takes another gulp of her drink before her gaze rakes over me. Her sultry green eyes set me on fire. She better stop fucking looking at me like that before I bend her over this bar. I'm already sporting a semi. "What's with the suit?"

"I own the hotel."

She snorts at my equally obvious lie. "Oh, good. Maybe you can upgrade my room then."

I swirl the liquid in my glass. "Meeting someone?"

She bats her lashes at me. "If I was meeting someone, I

wouldn't be sitting here with you. I like my men jealous and possessive."

Wouldn't know any other way to be. I take another gulp of whiskey. Already starting to catch a buzz. Abstaining from alcohol for hockey has turned me into a lightweight.

"What's your name?" I ask, because I'm not supposed to know.

A smile plays on her ruby lips. "Mystery."

So no real names then. That's fine. I'm used to that.

"What's yours?" she asks.

"Investigator."

This pulls a genuine laugh from her, and it's the most magical sound I've ever heard.

Her palm lands on my thigh, red-painted nails skimming along my pants and sending chills down my spine. "I think I have an idea to shake up our miserable evenings. If you want to come up to my room with me."

Jesus. This isn't at all how I expected tonight to go. Through text, she's the sweet, caring, funny girl. Not the seductive vixen. But I like this side of her.

No, I fucking love it.

I shouldn't go through with this. Not when I know exactly who she is and she has no clue who I am. Not when I know that we're already step-siblings.

"Don't worry. I'm not going to get attached or ask for your number or stalk you on social media." She squeezes my thigh. "I just want to get fucked."

Well, shit. Hard to say no now. Especially when my cock is rock-solid.

Fuck it. If Sienna wants me to fuck her, I'll give her every inch. I've daydreamed about a night with her for a while, and this may be the only chance I get once she finds out who I really am.

Drown in You

I let her pull me off the stool. "Where's your room?"

Chapter 5

Sienna

THIS IS QUITE POSSIBLY the second-worst decision I've ever made.

Maybe I shouldn't be inviting strange men up to the hotel room my estranged father paid for. But I don't care. I want a wild night of hot sex with a gorgeous stranger to make me forget.

And my god is he gorgeous. Blond hair—so dark you might almost mistake it for brown—curls adorably around his ears. He has a square jaw that I bet would clench particularly attractively when he's angry and soft gray eyes that betray the sorrows he's running from.

His dark suit is tight around his arms and shoulders, and I'm dying to rip his clothes off to reveal the hard, bulging muscles underneath. He's probably an athlete, but I'm not going to ask. If he says he's a football player, I might not be able to go through with this.

The instant he gave me that disposable camera, he reminded me of Ten, and even though it's ridiculous, it made me feel safe with him.

He presses a hand against the door above my head, forcing me to lean back and crane my neck to meet his gaze. His heady, musky scent floods my nose and I want to wrap myself in it like a blanket. Those gray eyes are no longer soft—they're electric.

"You sure you want to do this?" His low, rumbling voice turns the butterflies fluttering gently in my stomach into a full-blown butterfly tornado.

I'm sure as hell that I want to do this now.

I clear my throat and give a single nod. "Yes. As long as you wear a condom, I'm not looking for anything beyond getting dicked down for a night."

His brows lift, a few shades darker than his hair, and he lets out a surprised laugh. The kind of easy laugh that tells me he used to laugh a lot once. Before whatever it is that happened to him happened.

Even though he's a complete stranger—I literally don't even know his name—and I don't know the root of his pain, my heart aches for him. Juliet likes to call that my fatal flaw. I feel bad for other people too much, feel their pain as if it's my own. It gets me into trouble.

"I don't have a condom." The realization dawns on him as the words leave his mouth. Despair melts him adorably.

"I do." I duck around him and grab the giant box of condoms from my suitcase. I wanted to make sure I had a healthy supply while I'm attending Diamond University. I plan on fucking all my troubles away.

This major life change still doesn't feel real. A new home, a new university, a new family. Although *family* is a stretch. I barely know my father, let alone his new wife and stepson. Who knows if they'll even want anything to do with me.

Living in Wakefield was hell, but being here probably won't be much better. Thank god Juliet kept her word and transferred with me. Her parents are wealthy enough to buy her speedy enrollment into Diamond University. At least having my best friend around will prevent me from plummeting into the pits of misery.

She'll be so proud when I tell her I skipped my father's wedding reception to fuck a stranger in my hotel room.

I didn't intend to miss the wedding, no matter how anxious I was to attend. But my shitty car wouldn't start, which meant I couldn't leave until Juliet's dad brought me a new battery. By the time I got to Diamond, the wedding was already over.

And now I'd rather have sex with a complete stranger than face my father and his new family.

The man whose dick I'm about to ride steps closer, nodding at the box of condoms in my hands. "How many guys are you planning on bringing up here tonight?"

"At least a hundred."

He snorts and damn it, guys who get my sense of humor are my weakness. So are giant men in suits. This guy is checking all my boxes.

I shake the package of condoms. "More people come out of college with STDs than bachelor's degrees, so I wanted to be prepared. I'm on birth control too."

The side of his mouth lifts in a smirk. "When you prepare, you really commit. Do you go to Diamond?"

"Let's not do the whole thing where we pretend we want to get to know each other before you're inside me." I crack open the box of condoms and toss one onto the bed. "Please don't ask me my major or any of that crap. That's not the kind of pillow talk I'm looking for."

Silently, he saunters toward me with his hands in his pockets, and I already want to combust. What is it about men in suits that makes women go feral? If he was wearing a mask, I'd come in about ten seconds.

When he reaches me, he brushes back a strand of hair,

sending goosebumps down to my toes. "What kind of pillow talk are you looking for?"

Holy fuck. Maybe I'm actually going to get lucky with this one and not have a night of mediocre, forgettable sex. "You know, the usual, vanilla stuff. *Good girl, eyes on me, beg me, crawl to me, you can take it, I decide when you breathe.*"

He malfunctions for a second. I'm a book girl, so of course, everyone assumes I'm as innocent as I look. He should listen to my audiobooks. His brain would melt.

When he recovers, he closes the distance between us, hooking a finger under my chin. His gray eyes are hooded with lust, and I could stare into them all day if not for the overwhelming desire to see the rest of him without clothes on. "In that case," he murmurs, "be a good girl and take off my belt."

My thighs clench. *Oh shit.* What have I unleashed?

I bat my lashes at him and smile sweetly, unfastening the buckle with embarrassingly clumsy hands. A man has never made me this flustered in my life. Normally, I'm the one taking charge and giving instructions in the bedroom. Half the time, I feel like a teacher instructing an inept student on where to find the clitoris, proper tongue techniques, and what the female orgasm actually looks and sounds and feels like, and no, it's not impossible to tell. Certainly not impossible to tell when I come. The few miraculous times it happens with another person, I make a show of it.

Partially because it really does feel that good and partially to reward them for their efforts. The people pleaser in me never sleeps, even during the throes of ecstasy.

But this man doesn't seem like he'll need instruction. In fact, I hope he gives me more orders. I need a gorgeous man to boss me around in bed like I need air.

Finally, I manage to pull his belt from the final loop and drop it to the floor.

"Now the jacket."

My heart thumps harder, and I contemplate the physics of taking the jacket off a man well over six feet tall.

"What kind of pillow talk do you like?" I purr, craning up on my toes to slide his jacket off his shoulders.

"You know, the usual, vanilla stuff. *Harder, make me come, let me swallow, that's the biggest dick I've ever seen, I'm coming.* That kind of thing."

Jesus. I really hope it will be the biggest dick I've ever seen. I'm already so turned on and he's barely even touched me. I'm not sure if this buildup is amazing or agonizing.

Both. Definitely both.

Once I get his jacket off, I don't wait for further instructions. I loosen the tie around his neck and slip it over his head. I'd suggest that he could tie me up with it, but maybe that's not the smartest move with a complete stranger. I still don't know how much I can trust him yet.

He watches with hooded eyes as my fingers free every button down the front of his shirt.

When I peel the lapels apart, I nearly gasp. This man is a work of art, hard chest and abs chiseled from marble. My palms land on his bare flesh of their own accord, grazing over the velvety soft skin.

Disturbingly, I realize I probably look like a kid discovering candy for the first time and draw back.

"Did I say you could take your hands off me?"

Fuck, that voice. I'll beg him on my knees to narrate my favorite books if that's what it takes. I grin. "I thought you might want my hands elsewhere."

I drag my palm up his shaft, and holy fuck. There's no way all of that is fitting inside me. The tip alone is wide and intimidating.

A soft, low groan of pleasure rumbles from deep in his

Drown in You

throat. My stomach somersaults. I will do anything to get him to make that sound again.

"Take those off," he hisses, nodding at my tights like me still being fully clothed in front of him is agonizing. I know the feeling.

Maybe in the darkness, he won't notice the bruises from where Marcus and his friends kicked me in the legs. As long as I leave my dress on, he won't see the worst of it.

He tracks every centimeter as I slide my tights down. I'm already so wet and ready for him.

"Now the dress."

I reach for the fly on his pants instead. "I'd like to keep it on, actually." I'm sure he won't care once his dick is in my mouth.

He steps out of my grasp. "I didn't follow you up here because I didn't want to see you naked. Now be a good girl and strip for me."

Well, shit. It's hard to argue with a man who says horny shit like that. Not to mention it's almost impossible for me to deny anyone their request. If it's what they want, if it's what will make them happy, if they'll like me more because of it, I'll do it.

"It's not a pretty sight," I warn him. If he's too turned off to have sex with me because of my bruises, I'll revolt.

He glowers at me, but there's a playful edge. I'm not sure if he's normally like this in the bedroom or if he's just indulging me. Either way, I'll take it. "If you don't take that dress off now, I will."

Screw it, if he wants the dress off, I'll take it off. If the bruise on my face didn't send him running, I'm sure a few more won't.

I strip off the dress, down to my strapless bra and panties in front of him. Yet I feel completely nude under his burning gaze.

A muscle in his jaw feathers as his gaze lands on the

41

constellation of bruises. I was right—he is incredibly sexy when he's angry.

His voice is low and dangerous. "Who did this to you?"

My heart stops. He's just met me, and he already looks like he would burn the world down for me.

"I told you. I f—"

"Don't say you fell." His warning is sharp.

Realistically, I know a total stranger can't possibly care about me, but he almost convinces me he does. "What does it matter what happened? You can't do anything about it."

The wrong thing to say. His eyes cloud, and I'm about to fuck up this whole one-night stand before I even get him inside me.

"I'm fine now," I reassure him. "I'm safe."

Except I don't think I'll ever be safe, no matter how far I run.

He steps so close, our chests nearly brush. Well, my chest and his abdomen. "Was it a boyfriend?"

I shake my head. "No. Not an ex either. Or a parent. They're miles away, and there's no point in talking about them anymore. Especially since we're strangers and we'll never see each other again. So maybe we can stop talking about this and you can fuck me now?"

I invited him up here to forget, not to rehash all of the shit that brought me here in the first place.

Lust glazes his features again. "I'll fuck you when I'm ready to fuck you."

Judging by the erection that's as hard as a rock in his pants, I would've assumed he's as ready to fuck me as he'll ever be. Instead of flinging me onto the bed or guiding me to my knees to blow him, he drops to his own.

The sight of this enormous, sculpted man on his knees before me makes my heart skip. His wide, veiny hands slip around to the small of my back, calloused palms anchoring me in place as his lips brush against my stomach.

Against one of my bruises.

A casual one-night stand shouldn't make my chest squeeze painfully, but with every brush of his lips against my bruises, he does. My stomach, my ribs, my thighs, my shins. I shiver despite the burning heat of desire pumping through my veins.

My eyes sting at his tenderness, and I quickly blink back the tears because there's no way in hell I'm ruining this night by crying. I've never been more desperate to have a man inside me than this one, and I'm not going to screw it up.

His kisses are featherlight, yet each one sets me on fire. I want his mouth on mine.

When he rises and kisses the bruise on my shoulder, I grab his face and pull him to me.

Our lips meet in an unexpectedly gentle caress. I'm used to men only wanting to give me a few quick pecks or immediately sticking their tongues in my mouth.

But he's different. Like his lips are hugging mine. Reassuring them that they're here and they're not going anywhere.

Except when I moan and his mouth turns feral.

He grabs my jaw with both hands and tugs me closer, lips roaming over mine and exploring, tasting, luxuriating. He just had his first taste of chocolate and now he's going to inhale the entire box.

I've never failed to make a man come before, but this is the first time I've ever made a man devour me.

When he finally fists my hair and tugs my head back, exposing my neck to him, I whimper.

That unleashes him entirely.

He sucks on my neck, turning me to liquid in his arms. My knees are so weak, I can barely stay upright without hanging onto his huge biceps for dear life.

For the first time, my sounds aren't exaggerated for a man's benefit. Every moan and whimper and hiss that he wrings from me is a direct result of his expert mouth and hands on my skin.

He keeps one hand fisted in my hair while he leaves hickeys on my neck, and the other hand drifts to my panties.

My breath hitches. His finger trails along the waistband, goosebumps springing up at the contact.

"Are you going to tell me your name before I'm inside you?"

I'll tell him my name, my address, my date of birth, my social security number if it means getting him inside me now—

No. I need to get my shit together. "Let's keep it a mystery." I'm already embarrassingly breathless. "I don't want you stalking me on social media after this and begging me to marry you."

Not that I'm on social media anyway, but he doesn't need to know that.

I want sex, not a relationship. Plenty of guys think all they want is a fuck buddy, but most of them end up getting attached and wanting more. Or when you get bored and break it off with them, they take it fine at first until they're crawling back three months later when they can't get the memories of coming inside you out of their head.

But relationships aren't for me. They always end in heartbreak. Since the divorce, I had to watch man after man break my mom's already fragile heart. I picked up the pieces every time and reminded her to bathe and eat. I've witnessed the consequences of relationships, and I won't put myself through that. Sex is enough to satisfy me, and if I can't get that, some altruistic genius invented vibrators.

"Don't worry." He smirks, cradling my hips. "I won't stalk you on social media."

I shouldn't find it insulting that a man who barely knows

me doesn't want to be in a relationship with me, especially when I don't want one, but I can't help the way my spine stiffens.

"I'll have you know, I'm great at riding cock, and I'll definitely have you on one knee proposing by the end of the night."

"Prove it."

Before I can say another word, he grabs my ass and hoists me into the air. I squeal as he tosses me onto the bed.

He doesn't follow me. Instead, he takes off his pants and boxers, and it's my turn to watch every move he makes.

When he's fully naked in front of me, my mouth goes dry. Yeah, there's no way he's getting every inch inside of me. I'm a nursing student—I know the vagina only stretches to a maximum of eight inches when aroused.

But he can damn well try.

He climbs onto the bed with me, but he doesn't rip my panties off and slam inside me. Not yet. His enormous hands tug my strapless bra up over my head, and his throat bobs when he stares at my tits.

Why does every look from this man light me on fire?

He shakes his head. "I can't believe you almost didn't let me see you like this." His murmur is the quietest I've heard him yet. "You're more than a pretty sight. Way, way fucking more."

My turn to swallow the lump in my throat.

He sits with his back against the headboard and pulls me onto his lap to straddle him. But he's still not ready to fuck me. His hands drift lazily up to my breasts as if we have all the time in the world and not one night together. When he squeezes my tits, I gasp and he bites his lip. "Mmm. These are incredible."

A man has never revered my body like this. I'm starting to realize the stranger I invited up to my room may not be like any other man I've ever met.

Sometimes, I imagine meeting Ten would go something like

this. I have no idea what he looks like beneath his mask or if we'd even get along in person as well as we get along through text, but when it's just me and my vibrator, I like to imagine Ten and I would finally meet in person, he'd be the most attractive man I'd ever seen, and we'd find somewhere semi-private to fuck each other's brains out. Not that I'd ever admit that to him. We're friends and that's all we've ever been. We've never turned our conversations sexual or even romantic. Though we've never explicitly discussed why, we both value our friendship more than sexting and neither of us wants to do anything to screw it up.

Except I haven't heard from him since I mentioned my father's wedding and I'm starting to wonder if I did something to piss him off. He never goes more than twenty-four hours without responding to me, even during hockey season. But I can't shake the feeling that he's ignoring me, and I don't know what I did wrong or how to fix it.

The man I'm straddling wraps his lips around my hard nipple and I shove thoughts of Ten out of my head. I can't be thinking of him when I'm literally about to fuck another guy.

He sucks my nipple, making my eyes roll as I claw at his hair. "I can't wait to taste you everywhere."

Holy shit. Every word out of this man's mouth turns me to molten lava. "You don't have to do that," I gasp. "I'm plenty wet."

"I know you are," he growls, grinding my pussy against his cock, my panties the only thing separating us. I cry out when his tip hits my clit. Yeah, it's not going to take me long to come at all. Not with him. "But I want you dripping for me."

I rock my hips, desperate to relieve the growing ache between my legs. "Do whatever you want," I pant before quickly adding, "Within reason. I mean—"

Thank god, he stops my blabbering, flipping me onto my

back and kissing, sucking, and nibbling his way slowly down my body like he's entranced by every inch. I jerk and writhe beneath him.

When his head is between my thighs, he murmurs, "You're going to love this, sweetheart."

Sweetheart. It's not *good girl*, but it's somehow better. Especially with that slight Southern accent, barely noticeable for anyone not fixated on his every sound. Or maybe every word out of this man's mouth is better by default. He could probably read a grocery list and turn me on.

"You seriously don't have to," I offer one last time.

Most guys like to get in and get out during a hookup, especially a one-time thing like this. Guys only care about getting you off if they care about you, and most of them don't have the patience or the endurance to go down on a girl long enough to make her come. Or maybe it's just me. Maybe it's always taken me forever to get there because no man has ever turned me on this much before.

His brows furrow now, but he keeps his head between my legs, the flimsy fabric of my panties the only layer separating us. "You're not making me. I *want* to lick your pussy until you come."

My god. Why can't every man be as direct and pornographic as this one? Thank god he's the one I met at the hotel bar tonight and not some other schmuck who would have no doubt disappointed me.

While his fingers trace my panty line, making me gulp, his eyes blaze. "Are you going to try to stop me again? Or are you going to be a good girl and take it?"

I shake my head quickly. "I'm not going to stop you."

Some crazy part of me trusts him enough to tell him he can do whatever he wants to me, but the much smaller, smarter part of my brain chastises the horny part for even considering it.

If this was more than a one-night stand, maybe I would. If he was my fuck buddy, I'd be on his cock three times a day, just to experience all the different ways he would fuck me. After the way he kissed my bruises and demanded to know who left them on my body, he might even be boyfriend material. If that's something I wanted.

Juliet would probably date him, but I'd die of jealousy knowing the incredible foreplay she's experiencing on a daily basis while I'm stuck getting jackhammered by fumbling, inebriated frat bros.

"That's my good girl," he murmurs, drawing my panties to the side and baring my pussy to him. He hisses sharply, and I freeze. "You're *perfect*."

My pussy has definitely never been called perfect before. I nearly blurt that he's perfect, but if that doesn't scream this-girl-is-going-to-stalk-me, I don't know what does. So all I squeak out is "Thank you."

His head drifts closer, his soft breath hitting the wetness pooling between my legs. I stop breathing as I brace for contact.

But instead of licking me, he blows softly on my pussy.

I jerk, gasping at the unexpected pleasure from a little air. *Jesus.* It's like I've never experienced human touch before. Every move this man makes sets me on fire. By the end of this, I'm going to be a burnt husk in front of him.

He chuckles softly, getting far too much enjoyment out of my reactions.

"When I finally lick your pussy"—He kisses my thigh—"are you going to scream for me?"

I've never screamed in bed before. Moaned, yes, whimpered, yes, but never screamed. Yet I am fully convinced that I'm going to scream when this man finally makes me come. I've never been wound so tight with sexual tension in my life. My screams will probably bring the entire hotel crumbling down. "I might."

"Mmm. Let's find out." Without any more preamble, his tongue flicks against my clit.

I cry out, back arching. *Fuck.* This is exactly what I need. Him. I need more of him. Like air. More than air. "Holy fuck!"

His tongue digs against my clit harder before swirling. My heart hammers against my ribs, and I cling to his hair, loving that it's long enough to tug on. He lets me pull him closer, pressing his mouth harder against me.

When he dips a finger inside me, I cry out again at the stretch, at the exquisite feeling of being filled, and he groans. That sound alone is almost enough to make me shatter.

"*Jesus.*" His groan is agonized. "You're fucking soaked."

"I know," I gasp. "You did this to me."

He chuckles. "I'm going to do a lot more." He groans again when he slips a second finger inside me. My eyes sting from the stretch and I tug so hard on his hair, I'm vaguely worried that I'm going to yank clumps from his scalp. "You're so tight."

"I'm not sure how much you'll be able to fit inside me," I warn.

"We'll make it fit." His tongue returns to my clit before he wraps his lips around it and sucks.

Stars explode in my head, and I'm gasping and moaning as he sucks my clit hard and pumps his fingers inside me.

The orgasm comes on so fast, I don't have time to brace for it. My pussy throbs hard once, twice around his fingers before pleasure barrels through me.

Electricity bursts along my spine. I scream, just as he predicted, back arching and hands pushing his head to escape the overwhelming pleasure. But he doesn't ease up. His mouth only sucks my clit harder as he continues thrusting his fingers inside me through every wave of my orgasm.

I'm torn between begging him to stop and begging him to never stop.

The pressure from his mouth starts to lessen and the pumps of his fingers slow as I come down from my orgasm, heart still pounding. My mind is buzzing, but there are no thoughts in my head. Exactly what I wanted.

But about a thousand times better than I could've ever anticipated.

He slips the condom on while I recover. I expect him to return and fuck my limp body before he comes in three pumps, but instead, he sits with his back against the headboard and picks me up like I'm a pillow, dropping me onto his lap. His hard length presses against my pussy.

"If you wanted me to ride you, you should've thought about that before you made me come so hard, I lost all motor function." My arms are too weak to lift, and my legs are jelly.

"All I want is for you to let me fuck you."

My pounding heart skips. "That's all I want too. Please do it. Please fuck me." I grind against his cock in emphasis.

His low chuckle makes my thighs clench. "I've never really liked dirty talk before, but I do with you."

I wrap a hand around his shaft, stroking. God, he's enormous. "If you fuck me, I'll indulge you in all the dirty talk you want."

His gray eyes hood. "Put my cock inside you, sweetheart."

I smirk when he hisses as I grind his tip against my clit first. He made me suffer in anticipation, so the least I can do is return the favor.

I rub his tip down my slit, spreading my wetness over the condom before slowly sinking onto him.

My breath hitches, every muscle in my body stiffening at the burning stretch. I've barely gotten his tip inside me and I already feel so full.

His hands tighten on my hips. "Take it like a good girl."

I try to be a good girl, I really do. But when I sink lower and lower until finally reaching the point that I can't take any more, I reach down and find that I can still wrap my hand around the rest of his cock.

He smirks. "You've got a few inches to go, sweetheart."

"Some things are impossible and getting your entire dick inside me is one of them."

He shakes his head, fisting my hair like he did earlier, sending tingles of anticipation skittering down my spine. "You can take it."

With that, he yanks my hair back and drives his cock up into me.

A scream rips from my throat almost as loud as when he was making me come, and his thumb circles my clit wildly, sending shockwaves of pleasure through my body to loosen my taut muscles and stretch my pussy for him.

My nails bite into his bare shoulders, and I cry out when he thrusts into me again, the bursts of pleasure making my head grow lighter and eyes cross.

He circles an arm around my back to anchor me in place as he repositions us with his legs under him to give him some leverage. He thrusts into me once, twice, panting against my shoulder. "Bounce on my cock."

His order is breathless, desperate, so I muster up as much strength as I can and rock my hips up before slamming back down.

We both moan, hearts pounding against each other's chests.

I'm not sure why he wants to keep me on top instead of just flipping me on my back and finishing this in two seconds, but I'll happily go along with it. This angle is so deep and surprisingly intimate for two complete strangers, our bodies entwined and pressed flush together, our breaths mingling and his gaze boring into mine.

We fuck like two people who've known each other for a lifetime, not like two strangers who don't even know the other's name.

Whoever he is, he is no mortal man. He's a god.

"You're gonna make me come," he pants as I bounce on his cock faster. A warning and a plea.

I clutch him to me to breathe the dirty words in his ear. "I want to feel your cock throb when you come inside me."

His groan is abrupt and sharp, eyes rolling as the pleasure overtakes him. The arm around my back anchors me in place as I keep rocking against him, and I yelp when his cock gives a hard throb inside me. "*Fuck.*"

Even though most guys stop thrusting when they come, he doesn't stop me from rocking against him as he spills into the condom.

My movements get slower and slower, coming down from his orgasm with him as he did for me.

We're both sweaty and breathless, panting and clinging to each other.

Holy shit. That just happened. I just had the best sex of my life with a total stranger.

Too bad this is nothing more than a one-night stand. I could do this over and over, at least five times a day until I die.

He inhales a deep breath, and for some reason, just listening to this man breathe is sexy. "That's the hardest I've ever come in my life."

My chest floods with pride. He doesn't know it, but I have a major praise kink. My praise kink and my mask kink are forever at war over the horny part of my brain. "Me too."

I've lied to make someone feel good about themselves

before. To spare their feelings. Chronic people pleasers are notorious liars. We lie like we breathe air.

But I'm not lying now. That seriously was the hardest I've ever come in my life. The worst part is that's probably the last time I'll ever come that hard.

He tucks a strand of hair behind my ear with heartbreaking tenderness. "I knew this is how it would be with you."

I smirk, even as his words make my heart skip. "And when did you come to that conclusion? In the five minutes we spent getting to know each other before leaving for my hotel room?"

"Something like that."

In the ensuing silence filled only by our breathing, a ringtone blares from his pants on the floor.

I climb off him, immediately slipping under the covers. Reality hits us like a bucket of cold water as he slides out of bed, ditching the condom in the trash and checking his phone. "Shit. I better take this."

"No problem. Thank you for—" What the hell do I thank him for? Making me come? Fucking me? Making me forget for an hour the shitstorm my life has become? The longest I've gotten to forget in months. Finally, I manage, "Hanging out."

He gives me a small smile. "No problem." He quickly slips on his pants and shirt, not bothering with the buttons before he tosses his suit jacket over his shoulder and heads for the door. God, he's so sexy. A more beautiful man has never left my bedroom. He turns back to give me one final smirk. "Thanks for letting me . . . hang out."

I smile at the easy way he teases me. Being with him is easy. Easier than being with anybody else I've ever met.

Too bad.

Chapter 6

Luke

LOVE AT FIRST SIGHT. The stuff of fantasies. But here Sienna Carter is, waltzing into my life and making me fall in love with her the second our eyes lock.

She's always been a pretty girl, but pictures didn't do her justice. Years of friendship made me care about her, but meeting her in person—hearing her voice and laugh and moans, touching her, holding her, fucking her—that's what pushed me over the edge.

I've fucking fallen for her, harder than I ever thought possible.

In the hotel hallway, I've got a grin on my face when I answer Ma's call. "Hey."

"Oh, good! You're still up! I figured you were probably heading upstairs to sleep when you left the reception early. Can you come down to the hotel lobby?"

"Why?"

"I just want to go over the schedule for tomorrow morning again before we head up to bed."

Translation: She wants to threaten me again if I don't drop

her and Mike off at the airport and move Sienna's stuff into her dorm.

All I want to do is head back to Sienna's room and crash after the best fuck of my life. I fantasized about sex with her being good, but I never could've expected it would be like that. Thank god she had condoms. The second the door closed behind us, I knew if I didn't get to fuck her, I'd leave that room with the worst blue balls of my life.

Her moans, her whimpers, her taste . . . every second with her drove all the thoughts out of my head, inflated my ego to the point of no return. Her screams when she came almost convinced me she came as hard as I did.

I don't care if we're step-siblings now. She's mine.

Ma is talking in my ear again, and the magical tranquility of the past hour is gone. "Meet us in the hotel lobby."

"I'll be right there."

In the lobby, a few remaining stragglers from the reception amble up to their rooms or out to their cars. Ma waves to me and jumps up from her perch on Mike's knee before running to hug me, still in her wedding dress.

She looks really fucking happy, and she deserves to be. I just wish it didn't cost Sienna her favorite masked man.

Ma flings her arms around me, the fabric of her white dress crinkling and her flowery perfume burning my nose. I squeeze her back. She keeps her hands on my arms when she pulls back, beaming at me. "Someday, you'll find love too."

She has no idea I've already found it with my stepsister.

Behind Ma, Mike stands, a phone pressed to his ear. He strides over to us with a grin and ends the call. "Sienna got here late, but she's up in her room and she's coming down now to meet us."

She's about to get the fucking surprise of her life. They all are.

When the elevator dings behind us, Mike waves to someone over my shoulder.

Ma gasps, clutching her hands together with a grin. "Is that her?"

"That's her," Mike confirms.

"She's beautiful!"

Mike's shout echoes. "Sienna!"

Behind me, a cheery, soprano voice calls, "Hi!"

I turn in the direction of the clicking heels. When she spots my face, she halts and the bright smile slips away.

The soft, round face I was just caressing minutes ago. That I watched contort in ecstasy as I made her come with my mouth between her legs.

"It's so nice to meet you, Sienna!" Ma calls, and her voice kickstarts Sienna back to life. She plasters a smile on her face as she ambles toward us, far slower this time. "I'm Deb. And this is my son, Luke."

Sienna stops at my side, folding her arms tight across her stomach. Her gaze flashes to mine for a second before she glances away again. "Nice to meet you," she mumbles.

So that's how we're playing it. Pretending we haven't already met. Pretending I haven't already had my cock buried inside her.

Ma wraps her in a hug, and Sienna pats her on the back awkwardly before doing the same with Mike.

"I've missed you so much," he tells her.

I can practically hear the thoughts swirling in her head. *There's no way this is fucking happening. There's no way the guy I just hooked up with is my new stepbrother.*

Ma backhands my arm. "Well, don't just stand there, honey! Give her a hug. You're family now."

Little does she know, I've already given my new stepsister a warm welcome into the family.

Sienna stiffens when I step toward her, and her hands barely brush against my back as I hug her.

Her body is still as soft and inviting as it was when she was naked. I've seen my new stepsister naked. I've made her come. I've been inside her.

I can't wait to do it again.

"Welcome to the family, sis."

Chapter 7

Sienna

I'm dead.

If our parents find out how Luke and I really met, they'll ship me back to Wakefield in a heartbeat. Where Marcus and his henchmen will get their grubby hands on me.

As long as they're still in Wakefield, I won't survive a return trip home.

On our way to the airport, Dad asks me a million questions. He wants to know everything—my major, my hobbies, my future plans. Juliet would say he's had years to learn this information about me, but I'm glad he's actually trying. In the passenger seat, Deb searches through her carry-on for the millionth time. Miraculously, neither of them has picked up on the tangible tension between me and Luke.

Beside me, my new stepbrother is impossibly relaxed. Like he's not at all terrified about our parents discovering we hooked up last night. Not at all bothered by the fact that we both unknowingly fucked our new step-sibling.

This morning, he's in gray sweatpants that bring a lump to

my throat. He's gone from sophisticated man in a suit to college athlete in less than twelve hours, and his personality seems to have shifted with the wardrobe change.

Last night, the crease between his brows and the dip to his mouth told me he had the world weighing on his shoulders. Now, he's got a spark in his gorgeous—no, not gorgeous, average, painfully average—gray eyes and a pep in his step. I guess getting laid really turned his mood around. Learning he fucked his new stepsister should've soured it, but he somehow seems happier than our just-married parents who are literally in the honeymoon phase.

Overhead, static voices announce delays and gate changes. When we reach the escalator that will take our parents up to security and off to their gate, Deb turns to Luke with glassy eyes. She throws her arms around him, blubbering into his shoulder. "Stay out of trouble, and keep an eye on Sienna."

He flashes me a smirk and winks. "Don't worry. I will."

My stomach drops. What the hell is he doing? What if my dad saw him?

But a quick glance at my father confirms he's entirely oblivious, busy reviewing his gate information with his glasses resting on the tip of his nose. Even if my father saw him, he probably wouldn't think anything of a friendly wink. Except I'm fully aware that that wink was anything but friendly.

My father looks so different from what I remember. Brown hair lined with wide gray streaks, glasses with thick frames, and a hunch to his shoulders. Like gravity has been weighing him down more than the rest of us. Part of me can't help but hope that's the physical manifestation of his guilt.

But he's trying now. And despite the disappointment I've held onto for years, I want to mend our relationship too.

"Have a safe flight!" I squeak, partially wishing they could take me with them so I can get away from Luke and his lingering gaze.

"Thank you so much, sweetie!" Deb throws her arms around me with a big smile. She's sweet. Genuinely kind and warm. The type of woman I'm lucky to have as a stepmother.

Another reason why I don't want her to know what happened between me and her son last night. I just met her—I don't want her already thinking less of me. Already thinking I'm some succubus who lured her son away from her wedding reception to get laid.

Since Mom announced the news that I was moving in with my father, I've been playing out all the worst-case scenarios in my head, and none of them were this bad.

None of them involved fucking my new stepbrother before I even learned his name.

God, that was so fucking stupid. I'd blame it on the alcohol, but I was only buzzed. I knew exactly what I wanted last night: a distraction from the shitshow of the day, my life. Living away from my mom, moving in with my estranged father, joining a brand-new family, and being ignored by my best friend since I was fifteen—I needed something to help me forget.

I got what I wanted. At a steep price. Especially if our parents find out what we did and send me packing.

I can't let them find out.

Deb cups my face, the floral scent of her lotion wafting up my nose. "You call us if there's anything you need while we're gone. And Luke will be around if you need a ride anywhere or you want to come home for a weekend. Okay? Our home is your home."

She's so nice, my eyes almost sting. "Thank you. I really appreciate it."

"Of course, honey! You're family now!" She hugs me one last time, squeezing harder than I'd expect of a woman her size.

"My turn." Dad steps forward and wraps me in a hug. It's still uncomfortable, but I can tell he was sincere last night when he said how much he missed me.

Maybe I'll never understand how he could've left me behind after the divorce, but that doesn't mean we can't make up for lost time now.

When he pulls back, he hangs onto one of my shoulders while squeezing Deb's hand with a smile. "A lot of reunions happening lately. I'm a lucky man."

I smile politely at them. "What do you mean?"

"We dated a few years ago," Deb explains. "Way back when you kids were still in high school."

I had no idea. I glance at Luke. Did he know? His face doesn't give anything away. "That's so sweet."

"Why'd you break up?" Luke's voice is flat. For some reason, he acts like he doesn't want our parents to be together.

Deb waves her hand at him. "That's water under the bridge."

But Dad gives a sheepish smile. "I had a lot of growing up to do." He nods to me. "And I still wasn't really over Sienna's mom. I wasn't ready to love again."

Not over Mom? How can he say that when he left us? She's the one who's spent the past decade pining for him. But I keep my mouth shut. He's remarried and about to go on his honeymoon with his new wife. Now isn't the time to interrogate him about his previous marriage.

Deb opens her arms wide. "Last hugs so we can get through security."

Dad pulls me into a tight embrace again. "We'll see you as soon as we get back. Call if you need *anything*."

Luke tries to shake his hand like they're business partners, but Dad wraps him in an awkward hug before Deb throws her arms around him. Luke eventually has to extract himself from her hold and Dad guides her to the escalator. Neither of them stops waving and shouting they'll miss us until they reach the top.

A heavy palm lands on the small of my back.

I jump, gaze darting to Luke as I step out of his grasp. "What are you doing?"

His grin is wolfish. "We have the whole house to ourselves now."

My mouth falls open. He can't be serious. Our parents are literally still in sight, we just found out we're step-siblings, and he's implying we should go back to his house to fuck?

Maybe this is his demented sense of humor. This is what happens when you hook up with a guy you barely know while buzzed. You think he's this Greek god in bed, playing your body like you're a piano and he's a maestro, but when you wake up sober the next day and he opens his mouth, you realize what a giant fucking mistake that was.

Except I can't get that version of Luke Valentine out of my head. The version where he was the mystery man in my hotel room, not my new stepbrother. I'm still fantasizing about that version of him, still playing out last night in my head, even if I shouldn't be.

For that hour, he was kind of the man of my dreams. He *definitely* was.

But then the universe tossed a bucket of ice water on me and woke me the fuck up.

"Did you miss that whole conversation last night where we found out we're related now?" I wave to our parents as they disappear to the security gate.

My stomach twists. Aside from the strangers flittering past, I'm now completely alone with Luke.

He rolls his eyes, and I hate that every move he makes is sexy. *No, he's* not *sexy. He's not.* "We weren't raised together."

Oh my god. Seriously? That's where he draws the line? I turn on my heel and head for the exit, ready to get to Diamond University, move my stuff into the dorm, and stay as far away from my stepbrother as I can get. "It's still wrong."

"Barely." He's right beside me, his stride casual while I'm beelining for the exit. "A date then. I'll take you anywhere you want to go."

The moronic part of my brain softens at his proposition. But I shake it off.

It unnerves me how easily he can keep up with me. Like if I tried to run from him, he'd catch me in a heartbeat. "Even if it wasn't wrong, I'm not doing anything to risk being sent back to Wakefield."

That makes the cocky grin slip from his face. "Why? I thought you said you were safe now."

I'm not sure how much our parents have told him. Clearly, if he's asking, he must not know much, and I don't really feel like rehashing it. I'd rather not think about it at all, actually. The bruises on my body are reminders enough. "Let's just move my stuff into my dorm and then you don't have to worry about me anymore."

He'll be busy with his own classes and schedule, and we can avoid each other. Pretend last night never happened. That we didn't make the worst, best mistake of our lives.

Once we're out of the airport and under the bright January sun, Luke tugs me to a stop, the hard edges of his face still unfairly beautiful in the stark light of day. "I'll always worry about you."

The intensity in his gaze makes my heart stutter. "Why? You barely even know me."

"Because I'm your big brother now."

In the car, my tight muscles relax slightly when Luke keeps his giant, veiny hands to himself. One rests on the stick shift the entire ride, mere inches from my thigh. Luckily, winter weather means I'm layered up in jeans, a sweater, and a thick coat. No exposed skin to tempt him.

Not that he should be tempted by his stepsister. We agreed to a one-night stand. Don't most college guys get bored with a girl after fucking her? Especially gorgeous guys like him who are used to getting any girl they want. Maybe he's flirting just to mess with me.

I text Mom to distract my mind from my stepbrother's suffocating presence. She has a ten a.m. shift today, and who knows if she remembered to set her alarm.

SIENNA
Are you up?

Dropped Dad and his wife off at the airport. Heading to campus now.

Even though my father's new relationship is beyond my control, guilt gnaws at me for mentioning his new wife to Mom. A painful reminder that not only did he leave her—he found someone else. And she's still alone.

While I wait, I type out a text to Ten.

SIENNA
My life is officially a shitstorm.

After I hit Send, I stare at the messages waiting for his reply. Luke's phone buzzes in his pocket, but he doesn't bother checking it. At least he doesn't text and drive. He's retained *some* morals.

Despite not getting a response from Ten in days—the longest he's gone without texting me since we met online—I'm holding out hope that there's a perfectly reasonable explanation. He was on a trip somewhere and didn't have service. His phone died and he hasn't gotten a new one yet. Soon, I'll get a text from him explaining his silence, and I'll feel like an idiot for worrying and jumping to conclusions.

We've talked almost every day for five years. He wouldn't stop now. Not when I need him most.

When my phone chimes, my heart leaps with hope. But the text is from Mom.

> MOM
> I'm already showered and dressed. How are they? Nice?

My cheeks flush at the prospect of texting my mother anything about Luke.

> SIENNA
> Yep!

When the Diamond University campus comes into view, I can't help gasping. The sprawling brick campus is gorgeous, like a quaint town pulled straight from historic London. Dorm buildings, dining halls, class buildings, gyms. Fountains and quads and benches and ponds. I bet this campus is stunning in the spring when everything is in bloom.

"You like the campus, sis?" Luke's deep, sultry drawl shouldn't turn me on as much as it did last night.

My nose scrunches. "Ew, don't call me that."

"Why not? You said that's the reason you wouldn't let me take you out."

My cheeks burn with shame when my thighs clench. As soon as Luke pulls up in front of Nohren Hall, I fling the door open before the car has even fully come to a stop. I don't have much—Juliet is bringing most of our dorm supplies since she's the one with wealthy parents who can afford to buy her basically whatever she wants. So moving my stuff in shouldn't take long. Then Luke and I can part ways and hopefully not have to see each other again for a long time.

I grab as many bags as I can and beeline for Nohren Hall to get my room key. Luke takes his time grabbing a few boxes from the car, chuckling at my rush to get away from him. Glad one of us finds this situation amusing.

When we finally reach the dorm, I hold my breath, hoping Juliet is already inside. But the room is completely bare.

Damn it. I need her to run interference between us.

"Which bed is yours?" Luke asks, and I hate the way a shiver races down my spine at the seductive way those words leave his lips.

"This one." I toss my bags onto the mattress before he can get any bright ideas about this empty room with two available beds.

Inside my purse, the disposable camera rattles, bringing back a rush of memories from last night. Sitting beside him at the bar, squeezing his thigh, moaning with his head between my legs.

He smirks, perching on the edge of my mattress. "I'm getting flashbacks to your hotel room."

I fold my arms. He clearly doesn't understand the magnitude of this situation, and I need to make the boundaries of our new relationship crystal clear to him. "What happened last night was a mistake. It can never happen again. Like your mom said, we're family now. So no one can ever know what we did, and we're going to pretend it didn't happen. Okay?"

His brows furrow now, and I gulp. He's back to that commanding, looming man he was in my hotel room. Except this time, I'm nervous about what he might do next.

I'm finally realizing there's a lot about Luke Valentine I don't know.

He closes the space between us in two slow steps. My pulse echoes in my ears. "I'll never pretend it didn't happen. And I won't let you pretend either."

His hand brushes behind my ear, tender . . . until he slides it around my neck and tugs me closer.

I whimper.

"It *will* happen again, Sienna. That wasn't the only taste of you I'm getting. I know you want me, just as much as I want you."

Jesus. If he was anyone else, if he wasn't my stepbrother, I would let him get another taste. I would let him fuck me right here.

But this is our new reality, and we need to stay away from each other, no matter what he thinks he wants.

A thunderous knock on the door makes us jump apart.

When Luke swings it open, four giant men and a tiny girl hover in the doorway. They're all grinning at Luke, one of the giants barrelling into him for a hug and clapping him on the back. "Missed you, man!"

The one with his arm around the girl's shoulders nods to me. "You must be the new sister."

All six pairs of eyes fall on me.

The giant who hugged Luke brushes past him, a wide smile on his face as he extends a hand to me. "I'm Knox."

He's equal parts sexy and boyish with his green eyes, wavy hair, towering height, and a sprinkling of freckles across his nose.

"Sienna," I tell him.

His fingertips trail over the bruise at my temple. "What happened here?"

Behind him, Luke's temper flares.

"I fell."

"Hands off, Rockefeller." Luke's command makes Knox drop his hand with a chuckle.

Heat crawls up to my cheeks. How can he be this possessive of me? We had sex one time. His friends will get suspicious if he keeps up the jealous-boyfriend act.

"Sienna, this is Wes, Violet, Damien, and Finn." Knox points to each of them. "We play hockey together. Except for Violet. She's a puck bunny."

Violet sticks out her tongue at him and Wes scowls, squeezing her shoulders. "The hell she is."

Wes is definitely the kind of guy you don't fuck with. His dark brown hair is mussed and blue eyes glazed, like maybe the reason they didn't meet us by the front desk like we planned is because he and Violet were . . . preoccupied.

Violet is adorable with her shoulder-length brown hair and librarian-chic wardrobe. Her smile is warm and kind, and her eyes brighten when they land on the partially open box at the foot of my bed. "Oh my god, she's a book girl! I already love her!"

"Hell yeah." I'm a hundred percent sure we're going to be instant friends. As long as she doesn't spend too much time with Luke.

"You a puck bunny?" Knox asks. His eyes eat me up, his Cheshire grin warming my belly.

Behind him, Damien and Finn can't take their eyes off me either. They're both freakishly tall—all of them are—but Damien has the widest arms and shoulders, his eyes so dark they're almost black. Finn is leaner than the others, but he could be a model with those devastating blue eyes, sharp cheekbones, and midnight-black hair.

Luke glowers like he wants to kill all three of them for staring at me like I'm the next puck bunny in their lineup.

Maybe this is how I get Luke to stay away from me. Flirt

with his friends right in front of him, convince him I'm not interested. Then he'll get the hint and find some other girl. A girl who isn't related to him by law. A girl who wouldn't get sent back home to face the dangers awaiting her if she were to get caught in Luke Valentine's bed.

So I bat my lashes at Knox. He's gorgeous, so flirting with him won't be hard. "I am now."

Impossibly, his grin widens, green eyes lighting up. But behind him, Luke's brows sink.

I'm going to pay for that later.

WHILE JULIET and I walk to our first classes in Eureka, the aptly named building that hosts STEM classes, I'm dying to tell her every mortifying detail about this weekend. But I can't bring myself to confess to every horrifying turn my life has taken in the past seventy-two hours.

Thank god, Luke's friends managed to convince him to hit the ice with them after they helped me move in. The Devils. That's what they call themselves, and the name definitely suits them.

Juliet showed up shortly after they left, and I've managed to avoid Luke since, but I'm sure that won't last long. Insanely, he doesn't seem too keen on letting our one-night stand remain that way.

In the sunlight, the stud in Juliet's nose glints before we push our way into the building. She nudges me with an elbow. "So? How was the wedding reception? How's the new family? Are they a bunch of weirdos?"

I groan, following her to the stairs when we spot the line waiting in front of the elevators. "It was *so* awkward."

"How evil is the stepmonster?"

"Not at all. She's actually really nice. And my dad seemed really happy I'm here."

"He should be over-fucking-joyed." My father will have a harder time winning Juliet over than me. She smirks. "What about the stepbrother? Is he hot?"

My pulse picks up speed. "Ew. He's my stepbrother."

Juliet and I don't keep secrets from each other, and the guilt gnaws at me for keeping this one, but what happened between me and Luke can't get out.

"So? That doesn't mean you can't see whether he's hot or not. It's not like he's your actual brother." Of course I should've known the kinkiest girl I've ever met wouldn't bat an eye at a little taboo.

"I'd set you up with him, but he's an athlete." That would actually be the perfect solution to keeping Luke preoccupied with someone else, but ever since Marcus, Juliet has sworn off athletes.

"Damn. Maybe he has some sexy friends for us."

"He does, but they're hockey players too. The Devils."

She rolls her eyes as we approach my Intro to Statistics class. "All right, the first party we go to, we're finding some gorgeous guys and getting laid."

"Agreed." For the millionth time this morning, I check my phone.

Mom is already on her way to work after confirming with a video that she remembered to lock the door behind her and the house isn't on fire. I'm relieved she's doing okay without me, even if it makes me feel a twinge of disappointment that she doesn't actually need me after all.

But the real reason an ache settles in my chest is because Ten is still radio silent.

If he's not ghosting me voluntarily, something bad might've

happened to him. But I have no idea how to get in touch with anyone who might know anything.

We've shared the darkest parts of our souls, our greatest insecurities. I told him about how abandoned I felt after my dad moved away when the divorce was finalized, how exhausted it sometimes made me to carry the weight of Mom's sorrows and heartbreak on my shoulders, how sometimes I just wanted to be a kid again even though I love her and knew she needed me. I know how much he misses his dad who died only a year before we met, how he still harbors guilt over not being able to do more for him, and how he still has nightmares about that day. But what does all that matter when I don't even know his last name?

The only thing I haven't told him is about what I did last summer. I couldn't bring myself to confess to the worst thing I've ever done, not even to him. Ten was the one person in my life who didn't know what happened, and I wanted to keep it that way. To hang on to that past life, from before I ruined everything.

"Who's texting you?" Juliet asks. "Ten?"

I try not to flinch. "Nobody. I actually haven't heard from him in a few days. I think he's ghosting me."

"If he is, then he's a loser. Forget him." She shrugs like it's no big deal. Because Juliet doesn't know what it's like to experience rejection or insecurity. "Text me when you're done with class so we can grab lunch."

She strides off, boots smacking with every step. A couple of scrawny guys waiting for their classroom to open up watch every sway of her hips. She'd eat them alive.

While the professor in my Intro to Statistics class gives us an overview of the syllabus, I ignore the first buzz from my phone in my pocket. But when my phone vibrates again, I can't resist the temptation to check.

Even though I tell myself not to hang on to hope, the disappointment still deflates me when neither of the texts are from Ten.

The first is from Dad.

> **DAD**
> Hope you have a great first day, kiddo! Feel free to call whenever you want to tell me about your classes or if you need anything.

The other text is from an unknown number.

> **UNKNOWN**
> You're not getting away that easy.

My heart drops.

Fuck. This has to be Marcus. Or one of his former teammates. What if they're looking for me?

I screenshot the text, and even though at this point I'm not sure he'll even read my message, I send it to Ten.

> **SIENNA**
> What do you think the odds are that this is a wrong number?

My heart pounds. Even if I block the number, Marcus will text me from another.

Ten won't let this message go ignored. Even if he's pissed at me for some reason, he cares about me. He wouldn't have stayed my friend for so many years if he didn't.

He'll text me back. He won't let me deal with this alone.

But as the professor drones at the front of the lecture hall and the minutes tick by, my phone screen doesn't light up. He doesn't respond.

Maybe he actually doesn't give a fuck. I don't know when the hell everything changed between us or what I did wrong.

I thought coming to Diamond would be the answer to all my problems, but instead, my whole life is going up in flames.

I'm only a couple of hours away from Wakefield. Marcus could drive here in a single day. What if he somehow manages to track me down?

Maybe no matter where I go, I'll never be truly safe.

Chapter 8
Luke

OVER THE HISS of skates slicing through the ice and my hammering heart echoing in my ears, Knox shouts, "Ease up, Valentine! You're gonna kill yourself."

"Ignore him!" Damien yells. "Rockefeller is just afraid you'll be better than him."

While they argue, I ignore both of them, chasing the puck between the orange cones over and over. Beneath my helmet, sweat drips from my hair.

But no matter how hard I push my body, I can't get the image of that screenshot Sienna sent me out of my head.

Some prick threatened her. And other than tracking down who the phone number belongs to, there's nothing I can do for her. No way I can protect her. And I couldn't even respond to her. Had to keep being the douchebag who ignores his friend when she needs help.

I'm fucking tired of feeling helpless. Like I can't do anything to protect the people I care about. Not Pop or Chloe or Sienna.

"Bring any puck bunnies home last night?" Knox asks.

Drown in You

I finally take a break, skating to the wall and leaning against it while I catch my breath. My lungs heave, starved of oxygen. "Who I fuck is none of your business."

"What I don't get is how he hasn't been balls-deep in his hot stepsister every night," Damien calls.

My fists clench. "Shut the fuck up, Vanderbilt. We don't talk about each other's sisters, remember?"

I would've been balls-deep in Sienna after a romantic candlelit dinner if she wasn't so set on avoiding me. As if finding out we're step-siblings somehow negates the mind-blowing night we shared. How can she just avoid me like nothing happened? I know when I've made a girl come, and she did. Hard. Every kiss, every moan, every breath—we were in sync from the moment we walked through that door together. We knew exactly what to do to each other because we know each other better than anyone else does. We're meant to be, and she'll learn that soon enough.

"And moms," Knox adds. "You know how hard it is for me not to talk about how much I want to bone Damien's mom every game?"

Damien punches his arm before turning back to me with a salacious grin. "I'm just saying, I wouldn't let the whole step-sister thing stop me. Not like you two grew up together. You can fuck her, just don't marry her."

I don't care who the hell our parents are married too—they're not stopping me from marrying her. She's mine. But if keeping my mouth shut means she'll stay here with me, that's what I'll do.

Now that I've finally had Sienna in my arms, I'm not letting her out of my sight. I've failed too many people I care about. I won't fail her.

Finn takes my place at the orange cones, chasing the puck as he darts between them. He's the best offensive player on our team. Usually, we don't hear a word out of him, and when we do, we're lucky if it's a full sentence. Yet the puck bunnies love him.

"Tell him, Ashby!" Knox calls.

Finn shrugs, keeping his eye on the puck. "I'd make my stepsister scream."

The other Devils hoot, and I shake my head. "Good thing you assholes don't have sisters."

"I have a hot cousin." Damien smirks. "I might give her a ride too."

Knox shakes his head. "Too far."

"You assholes training or gossiping?" Wes barks. He's not usually late for practices and workouts, but when he is, you can guarantee it's because he was fucking Violet Harris.

I screwed things up with Violet too. I believed an asshole like Trey Lamont over her. I'm partially to blame for him and a few of the other Devils kidnapping and attacking her. If I hadn't believed Trey, if I hadn't resented her for Chloe's death, I would've seen that Violet was a victim, not a villain.

Since last semester, I've been trying to make amends for the way I treated her. The way we all treated her. Wes led the charge until Trey took over, but I played a role. I could've stood up for her, I could've refused to participate, but I didn't. I wanted my sick, twisted revenge on Violet too.

But instead of getting back at me, she's forgiven me. I get what Chloe saw in her. Why they were best friends. Now that she's lost Chloe, I'm trying to be the friend Violet deserves.

"We were just discussing how Valentine won't fuck his stepsister." Knox winks at me.

God, I fucking hate them. They're lucky they're like my brothers. I'd love to tell them exactly how hard I already fucked my stepsister, but Sienna will never forgive me if she finds out I spilled our little secret.

Drown in You

Wes steals the puck from Finn, aiming it at the net. It sails right in. "If Violet was my stepsister, that wouldn't stop me."

I'VE GOT a full schedule and other shit to do, yet here I am, stalking my stepsister around campus.

From the balcony above her head, I watch her at a table in the University Center. Her laptop is charging while she types away, fingers occasionally drifting from the keyboard to rip off a chunk of a breadstick and dip it in tomato sauce. Every time she sucks the red liquid from her finger, my cock twitches.

For some reason, everyone is keeping the cause of her arrival a secret. But like Ma said, we're family now. So no more keeping secrets from me. Who gave her those bruises? Who is she running from? Why didn't she tell Ten? What else has she kept from me?

Whether they like it or not, I'm finding out.

Below the balcony, Sienna remains blissfully unaware of her stepbrother tracking her every move.

Behind me, Finn hunches over his laptop at our round table, actually doing the classwork we need to get done before practice this afternoon. The bullshit work for my Intro to Nutrition class can wait—this is more important.

"How do you track somebody's phone?"

Finn doesn't respond to my question. He keeps typing on his laptop, and I'm about to ask if he heard me until he points at his screen. He's pulled up a step-by-step guide on how I can track Sienna's phone. Only issue is I need to get my hands on it.

"Thanks." I clap him on the shoulder. "You know, you're my favorite person with selective mutism."

That manages to get a rare grunt of amusement out of him before I grab my shit and take off down the stairs.

As soon as Sienna leaves her seat to throw away the empty box of breadsticks, I make my move.

Her phone peeks out of her bag. All I need to do is install a GPS app and share her location with my phone. Then I'll be able to find her wherever she goes.

But when I grab the phone, her screen is locked. *Fuck.* I try a few of the usual suspects, but Sienna is smart enough not to make 0-0-0-0 her passcode.

Wait. I bet—*yes*. I grin at the screen as it unlocks. 1-0-1-0. Ten-ten. That's my girl.

My thumbs sweep across the screen to download the app and enable location sharing.

When I spot her heading my way with a wary grimace, I tuck her phone behind my back.

I like her like this. More toned down than the sexy seductress I met at the hotel. Not as try-hard as the selfies she used to post on social media. Her distressed jeans don't reveal any bare skin beneath and her sweater is loose over her chest, concealing her perfect tits. The long sleeves of her cardigan cover any bruises that may still be lingering underneath and the hem hits below her ass, giving none of the guys here anything to ogle. But I do anyway.

Not staring at her is impossible. She's got the kind of round, innocent face that makes you want to protect her. Bright, wary green eyes that make you want to chase her because she'll make the most beautiful prey. And pouty lips that make you want to slide your cock between them. That make you want to say something, anything, just to make her smile.

No, Sienna will never hide from me now.

"Luke." Her voice is curt as she slides into her chair, already dropping her gaze from me to her bag.

"Hey, sis." I love the way the nickname drives her insane. She wants to rip my head off and I'd love to see her try. Not really a fan of the new legal status of our relationship myself, but getting her riled up makes blood pump to my cock.

Her brows furrow when she digs through her bag, frantic.

"Looking for this?" I hold her phone up and out of reach when she grabs for it.

"How did you get my phone?" Her eyes narrow, and I shouldn't be getting off on her anger this much.

"Maybe you should be more careful about leaving valuables lying around where anyone can take them."

"Gee, thanks." She holds out her hand. "Please give me my phone back."

"Why are you so paranoid?" I flick a brow up at her. "Hiding something? Nudes?"

God, I hope so. I'll send them to my number right now.

She folds her arms over her chest. "No, but it's my phone, and I deserve privacy."

"We're family now, sis. There's nothing private between us." I lean closer to murmur in her ear. "Not anything inside your phone. Or beneath your clothes."

Sienna snatches the phone from my grasp, her fingers grazing my skin. The brush of contact is too short-lived. I need more. I've never craved someone the way I crave her.

"What are you even doing here?" Sienna snaps. "Are you following me?"

"Ma said to keep an eye on you."

"Pretty sure she didn't mean *stalk* me. Don't you have something better to do? Class or practice or something? Maybe a puck bunny to bang with your buddies in the locker room?"

"Not my style. I'm a one-woman-at-a-time kind of guy."

She sighs. "I really don't know why you're being like this. Sure, we had a great time that night, but—"

"We had an *amazing* night, Sienna. A night I can't get out of my head."

That shuts her up.

If only she knew that the night in her hotel room wasn't just a random one-night stand—it was the culmination of years of suppressed attraction and the best friendship either of us has ever had.

She can't know that I'm the masked man she's been talking to for years—she never can—but maybe if she did, she wouldn't be fighting me so hard on this. If our whole relationship hadn't been built on a lie, maybe she wouldn't give a fuck about our parents' marital status either and she'd fall for me the way I've fallen for her, no matter what anybody had to say about it.

"You know the last time I slept through the night? The last time I didn't have any thoughts in my head except about the girl in bed with me?" I step closer, forcing her neck to crane so she can meet my gaze. Her jasmine scent is intoxicating and I want to wrap her around me. Wrap those thighs around my face and breathe her in, get another mouthwatering taste. "You gave me that. I can do the same for you if you let me."

Her nostrils flare, even as her eyes soften. "Sex is off the table ever since we found out our parents are married. But if you need someone to talk to—"

"We don't need to have sex on the table. We can do it on the floor, in our beds, on the couch, in the shower—"

"Stop." Sienna jumps up from her seat, chair squealing against the shiny floor. She stuffs her laptop and phone in her bag, swinging it over her shoulder. "I told you, this isn't happening."

I cup her chin before she shakes me off. Her gaze darts around the room at the nearby students too engrossed in their own work and lives to notice us, but to her, we're under a spotlight. "And I told you it is."

"So, what?" She blinks at me, angry tears shimmering. "You're going to force me?"

Her voice wobbles, but she can't possibly believe I would ever force her. That I would ever have to. When I have Sienna again, she will be a willing and eager participant. "This isn't just about sex, Sienna. This is way more than that. And I won't need to force you. You'll be begging for it."

She scoffs, rolling her eyes even as she gulps. "Yeah, right."

When she's about to walk away from me, I pull her back and lean down until my mouth brushes against her ear. She shivers. "I can't wait to hear you beg for my cock, sweetheart."

With that promise looming over her head, her green eyes widen. She doesn't know what to expect from me. She can't predict my next move. I like that.

Chapter 9

Sienna

IN THE DINING HALL, Luke sits with Violet, Juliet, and a few of his giant teammates, the Devils. The intimidating, hulking, slightly terrifying, devastatingly handsome group of hockey players.

Wes Novak, Knox Rockefeller, Damien Vanderbilt, and Finn Ashby. Violet has apparently already locked Wes down, and I can't blame her. His dark brown hair and blue eyes are striking.

Luke tracks my every move with predatory focus. Somehow, he can sense me as soon as I enter a room, sharp gaze lasering in on me through the sea of faces.

This isn't just about sex, Sienna. This is way more than that. How could he say that when we've barely known each other for more than five seconds? Sure, the sex was incredible, but I'm not egotistical enough to think that night could've been enough to make him fall for me. Maybe he'd really say anything to get in my pants again. He's probably more turned on now that I'm the forbidden stepsister, like every other guy browsing a porn site.

Drown in You

I need to get better at avoiding him. This campus is big enough that I should be able to stay away from him easily. Tonight, I screwed up.

"Sienna!" Violet waves.

I lift my chin and head for their table, the Devils' eyes on me every step of the way. My stepbrother's rapt attention makes my cheeks burn.

When I aim for the last open seat next to Juliet, Knox moves down. Forcing me to sit between him and Luke.

I plaster on a smile, pretending I'm grateful for the gesture and not fantasizing about kicking him.

"Glad you could join us, Sienna." Knox grins at me.

"Thanks." I dare a glance at Finn and Damien—they're both watching me like hawks. I guess they've gotten their fill of ogling Juliet. Or maybe they're fantasizing about us both.

I don't dare give Luke a fraction of my attention.

When I set my plate down, I tell Juliet, "I see you've met everyone."

"We ran into each other in the library." Violet beams at Juliet like this is the best possible news. "I introduced her."

Juliet and Violet. Their names are so similar and yet they couldn't be more different. Juliet has long, black hair mixed with shocks of red, while Violet has cropped, simple brown locks. Violet is short and tiny, while Juliet is nearly five-eight and regal with enviable curves. Juliet has a stud in her nose, multiple rings in her ears, a piercing through her eyebrow, and tattoos on her arms and who knows where else while Violet's skin is entirely unblemished. Violet has a cute librarian kind of look while Juliet is a goth queen. Yet somehow this new friendship blossoming between the three of us makes sense.

"*You* went to the library?" I raise an eyebrow at my best friend. I've been trying to get her to listen to my smutty audiobooks for years, and now we transfer to Diamond University and she's suddenly a reader?

Juliet rolls her eyes, rimmed with dark liner. "For research. I'm doing a project on serial killers."

"Every project you do is on serial killers."

"*Every* project?" Knox lifts a brow, amused.

Damien leans forward, elbows on the table. I don't think he ever smiles, but there's a spark in his dark eyes. "Sounds like we got a little psycho on our hands."

Juliet tosses her braid over her shoulder. She's used to attention from guys. As intimidating as the Devils are, they don't faze Juliet. "I'm obsessed. Sue me."

"Is your roommate eating with us?" I ask Violet.

She nods to the Devils. "They're my roommates. I was supposed to share a dorm with my roommate from last semester, but she transferred to Harvard because she's brilliant. So I'm staying with Wes in his room."

Speaking of her boyfriend, his gaze is locked on her and he smiles when she catches his eye. I've just met them and they're already the cutest couple I've ever seen.

Knox groans. "Yeah, and it sucks for the rest of us."

"Like you three aren't louder than us," Wes says.

Juliet's eyes light up. "What?"

"Not like that," Damien growls. "We like sharing our puck bunnies."

"Who? You, Knox, and Luke?"

For some reason, my stomach twists at the mention of Luke. At the thought of him with Damien and Knox and some girl, all of them taking turns fucking her. Is that how he's been spending his nights after practices?

"Me, Damien, and Finn," Knox corrects. "Luke doesn't share."

I nearly jump when a finger brushes against my knee,

stroking gently over the small patch of skin exposed through my distressed jeans. At my side, Luke's face remains impassive. No one would have any idea he's touching his stepsister under the table.

I'm about to leap out of my chair with some excuse to get the hell out of here when Knox says, "We're going to the bars tonight. You two should come with us."

"Yeah. Come," Damien adds, voice dripping with innuendo as he eye-bangs my best friend.

Juliet ignores him, but she nods at Violet. "If you'll be there, we're in."

"I'm not," I blurt. When all eyes turn to me, I add quickly, "I'm not . . . feeling great. I think I'll skip it tonight."

A night out with new friends and a few gorgeous hockey players actually sounds like just the distraction I need, but not if Luke will be there. He's the reason I need a distraction in the first place.

Under the table, his hand squeezes my knee, but I refuse to look at him to determine whether it's a warning or a threat.

If Luke will be there, I need to stay far away. Especially where alcohol is involved. Last time, we gave in to our inhibitions. Far too easily and quickly.

"What? No, you can't!" Juliet leans across Knox to grab my hand. Her boobs nearly brush his arm, and he doesn't mind at all. "You have to come with us. It won't be any fun without you."

"As long as I'm there, it'll be fun," Knox objects.

"*Please*, Sienna."

Damn it. She knows exactly how to appeal to my people-pleaser side.

"We need another girl to balance out all this testosterone," Violet adds.

Beside her, Wes nods. "That's true."

"Drinks will be on us," Damien promises.

Great, now they're ganging up on me. I force a smile. "I guess I can come for a little while."

They all launch into plans for meeting up. Luke's finger on my knee resumes its casual strokes back and forth across my skin. Shivers race down my spine, nipples peaking beneath my bra.

I try to cross my legs to move out of his grasp, but his palm keeps me rooted firmly in place. That shouldn't cause a flood between my legs. Not from him.

Luckily, everyone is distracted when he leans over and murmurs in my ear. "Don't worry, sweetheart. I'll protect you."

Like it's other men I'm worried about at the bar.

No, the only man I'm worried about getting his hands on me is my stepbrother.

Violet stands with her empty plate. "Sienna, want to grab dessert with us?"

I've barely even touched the food on my plate, but I leap to my feet. "Yes!"

As soon as Luke's hand is off my knee, my racing heart slows. Violet waits until we're out of earshot near the dessert bar before she grins at me and Juliet. "So which of the Devils do you have your eyes on?"

I'm about to sputter that I'm not checking out any of them, I'm not interested in dating anybody, and as a matter of fact, I'm celibate.

But thank god, Juliet answers first. "None of them could keep up with me and all the kinky shit I'm into."

Violet's grin widens. "Like what?"

"Masks, choking, blood, somnophilia, degradation."

"The vanilla stuff," I add.

Violet gives a short laugh. "I know the perfect guy for you, but he got expelled last semester."

Juliet quirks a dark brow. Her interest is piqued. "What'd he do?"

"Spiked girls' drinks, cut me with a knife, and nearly killed my boyfriend."

Oh fuck. I guess it's a good thing he got kicked off campus. The other Devils are already intimidating enough, let alone a guy like that.

"Holy shit." Juliet's blue eyes widen, but there's a spark of interest. She is absolutely twisted. "Is he in prison?"

"Of course not." Violet's mouth sours. "Daddy's money got him out of trouble. I won't be surprised if he ends up back here. I just hope I graduate before then."

My body temperature spikes. Damn. I hope I do too. I left Wakefield to get away from guys like that.

"Minus the trying to kill someone thing, he sounds like just my type," Juliet concedes.

"Please." I roll my eyes playfully. "You'd love a murderer for a boyfriend."

"*Serial killer*," Juliet corrects. "And it's called hybristophilia, thank you very much." She leans around me to blatantly check out the Devils. "Out of the ones who are still on campus, though, I'd say Sienna's stepbrother is the cutest."

I wish I didn't agree with her.

"What about you, Sienna?" Violet smiles at me.

I blurt out the first name that pops into my head. "Knox."

He flirted with me pretty blatantly. If I wanted someone to help me forget about my night with Luke and get him to leave me alone, I'm sure an hour alone with Knox would do the trick. His charm and cocky grin only add to his appeal. He knows how to stroke an ego, that's for sure. He'd probably be plenty of fun in bed.

The other two Devils are viable options too. Damien wears a permanent scowl, a line etched between thick brows pulled down over black eyes. He would probably throw me around like a ragdoll and I would love every second. Finn is silent but his looks are devastating and he's most likely the type to make you see God when he gets his hands on you. I could fuck any of them and have a great time, and by the way they all stared at me when we met, I have no doubts they would let me.

But I'm not sure a wild night with one of them would be enough to push Luke away. He might even become more possessive. And as much as I hate to admit it, I doubt a night with any of them would come close to my night with Luke.

"I don't blame you." Violet beams. "He's single. I'm not sure he's looking to commit to anyone, though."

I wave her off. "I'm not either."

I've never wanted a relationship, and I certainly don't want one now.

Juliet lifts an invisible glass of champagne. "To staying single and fucking happy."

"So what's it like being Luke's new stepsister?" Violet asks.

Ugh, I wish she had asked me anything else. I'd rather talk about the weather than about Luke. "It's . . . kind of awkward. The whole situation is." Biggest understatement of my life. "I'm not really close with my dad, so I kind of feel like an outsider."

"It'll get better. Luke is a really good guy when you get to know him. He's just been dealing with a lot since Chloe."

Chloe. She must be his ex. Maybe it was thoughts of her haunting him the night we met. "What happened with Chloe?"

Violet sighs, soft brown eyes turning somber as she grabs a cookie. "She died. It happened at a party last summer. Chloe's drink got spiked, and I . . . pushed her in the pool. She drowned."

Juliet mutters, "Shit."

My hand flies to my chest. "Oh my god. I'm so sorry."

I can't imagine the burden Violet has had to bear since that night. Losing her friend and possibly even feeling responsible.

She manages a small, thin-lipped smile. "Thanks. Wes and I have had each other to lean on, but Luke . . . he won't really open up to anybody. I worry about him, honestly."

"I'll get him to crack." Juliet studies Luke like he's a specimen under a microscope. "I'm a psych major."

"So they were friends?" I have a good feeling I already know the answer, but I want confirmation from someone who obviously knows Luke better than I do.

Violet doesn't answer right away. She keeps her attention on the dessert bar. "They were kind of more than that. They went out on a date and kissed once, but that was it."

Juliet shovels a peanut butter cookie into her mouth. "You think he's still hung up on her?"

For some reason, my breath catches.

"Not exactly." Violet glances to the table where Wes is staring at her, and Luke is staring at me.

The knot in my chest tightens.

The other Devils are all enraptured by a girl with platinum-blonde hair that drifts past her waist. She's small, shoulders hunched as she aims for an empty, secluded table in the corner and eats alone. An ethereal beauty, even from this distance. They really are insatiable.

"I think he feels guilty for some reason," Violet says. "He's hard on himself. But I get it. I felt a lot of guilt over Chloe's death too, for a long time. We were all there that night, but none of us saved her."

Juliet's gaze flashes to me. At the guilt she knows still weighs on me over what happened to Marcus. Maybe my new stepbrother and I have more in common than I thought.

Chapter 10

Luke

At the bar, the girls still haven't shown. My foot bounces against my stool as I clutch the drink in my hand, ignoring the puck bunnies fawning over Finn, Damien, Knox, and me. They all know better than to bother with Wes. He's only got eyes for one girl, and now, so do I.

My phone buzzes in my pocket. A text from Sienna to Ten.

> SIENNA
> Going out tonight! I miss you.

She follows up the text with a photo she snapped in the mirror. My mouth waters at that little black dress hugging her every curve. She knows exactly what she's doing, trying to bait me into responding. I wish I could. Wish I could tell her how gorgeous she is, no matter what she's wearing. But she'll just have to settle for hearing it from me in person.

"Finally!" Wes calls, leaving my side to meet Violet.

Behind her, Juliet is dolled up in a skimpy, all-black outfit, and Sienna—

Fuck. *Sienna.*

Drown in You

The little black dress she squeezed into leaves little to the imagination. She's even more gorgeous now that I can see the way she moves in it. Judging by the way her gaze shifts from confident to cautious when she spots me, she didn't pick that dress herself.

Sienna grabs her friends, dragging them to the dance floor with the few people hammered enough to dance in public. Wes follows without hesitation, happy to grind against Violet's ass.

A small smile crawls across my lips. Sienna thinks she can avoid me tonight. She'll learn soon enough that she'll never escape me. That she won't want to.

Knox grins when the girls form a circle to dance together and smacks his glass down on the bar. "That's my cue."

I clap a hand on his shoulder, keeping him rooted in place. "Keep your hands off my sister."

He smirks at me. "Relax, Valentine."

At a nearby booth, Damien whispers in the ear of the redhead on his lap, and Finn rests a casual hand on a puck bunny's hip while she grinds against him.

On the dance floor, Sienna is magnetic. Her movements are awkward and choppy, but she's grinning. My watchful gaze is forgotten as she loses herself in the music and laughter. A glimpse of that girl she was when we met at the hotel—confident, bold, bright. She's good at hiding the pain underneath. So good at compartmentalizing, you'd almost think she wasn't a girl who'd been beaten and chased out of her hometown. The kind of girl who hides her dark secrets beneath humor and smiles.

I can't take my eyes off her. I haven't been able to since we met. She's more enchanting than I ever imagined.

Once she finally leaves the dance floor, fanning her flushed cheeks, she tries to ignore me. Pretends I don't exist.

I slide over the drink I ordered for her. "Reminds me of the night we met."

Her nose scrunches at the glass. "How do I know you didn't spike this with something?"

My jaw clenches. She must not have heard about what happened to Chloe. "I'd never do anything like that. To you or anybody."

She blanches at the sharp edge to my tone, grabbing up the glass but still refusing to take a sip. "Okay. Good."

"Relax. It's water. Figured you could use some after all that dancing."

Finally, Sienna takes a hesitant sip. Relief washes over her when she discovers I'm not lying, and she downs half the glass. She takes a seat, leaving a few empty stools between us. "Please tell me you didn't watch me dance."

I move to sit right beside her, her intoxicating jasmine scent drifting up my nose, and she stiffens. Her bare thigh is prominently on display, begging to be squeezed, kissed, sucked. "How could I not watch you dance in that dress?"

She rolls her eyes, even as my words make her throat bob.

Now that she's inches away, I rake my gaze over every inch. Where the neckline plunges to reveal her cleavage, where the hem stops just below her ass, where the fabric cinches in at the waist and hugs over her hips. She's beautiful in that dress. In everything. In nothing.

Sienna takes another gulp of her water, keeping her gaze fixed on the alcohol behind the bartender. "You should find a girl who isn't your stepsister to hook up with tonight. Some other girl who can help you sleep through the night." She gestures around the bar. "There are plenty of options."

If only she knew she's not just my stepsister or some girl. She's everything. Everything I didn't know I've been waiting for.

Drown in You

At the booth, the redhead who'd been in Damien's lap now has her hand on his chest and some other guy's. Probably a boyfriend or a jealous ex. Damien is ready to rip the guy's head off for her. He'll do just about anything for a night with new puck-bunny pussy.

Sienna would never grind against some other guy while her boyfriend was ten feet away.

I shake my head. "There are no other options. There's only you."

For a second, she preens at the praise before she buries the joy back down. She loves my flattery, even if she doesn't want to admit it. "You shouldn't say things like that to me."

If it was Ten saying that to her, she'd love it.

Damien and the jealous boyfriend stomp toward the exit, taking the fight outside. The redhead protests at their backs, even as she grins, loving that two guys are about to fight over her.

I grit my teeth. I don't want to leave Sienna at the bar alone, but right now, Damien needs me more than she does.

"Don't drink anything anyone gives you," I warn her before I follow the group outside.

In the cold, the redhead shivers in her tiny skirt and top while the guys swing fists and land punches with sickening thuds on each other's arms and jaws. Damien's buzzed enough to be pissed but not stumbling drunk like his opponent. He doesn't need my help, and I'm not jumping in to catch an elbow to the gut or a fist to the face if I don't have to. Hockey fights are hard enough on the body—I don't need to get into fights off the ice too.

Once the dude is laid out, the redhead gloms onto Damien's arm. He shakes her off. Already lost interest.

I clap him on the shoulder as he heads back for the door. "You good?"

"Great. Knuckles barely even hurt."

A loud burst of laughter greets us when we head back in, carrying over the thumping music. I'd recognize that high, musical laugh anywhere.

Who the fuck is making her laugh like that?

Chapter 11

Sienna

KNOX IS PRACTICALLY DROOLING over the sluttiest dress Violet and Juliet plucked from my closet.

Tonight, Juliet is a goth princess in a short black skirt and top that barely qualifies as a shirt, stopping just below her boobs. Tights with a rose pattern cling to her legs and all she needs to complete the look is an onyx crown. Violet has traded in her long, flowing skirt for a sinful red dress that hugs her every curve. Wes-approved, I'm sure.

Though I initially protested because I didn't want to find out how Luke would react to seeing me in this dress, I'm glad they pushed me to wear it. As soon as Luke left the bar with Damien, Knox beelined for me.

"Sienna waits for you!" He beams, leaning against the bar next to me, so close his heavy cologne fills my nose. His boyish face is already flushed. From alcohol or dancing his ass off, I'm not sure. Could be both. "Get it? Sienna waits for you? Like Vienna by—"

I giggle. "I get it."

I take another gulp from my water. I shouldn't be touched

that Luke ordered me a glass of water after noticing how much I sweat my ass off on the dance floor.

I'm painfully aware of his absence and that he could return at any moment while Knox regales me with a hilarious story from their practice yesterday. I clutch at my stomach, the laughter making my abs ache until someone yanks my arm.

"Come on." Luke wrenches me away from Knox, jaw hard and gray eyes blazing. "We're going home."

"Don't be like that, Valentine," Knox protests.

"Let me go!" I try to pull out of his grasp, but it's like fighting stone.

As he tugs me toward the door, I catch my friends' eyes. Violet waves and Juliet mouths for me to text her.

I'll definitely be texting her to come rescue me from wherever Luke plans on locking me up.

Once we're outside, the freezing January air pierces me to the bone. I finally manage to wrench out of his iron grip and clutch my arms to my shivering body. "What the hell, Luke?"

He rounds on me. "Why do you hook up with guys you barely know?"

His sharp tone momentarily withers me. But who the hell is he to judge who I hook up with? Not that I was even hooking up with Knox. We were literally just having a conversation. I don't owe Luke Valentine any sort of explanation.

I narrow my eyes at him even as my teeth chatter. "Why do you hook up with girls you barely know?"

He's a big fucking hypocrite considering he hooked up with me the night we met.

"I don't." He steps closer, and I'm forced to lift my chin to meet his gaze. But I'm not backing down. Not this time. I'm done letting my stepbrother intimidate me.

When Luke followed me up to my hotel room, I assumed

Drown in You

one-night stands were a regular experience for him. It never occurred to me that we were both behaving out of character.

"I've never done anything like that either," I admit. "I at least know their names first."

"So why did you?"

Maybe I should end this conversation here. We should be pretending that night never happened, not rehashing it right in front of a bar where any drunk college student stumbling past could overhear.

But his gaze is heavy, simmering with a quiet need to hear the answer.

"I think . . . I think I was willing to that night because I didn't want to be at my father's wedding. And I was lonely and lost and I don't know." I'm blabbering now, teeth chattering as I study the few inches of space between our feet. Between his expensive boots and my old heels with exposed toes about to fall off.

The stress of everything with Marcus and the move and the new family, the sting of rejection when Ten kept ignoring me, it was all too much for one night. I needed an escape, and Luke gave me that.

"For some reason, I felt like I could trust you. And when it was happening . . . it was like I'd known you way longer than ten minutes."

He put that disposable camera in front of me and reminded me of the best friend I had. Of the friend I was missing. Even though I've only known Luke for about a week, something about him is weirdly familiar. Like we knew each other in a past life and our souls still remember the connection we shared.

But in this life, we're step-siblings and nothing can happen between us.

His finger hooks under my chin, tilting it up to force our eyes to meet. "It lasted a lot longer than ten minutes."

God. As if I could forget. No matter how much I wish I could.

"Come on." He leads the way to his car, and I'm grateful when he doesn't grab me by the arm or the hand. "I'm taking you home."

I could run back inside. Refuse to leave with him. Unless he wants to pick me up and drag me kicking and screaming, he can't force me. But I'm freezing, my limbs are drained, and my warm bed sounds perfect right now.

As we head for his car, I spot a red Cadillac parked along the sidewalk a few vehicles down.

My heart stops. The same car Marcus drives.

But no, he can't be here. He wouldn't follow me all the way to Diamond. His goal was to drive me out of Wakefield—he accomplished that. Besides, he wouldn't have any way of finding me. I wiped my existence from the internet, and there's no way Juliet's parents would've told him where we are.

I take a few deep breaths to try to slow my racing heart.

"What?" Luke frowns at me from where he stands by his car, door propped open for me.

I shake my head and force a smile. "Nothing."

In the car, I pull out my phone. No texts from Ten. I hate the way my heart still sinks with disappointment every time. I was hoping that photo in my dress would get him to respond. He'd at least tell me to have fun or be safe. But he's still ignoring me.

A hint of frustration joins the disappointment. I didn't do anything wrong, and there hasn't been a time I've ever needed him more. Yet this is when he chooses to abandon me, even after he knows how much my dad's abandonment screwed me up. He's always been my rock, but right now, he's being a shitty friend. But if I call him out on it, I'm terrified I'll only drive him further away.

Drown in You

Luke cranks on the heat, and I bite back my gratitude. He's blasting the heat because he's cold too—it's not just for me. He nods down to my phone. "What's wrong?"

"Nothing." But he keeps staring at me. We're not leaving until I give him an answer. "I just haven't heard from a friend in a while."

"What friend?"

I brace myself for his jealous streak. Not that he has any right to claim any sort of possession over me. I've known Ten way longer than Luke. "His name is Ten."

Luke flicks the turn signal and pulls away from the sidewalk. "Sounds like a dick."

I snort. "You don't even know him."

"Tell me about him."

That's not at all the response I expected. I would've assumed Luke would demand that I hand my phone over so he could delete and block Ten's number. "He's really funny." I smile just thinking of all our corny inside jokes. "He always knows the right thing to say. He wears a mask, so I don't know what he looks like, but I know him better than anybody. He's basically been my rock since I was fifteen. I tell him almost everything. Even more than I've told Juliet."

"Almost everything?" Luke lifts a brow. "What haven't you told him?"

"If I didn't tell him, I'm not telling you."

In the darkness, with the glow of the streetlights passing, Luke is impossibly handsome. Still the most gorgeous man I've ever seen. "If he was in front of you right now, what would you say to him?"

God, there's so much I want to say to Ten. I want to smack him and scream at him for making me worry, for driving me crazy, for making me doubt myself the way my father did. But I also want to throw my arms around him and thank him. Thank him for being there for me every time I needed someone these past few years, thank him for reassuring me that my dad leaving me behind wasn't my fault, thank him for always making me feel loved and worthy.

"I'd tell him he's an asshole for ghosting me," I say. "And that I missed him and he better never do it again. And he owes me, like, ten dozen flowers."

"Would that make you feel better?"

"Worth a shot." I need to change the subject. Talking about Ten is bringing the familiar prickle of tears to my eyes. "So have you talked to your mom lately?"

"Yeah, she texts and calls every day."

It's actually kind of sweet that Luke talks to his mom every day. I grit my teeth. It's annoying that anything he does is sweet. "So does my dad. My mom calls me every day too, but she's not living it up in Europe."

Luke averts his gaze from the road to give me a small smile. "I'm glad your dad's trying to fix things with you."

His sincerity throws me. He cares more than I'd expect for someone who's still little more than a stranger. "Yeah. Me too."

"You deserve a dad who does more than send you cards and call you on your birthday."

My spine stiffens. "How do you know about that?"

Luke hesitates for a second, concentrating on the road in front of him. "He mentioned it. Pretty sure that's his biggest regret—missing so much of your life. And it should be."

For a twisted stepbrother entirely too possessive of his stepsister, he's also thoughtful and sweet. Those may be the worst things about him.

"My biggest regret is being the reason he left. One of my biggest regrets, anyway."

Luke's jaw clenches. "He didn't leave because of you."

"Why else would he have basically disappeared from my

Drown in You

life? I was too loud, talked too much, couldn't sit still. He and my mom never fought about anything. Then they got a divorce, and he was never around. So I pretty much know he left because of me."

"That's ridiculous."

For the first time since sliding into Luke's car, I glare at him. His attention is fixed on the road, leaving me to admire his profile. The hard, square jawline, the full lips, the dark blond hair curling in wisps around his ears. For a moment, I remind myself that I can't be attracted to my stepbrother. "How is it ridiculous?"

Luke's brows bend into a deeper frown and he slows when we approach the intersection near campus. "You weren't too wild or too loud or too much. That's called being a kid. And kids don't cause divorces—adults do. Your dad taking off and not being around for ten years isn't your fault. That's on him."

His words warm a cold part of my chest that even the heat blasting from the vents can't reach. They're oddly reminiscent of what Ten said to me when I confided in him about the divorce and the lack of a relationship with my dad. *It's not your fault. If he's not around, then he doesn't deserve you.*

Since my parents' split, I've lived with the gnawing guilt that I'm the one who drove him away. That if not for me, Mom wouldn't be left crying on the couch most nights. She wouldn't be hopping from man to man, trying to find the love she once shared with my father.

Luke wasn't there. Ten wasn't there. Neither of them knows the whole situation. But every part of me longs to believe them.

When Luke coasts through the intersection, passing the road that leads to Diamond University, I elbow him. "Hey! You missed our turn."

"We're not going back to Diamond," he says simply.

My heart skips. "Where are we going?"

"I told you. I'm taking you home."

"What? Back to Wakefield?" My voice goes up an octave. Is this his way of punishing me for daring to flirt with Knox? He's going to threaten to send me packing? Back home to face Marcus and his henchmen?

"No, back to *our* home, Sienna." His molten gaze melts me. "We need to check on the house and Bud."

"Bud? Who's Bud?"

"My dog. *Our* dog," he corrects with a smile.

My mind is whirling. "You have a dog? Who the hell has been feeding him and taking him outside this whole time?"

Luke shrugs. "Neighbors. The housekeeper. He's had plenty of care and attention, trust me."

"So why do we need to go back?"

"Because I told the housekeeper we'd be there. Give her a day off."

My nails bite into my palms. "Okay. Why do *I* have to be there? Can't you just go alone?"

Spending a night with Luke in his house without our parents is the worst possible idea. There will be no one around to distract us. No classes or practices to rush off to. No friends or roommates to barge in.

Just me and my stepbrother. Alone.

His wolfish grin brings a lump to my throat. "Because we're family now, sis."

Chapter 12

Luke

Sienna gapes as I lead her into the house until Bud barks and runs up to us, tail wagging so hard his whole ass shakes.

"You are so *cute!*" She drops to her knees, giggling while Bud licks her face as she pets him.

He already loves her. We both do. "Ma has a bedroom ready for you."

"It's cute the way you say *Ma*." The words are out of her mouth before she can think better of them.

"Yeah?" I smirk down at her.

"It's just that little hint of Southern accent that sneaks in. Don't get a big head about it." She finally straightens, even as she continues scratching between Bud's ears. "Your house is huge."

"Ma's a judge. She makes good money."

Not to mention my pops left her a million-dollar life insurance policy. She cried when she found out. Not from relief or happiness but because no amount of money could replace him. Nothing ever would.

Sienna's attention drifts to a framed photo hung on the wall among Ma's extensive collection. A wall devoted to memories. To ghosts. Her finger trails over the frame. "Is this your dad?"

I swallow the lump in my throat. A photo of Pop and nine-year-old me covered in mud we'd been flinging at each other. Ma snapped the photo while we were mid-laugh. Still one of my favorites of us. "That's him."

"You look *just* like him." She smiles.

"Yeah." I clear my throat. "You want to see your room?"

Sienna gets the hint and drops the subject, nodding. I lead the way upstairs, Bud's paws clicking behind us.

When I open the door to her new room, her face lights up. There's nothing in the world better than seeing her happy. "Wow. Your mom really outdid herself."

She skims the white bedspread made of the softest Egyptian cotton and the matching silk pillowcase before hugging the blackout curtains like they're her long-lost best friend. Now I'm jealous of fucking curtains. She swings open the double doors that lead to a walk-in closet before yanking on the bathroom door and gasping. "I can have my own bathroom?"

"Your own bathroom, your own room, your own TV." I wink at her. "But we're sharing a bed."

She whirls on me, scowling even as her eyes are wide. "Luke, no—"

"Come join me in the hot tub."

Her lips purse and she folds her arms. "It's thirty degrees out."

I shrug. "Best time to use the hot tub."

She shakes her head, grabbing the door and moving to shut it in my face. "No. I'm going to bed—"

I slap a palm against the door, bracing it open with ease. "I'll keep my hands to myself. Promise. At least until you beg for them all over you."

"I won't." Her throat bobs as she scrambles to come up with another excuse to avoid me. "I don't even have a swimsuit."

I smirk. "You have a bra and panties."

She rolls her eyes. "I'm not stripping down to my underwear in a hot tub with you."

"What's the difference between that and a bikini?" She doesn't have a quick response to that. "Exactly. So come on—get your ass downstairs. The hot water will help you relax before bed."

Without waiting for her to protest again, I leave her room to grab towels.

By the time I've been in the hot tub for ten minutes, Sienna still hasn't showed. I'm about to head upstairs and drag her out when she finally makes an appearance.

My heart drops. She's swapped her dress for my jersey, the hem reaching nearly to her knees.

"I hope you don't mind I borrowed one of your shirts." She scurries over to the hot tub across the frozen deck.

Jesus. She has no idea the effect seeing her in my jersey has on me. Beneath the bubbling water, my cock stiffens. The outline of her bra shows as she sinks into the water, and I wish she was naked beneath my jersey.

Silence falls between us as I fail to swallow the rock lodged in my throat at the sight of her. She briefly meets my gaze until her bashful green eyes flick away again, her fingers twirling around the end of her hair with restless energy.

I love how nervous I make her. How much she worries about what I'll do to her. About what she wants me to do to her.

"What's your major?" she blurts.

I should've braced myself for questions. She already knows Ten's major, but if I lie to her, she can easily find out the truth. Then she'll wonder why I lied in the first place and put the pieces of the puzzle together. I already slipped up in the car earlier. Nearly panicked when she asked how I knew her dad only sent her cards and called her on her birthday for years. I've gotta be more careful. "Kinesiology. I'll help athletes recover from injuries. Once I'm forced to retire from the NHL."

Hockey is hard on the body. Most players don't stay in the game past forty. I've known my backup plan since junior year of high school.

"Oh, really? That's Ten's major." A little smile flickers on her lips as she thinks of him. Me. "Why do you want to do that?"

I can't tell if she genuinely wants to know or if she's just making conversation to avoid awkward silence. It's adorable how she blabbers when she's nervous. That's one thing I didn't expect from the girl I met online. Even though I've known her for years, there's still so much left to learn.

So many secrets she's still keeping from me.

I rack my brain, trying to remember what I've told her as Ten. If I give away too much, she'll grow suspicious. For now, she's still in the dark. I need to keep her that way. "My pops was in the NHL. Then he got injured and couldn't play anymore. Not even recreationally. It always bothered him that we couldn't play together."

But that never stopped him from driving me to every practice and game. Never stopped him from being the loudest parent cheering from the stands. Never stopped him from volunteering to coach or to get up at the ass crack of dawn when I wanted to hit the ice for fun. Even if he couldn't be on the ice anymore, he never stopped smiling when I was.

That's the kind of dad Sienna deserves.

"That's . . . actually kind of sweet of you." The words leave Sienna's mouth with a bitter edge. Almost like she resents having to admit it out loud.

"Says the nursing major."

She lifts a brow. "How do you know that? Uncover that information while you were stalking me?"

For a second, I panic. Keeping track of what she's told me as the anonymous masked man and what she's told me since we met in person could quickly become a big fucking mess. "Mike asked you about your major on the way to the airport."

She nods. "Right. The horribly awkward car ride."

"Why nursing?" That's something someone who barely knows her would ask. Someone who hasn't already discussed with her at length the different majors she was considering senior year of high school. Nurse, doctor, vet, teacher. Unlike me, she hasn't had her life planned since she was sixteen. But it felt good, being the person whose opinion she cared about most. She trusted my judgment, trusted I'd encourage her toward the right path.

"I've always taken care of people," she says casually. "It's what I'm good at."

She'd be a great nurse. Caring, kind, empathetic. Not to mention every guy fantasizes about waking up in a hospital to a nurse like her.

Sienna bites her lip before asking, "What happened to your dad?"

Fuck. I really, really don't want to think about that. I've spent years trying to shut out the memory of my father's final moments, trying to preserve only the happy ones. The ones where he's smiling, laughing, cheering me on.

I've never shared the details of Pop's death with anyone. Not my friends, not Chloe, not even Sienna. All she knows is that Ten was there when his father died.

But for some reason, I want to tell her now. She wants to know, and maybe if I confide in her about this, she'll finally tell me why she's really here.

I shift on the slick bench, propping my elbows behind me

onto the cool, dry concrete. "He was driving me to hockey practice. He started having chest pain and swerving on the road." My stomach constricts, the memories rushing back. "I grabbed the steering wheel and jerked the truck to the side of the road. I managed to bring the truck to a stop and called 911. He passed out while the dispatcher told me the paramedics were on their way. They didn't get there in time."

Pop?

Pop. Pop!

I shook him. Expected him to come to, for his eyes to flash open any second.

They never did.

I'm glad you were the last thing he saw. That's what Ma told me at his funeral. As if I should've been grateful I witnessed my father's death. That I was right there, holding his hand, and still didn't save him.

"When the paramedics finally showed up, he was already gone."

Sienna scoots closer, green eyes soft with concern and maybe even pain. Almost as if she can feel my hurt like it's her own. Her hand starts to reach out, a girl used to providing comfort, but she withdraws it. She's always been so good at comforting me. The best.

She'll never know how many times she's saved me.

"I'm sorry, Luke," she murmurs. I can barely hear her over the bubbling water. "That's awful."

I nod. "It sucked."

"I bet you really miss him."

I'm forced to drag my gaze away from her and up to the lone, full moon in the dark sky before she catches a glimpse of the tears stinging my eyes. "Every day."

She inches over again. If she gets any closer, her bare leg will brush against mine, and I'm not sure I'll be able to hold

Drown in You

myself back. If I'll be able to stop myself from burying my cock inside her and driving all the painful thoughts away.

"Ten lost his dad too. So I know how much that can hurt."

I clear my throat, finally able to meet her eyes again. "What's the deal with you two?"

"Me and Ten? We're just friends."

"You sure?"

She rolls her eyes, but a blush creeps up to her cheeks. "I don't even know what he looks like. And he lives in California."

"And what if he moved here for you? Would you date him?" I'm not sure what I want her answer to be. We're the same person, but she doesn't know that. Which version of me would she choose?

"I don't know." She chews her lip. "I'd probably be too scared to screw up our friendship."

Disappointment wedges in my chest. Even if I came clean now, she still wouldn't want me.

"Luke." Sienna inches closer again, hesitant. "What happened with Chloe?"

My spine goes rigid.

Chloe. How the fuck does she know about Chloe? Violet must've told her. I've never mentioned Chloe to Sienna. I can't remember the last time I spoke her name out loud. Certainly not since Sienna showed up.

She doesn't get to know about Chloe when she's still keeping so much from me. I've admitted plenty to Sienna tonight. Now it's her turn.

"Why are you really here? Why did you leave Wakefield?"

Her mouth falls open as she debates whether she's finally going to tell me the truth.

A ringtone pierces the silent darkness around us.

Sienna jumps out of the hot tub, the water sloshing. My soaked jersey clings to every delicious curve of her body. She dries her hands with one of the towels before wrapping it around her shoulders and answering the phone. "Hey, Mom! No, I'm actually not at the dorm. Luke brought me to Dad's house."

She glances back at me only briefly before heading inside.

Leaving me alone with nothing but the silence and the water and the moon. Nothing but me and a drowning girl I can't save.

AFTER SHE GETS off the phone with her mom, Sienna snaps a photo of Bud and sends it to Ten.

> SIENNA
> I know you're a dog person. I met the sweetest pup today. Isn't he so cute?

When is she going to tell Ten about me? She'd never admit to what we did when we met or the fantasies she has about me, but she hasn't even mentioned my existence. Ten knows about everyone else. Do I mean that little to her?

I give her an hour alone before I sneak into her room and watch her sleep with a mask covering my face.

Beyond the soft glow of the nightlight, Sienna doesn't shift in her bed. Her eyes don't spring open to find a masked man watching her. Part of me hoped she'd wake up the second I snuck in here. Open that pretty little mouth to scream so I could shove my cock in it.

But she's oblivious. Chest rising softly with each deep, slumbering breath. Maybe sleep is the only time she finds any sort of peace now.

She could find it with me if she let herself.

Drown in You

My balls tighten, every inch of me longing to close the distance between us, slide my mask up, and bury my mouth between her legs. Eat her hard while she stirs slowly from sleep, make her come while she's still wondering whose head is between her legs, and get her screaming on my cock when she finally realizes it's me. There's nothing in the world I want more than to be the one who makes her moan, smile, laugh, scream.

If Ten is going to disappoint her, then I need to do everything I can to make up for it. Be the guy she wishes Ten would be.

I slide my hand past the waistband of my sweats and pull out my cock, the vein on the underside of my shaft already pulsing.

With a stroke down to the base, I imagine Sienna blinking awake. Eyes adjusting to the darkness to find her stepbrother in a mask jerking off to her sleeping form.

She'd protest, order me to get out. But I wouldn't. I'd saunter over to her bed, grinning as I watched her throat bob. Her eyes would pop wide open when I slid my hand into her hair to keep her head in place and shoved my cock past her lips. The protest would build in her throat, but she wouldn't be able to voice it around my dick filling her mouth.

My shaft would drag along her slick, soft tongue before hitting the back of her throat. Her gag would vibrate down my cock all the way to my balls. I'd have to fight off the orgasm rapidly building up as I rocked my hips back before driving my cock into her throat again. Again and again and again.

Then I'd rip off her panties, flip her on top of me, and eat her soaked pussy while she eagerly sucked my cock, both of us desperate for our own release and each other's.

Her gurgles would fill my ears and then her screams as her

pussy pulsed, and I'd spill every drop of hot cum down Sienna's throat—

My pants echo beneath the mask as I pump my cock. I grab the nearest item of clothing I can find.

Sienna's silky, black dress.

I wrap the fabric around my tip just before the cum explodes out. Bite back my groan, head tipping as I stroke my cock through every wave of my orgasm.

Cum covers Sienna's dress. The proof of exactly what she does to me.

Heart hammering, I drop her ruined dress on the floor. She's still sound asleep. Blissfully unaware of what her stepbrother just did in her room while she slept.

Sienna has no idea the effect she has on me. But she will.

I sneak closer, tempted to brush back the hair on her cheek. On her bedside table, the contents of her purse spill out. Her phone, her wallet, a tampon, lip balm . . . and the disposable camera.

She could've thrown it away by now. Ridding herself of all the memories of that night. But I mean more to her than she lets on.

S*** *means everything to me.

Chapter 13

Sienna

WHEN I SHUFFLE into Luke's enormous kitchen the next morning, the room is already filled with the delicious aroma of fried eggs and bacon. In front of the stove, a shirtless Luke flips strips of frying pork in a sizzling pan. But that's not what stops me in my tracks.

Dozens of flowers are bundled in bouquets, some on the table, others on the counters. Roses, lilies, tulips. "What are those for?"

Luke gives me a half-smile. "You said ten dozen flowers would make you feel better."

"That . . ." I can't come up with sufficient words to thank him. Even if the flowers didn't come from Ten, the gesture warms my heart. Just like when he knelt before me and kissed the bruises that dotted my bare skin. "That is . . . actually sweet. Thank you."

"Don't act so surprised. My last name is Valentine, after all."

I can't help but laugh at his cheesiness. "I won't be able to fit them all in my dorm."

He shrugs. "Leave some here; take some with you. They're yours. Do what you want with them."

"What am I supposed to tell people?" I skim a finger over a silky petal. My stepbrother bought me *ten dozen* flowers. How am I supposed to explain that?

He smirks. "Tell them any guy who thinks he has a shot with you better treat you as well as your stepbrother."

I flush. Luke Valentine leaves me speechless more than anyone I've ever met. "I'll send a bouquet home to Mom and leave some for Deb."

"Go for it." Luke nods at my clothes with a spark of amusement in his eyes. "Nice outfit."

"I couldn't find my dress." I left it in my room after slipping on Luke's jersey last night. But when I looked for it this morning to slip it back on, it was gone.

Part of me is relieved. After the way Luke looked at me last night when he saw me in that dress, if he saw me in it again this morning, he would've made me his breakfast.

I forgot to toss my underwear and his jersey in the dryer last night, so now I'm in the T-shirt and gym shorts I stole from his laundry. They're ridiculously oversized, the shirt reaching past my butt and the shorts hitting my calves, but he somehow still eats me up the way he did when I showed up to join him in the hot tub.

"It's in the trash."

I frown. "Why?"

He flashes a wolfish grin. "You really want to know?"

God. What the hell did he do to it? I shake my head. "No, I really don't."

With his fork, he points at a few plates on the table. "We've got scrambled and fried eggs, and butter, jam, or peanut butter for toast. Take your pick. Bacon will be ready soon."

Luke Valentine made breakfast for me. He bought me ten

Drown in You

dozen flowers. My new stepbrother is making it difficult to keep pushing him away.

"You should put a shirt on," I tell him. "The bacon fat could burn you."

He winks at me. "Thanks, Doc."

But he doesn't leave his spot in front of the stove. I huff and collapse into a seat at the table with my back to him. If he's going to walk around this house shirtless, then I simply won't look at him. He obviously knows at this point that I have a thing for muscular men. But I won't let him get to me.

Honestly, I'm shocked he didn't try sneaking into my room last night. My bedroom door doesn't have a lock, and I was certain that as soon as I got off the phone with Mom, he'd be sauntering in to fulfill his promise to share a bed with me. But he didn't.

Somehow, I managed to sleep more peacefully than I have in months.

My phone buzzes with a text from Juliet.

JULIET
I slept so much better without your snoring!!!

"Asshole," I grumble.

"What?" Luke sets the plate of bacon in front of me.

"You didn't hear me snoring, did you?"

"Oh, that was you? I thought someone was running a chainsaw."

I roll my eyes. "Ha ha."

Without another word, Luke leaves the kitchen. Is he going to let me eat alone? A confusing mix of relief and disappointment stirs in my belly. I should be grateful he's giving me space. It's what I've been asking for since we found out we're stepsiblings.

But I can't help the guilt that eats at me from our conversation in the hot tub last night. I asked him about how his father died and then about Chloe. Forced him to relive those painful memories. He told me about what happened to his dad, the heart-wrenching details of being at his father's side as he took his final breath. Unable to save him. Unable to do anything for him. Asking about Chloe was pushing it. He avoided the question entirely, changing the subject to my sudden arrival.

Thank god Mom called. Nothing good will come from Luke finding out the truth.

Drool hits my bare foot. Beneath the table, Bud wags his tail and blinks adorable, big brown eyes at me. I laugh and slip a slice of bacon beneath the table. "Don't tell Luke."

"Don't tell me what?"

I jump at his booming voice as he strides into the room. Seeing him barefoot in nothing but gray sweatpants makes butterflies flutter in my stomach.

He purposely left his sweats hanging low on his hips, proudly displaying the mouthwatering *V* that descends into his waistband. The Adonis belt. As a nursing major, I've been required to study male anatomy, and Luke Valentine is the best specimen I've ever seen.

I scramble for the orange juice in the middle of the table, tempted to drink from the jug but managing to pour a glass before chugging. "I shared my bacon with Bud."

"Careful. If he likes you too much, he won't let you leave." Luke sets a laptop down on the table in front of him, propping it open. The screen prompts him for a password. "What do you think Mike's password is?"

"Why are you trying to get into his laptop?"

"To dig up dirt," he says simply.

At least he's honest. I wish I could be as blunt and honest as he is. "I'm not helping you snoop on my father."

Luke glares at me. "He screwed your mom over, didn't he?

Left her with a kid to take care of all on her own? Left her heartbroken. You think my mom deserves to go through that?"

Well, damn. That's hard to argue with. My father may be trying to make amends now, but if Luke thinks he's hiding something, I don't want Deb getting screwed over. I don't want her to go through what my mother has been going through for years.

"Click on the hint." When he does, the hint prompts him to enter my birthday. I can't help but smile that Dad made my birthday his password. "Oh, it's—"

Luke's fingers fly across the keyboard, and he's in, going straight to my father's saved documents.

The back of my neck prickles. "How did you know my birthday?"

He doesn't answer right away, and my mind whirls with all the possibilities until he finally says, "Just did a little light stalking."

With access to my father's laptop, Luke's search keeps his attention. I stuff eggs and bacon into my mouth, trying to suppress the insane thoughts swirling in my head.

What if Luke is Ten? He knows my birthday; he knew my dad only sent me cards and called me on my birthday for years. They're both into hockey, they share the same major, and both lost their dads. Our parents dated years ago, and he seemed weirdly interested in Ten but not jealous. He gave me the ten dozen flowers I wanted from Ten and a disposable camera when we met, days after I told Ten I wanted one, and the way he kissed my bruises that first night . . . it was like he already cared about me. Already knew me.

I shove the thought away. It'd be easy for him to find out my birthday, and plenty of hockey players plan to become kinesiologists or physical therapists. Lots of people lose a parent when they're young, and my father told him about the cards and birthday phone calls. He gave me flowers and kissed my bruises because, despite his possessive streak, he's also surprisingly sweet. And the disposable camera was nothing more than a coincidence—a cute, vintage wedding favor for the guests at our parents' reception.

Ten lives in California. Hell, he has a phone number with a California area code. Besides, Luke would've told me he was Ten when we finally met. The odds of them being the same person are ridiculously low. I'm only imagining they are because I miss my friend. Nothing more than wishful thinking.

My phone buzzes, but it's not Juliet this time. It's not Mom or Dad either, and of course, it's not Ten.

It's Marcus.

This time, he's included a photo with his message. My stomach drops.

A dark image that displays a line of knives and rope.

UNKNOWN

I've got plans for you.

"Sienna? What's wrong?" Luke asks.

Heart racing, I force a smile and tuck my phone into my shorts pocket. Luke's pocket.

"Nothing. I'm fine." I stand, stuffing a slice of bacon in my mouth even though I've lost my appetite and beelining out of the room. "I'm going to grab my stuff so you can take me back to campus. Juliet needs help studying."

"Sienna!"

But I don't stop. I can't let him see the tears pooling. I can't let anyone see Marcus break me. Not again.

Drown in You

Violet works behind the front desk in the library while I sit at a table across from Juliet. She's working on a profile of a serial killer for one of her psychology classes, and I've never seen her work this hard on anything.

I love my best friend, but she disturbs me.

I snap a photo of her with my disposable camera. She narrows her eyes at it. "Where the hell did you get that?"

"Luke gave it to me during the reception." I stuff it back into my bag, suddenly self-conscious. I have a camera built into my phone. There's no reason for me to be carrying around a cheap camera and using it to take grainy, shitty photos.

"How was your weekend with your stepbrother, by the way?"

Thank god Juliet's gaze drops back to her laptop screen so she doesn't see me blush. "It was fine."

When she goes back to typing notes, I pull out my phone. I start and stop five different messages to Ten. I don't know what to say to him. That's never happened before.

"Who are you texting?" Juliet asks.

"Ten."

She lifts a pierced brow. "I thought you said he ghosted you."

"He did."

"And you're still texting him?" She snatches the phone from my hand and scrolls up the wall of texts from me, all with no response. "I love you, but this is officially pathetic. Do I need to stage an intervention?"

I grab my phone back, shoving it into my bag. "I already know how pathetic it makes me look. And feel. But I can't let him think I gave up on him. I can't let him think I don't care anymore."

"Why not? He obviously doesn't care about you."

I flinch, but if there's one thing I can count on Juliet to be, it's honest. Even if her bluntness can sting.

"Why does it matter to you how he feels when he obviously doesn't care how he's making you feel? Do yourself a favor: stop texting him. You deserve better friends than that. That's why you have me."

Maybe she's right. Ten could be ghosting me simply because he doesn't want to talk to me anymore. He could be waiting for me to finally get the hint—the same thing I did to my dad when I ignored his texts for months.

If he wanted to talk to me, he would. Just like my father did when he wanted to mend our relationship.

I have other friends. I have my family. So why am I still so hung up on Ten when he clearly doesn't want anything to do with me anymore?

Juliet smirks and folds her hands under her chin. "And as your best friend, you have to tell me: did you fuck your stepbrother last night?"

My mouth falls open, and I reach across the table to smack her shoulder. "Juliet!"

"What?" She rolls her eyes. "Tell me you haven't thought about fucking him."

If she only knew the truth. Thank god she doesn't. "If you think he's so fuckable, why don't you do it?"

Juliet shrugs, turning her attention back to her laptop. "Put in a good word for me and I will."

A surprising twinge of disappointment buries itself in my chest. What if I set them up and Luke actually takes her up on it? I should be glad his attention would shift to someone else, someone who isn't related to him, but I'm not anywhere near as relieved by the idea as I should be. "Will do. I'm going to head back to the dorm."

Juliet nods. "I'm going to stay and keep working on this.

Call security if I'm not back in the dorm by two. Or send your stepbrother to come rescue me."

I can't get Luke out of my head.

The memory of his fiery eyes when he dragged me away from Knox and the bar. How his bare chest and shoulders glistened under the moonlight while he waited for me in the hot tub. How those gray sweatpants hung on his hips while he made me breakfast. How I couldn't stop fantasizing about him sneaking into my room to have his way with me.

When I curl up in bed for the night, my thighs clench together, trying to relieve the persistent, dull ache between them.

He's my stepbrother. Even if we didn't grow up together, I shouldn't want him. Our parents are married. We'll attend the same family reunions and holiday parties. There's no future in which Luke and I can be fuck buddies while our parents are married. Especially not when my stay at Diamond University hinges on my father and stepmother letting me live here.

But the horny part of my brain is fully ignoring the rational part tonight. Even if logic tells me I shouldn't want Luke, that I should stay as far away from him as I can, my libido screams otherwise.

After thirty minutes of tossing and turning, alternating between chills and sweats as the memories of our night in the hotel room plague my mind, I give up and grab my phone. I find one of my favorite smutty audiobooks and navigate to the chapter in which they bang in the bathtub. Not sure I would let Luke shove my head underwater while he fucks me, but I'd definitely let him do everything else.

I grab my vibrator and push it down my pajama bottoms. As the sultry voice of the narrator fills my ears, I crank up the pressure on my vibrator, the drone nearly drowning out the audiobook.

Pleasure zips through my clit and down to my toes. Even as I try to concentrate on the story, Luke's face keeps popping up.

We're the ones in the bathtub. He's taking his time massaging me. Kneading my erect nipples, sinking his thumbs into the knots at my shoulders, slipping his fingers between my slippery thighs.

Then he's instructing me to get on my hands and knees. I do as he says, the water sloshing, my bare ass cool outside the warm embrace of the bath water. But not for long as his huge hands rise to caress my cheeks.

Until he's nudging his hard cock at my entrance—

The door creaks open.

I gasp, sitting straight up in the darkness and fumbling to simultaneously turn off my vibrator and the audiobook.

Shit. Juliet is back.

Oh my god, oh my god, oh my god. Even if we're best friends, we don't need to be *this* close.

In the darkness, it's not Juliet's slender form entering the room.

Luke's gray eyes gleam. "Hey, sis. What are you up to?"

Shit. I've never been caught masturbating before, and it's more mortifying than I imagined.

I clutch the blanket to my chin. "How the hell did you get in here?"

He holds up a key card before shutting the door behind him and plunging us into full darkness. My pulse picks up speed. "Got your roommate's key."

"*Stole* it, you mean. Just like you stole my phone."

He shrugs. "I gave it back, didn't I?"

Drown in You

My stepbrother is a kleptomaniac stalker.

I leap out of bed, the space between my legs soaked. Heart racing, I dart past him and reach for the doorknob. "Get out—"

Luke grabs me by the shoulders and pushes me into the wall, my body slamming flush against the plaster.

My breath catches, and as my eyes adjust to the darkness, I note the fire in his gray eyes. He's leaning over me exactly the way he did that first night, a palm planted above my head. "I can do a lot more for you than that vibrator can."

I try to push him off, but he's a brick wall. He doesn't budge. A strange mix of fear and desire pools low in my belly.

I didn't stop my vibrator or the audiobook in time. He knows exactly what I was doing when he waltzed in here. I can't let him know he was the one I was fantasizing about. His ego is inflated enough, and he'll mistake my private fantasies for what I really want.

My heartbeat stutters. We're alone in my dark dorm. He could do anything to me, and I can't stop him.

"You need to leave." I try to make my voice strong, commanding, but the words come out in a whisper. "Now."

He spins me, and I gasp as he shoves me against the wall again, my back to him this time.

"Luke—" My voice wobbles in the tense silence.

His huge hands land on either side of my head with twin thuds. My heart stops.

He closes the space between us, torso brushing against my back. His hard cock grinds against my ass. I can't breathe. Can't speak. I'm frozen, anticipating his next move with bated breath.

Please touch me. Please fuck me. Please.

What the hell am I thinking? I can't do this with my stepbrother. I try to wriggle out from under him, but he only presses into me harder, flattening me against the wall. His throaty groan sends goosebumps down my arms.

He bends, soft lips and hot breath hitting my ear. "You want me, Sienna. Take what you want. I'll give you everything."

I swallow down the rock lodged in my throat, wondering what he means by *everything*. "It's wrong. And we need to stay away from each other."

To my shock, Luke pushes off the wall, leaving my body cold in the darkness without his warmth.

I spin to face him, heart still pounding and knees weak with relief. Or maybe lust.

But he doesn't disappear out the door. Not yet. My stepbrother jerks my chin up. "It's too late for that. I'll never be able to stay away from you. Now, run."

"What?" My mind scrambles to process his order.

"*Run*, Sienna. If you can hide from me, I'll let you go. For tonight. And if you can't . . ."

My chest clenches. There's no fucking way I can outrun Luke Valentine. He's a hockey goalie in the best shape of his life. There's no *if*.

He *will* catch me.

"And if I can't?"

He flashes a sultry smile. "Then I'll do everything you want me to do to you."

My stomach flips. That's simultaneously exactly what I dreaded he would say and what I hoped he would. "There's nothing I want you to do to me."

"You can't lie to me." He squeezes my chin. "I know what you really want."

I jerk out of his grip. "What will people think if they see you chasing me around campus?"

If he really wants me the way he claims, he wouldn't do anything to jeopardize my ability to stay here.

"They won't know it's me." He pulls out a mask before slipping it over his head. It's nothing like the masks Ten wore—the Ghostface mask, the purge mask, the Jason mask. All of which became my favorites.

This one is unlike any mask I've ever seen. Dark gray with slanted eyes like he's permanently daring the world to fuck with him. A few small holes allow air to pass through in front of his mouth, and jagged crimson lines strike up his forehead from between his eyes like lightning bolts.

Like a devil's horns.

"This is your last warning." From beneath the mask, his voice is more ominous. Every hair on my body stands up. "Run before I catch you."

I don't bother waiting to see if he's a man of his word—I spin, yank the door open, and take off.

The first escape I find is a door to a stairwell. I sprint for it, the door to my dorm clattering shut behind me and echoing down the hall. His pounding steps follow.

He's going to catch me before I've even hit the bottom of the staircase. He's going to fuck me right there, for anyone to walk in and see.

As much as I hate to admit it, being chased and fucked by a masked man is among my top five fantasies. But not if that masked man is my stepbrother. All it would take is his mask falling off while he's thrusting inside me for everyone on campus to find out exactly what kind of relationship the new step-siblings have.

I grit my teeth. No, I won't let him ruin this for me. I won't let him catch me. I'm not an athlete or a runner, but I'm going to run harder and faster than I ever have.

Like my life depends on it. Because it does.

Heart thundering, I jump down the stairs, risking a sprained ankle as I skip steps to descend the staircase as fast as I can.

The door at the top of the staircase squeals open. *Shit, shit, shit—*

My joints are already aching from every hard smack of my feet against the tile. Above me, the echoing boom of Luke's footsteps doesn't follow.

I dare a glance up. He's taking his time striding down the steps, as if he has all the time in the world. As if catching me will take no effort at all. "Better run faster, sis."

My fist curls around the banister as I clench my teeth. *Prick.* He really thinks I won't be a challenge.

I'll show him.

Once I finally hit the landing on the first floor, I'm already breathless, lungs aching and heart straining against my ribcage. Maybe he's right not to worry about catching me.

No. I won't let him get in my head. Won't let him get his hands on me. I'm *not* letting my stepbrother fuck me against some tree or in the dirt. He may be bigger, faster, and stronger, but I'm smart. I don't have to outrun him—I just have to hide from him. Long enough that he'll give up and head back to the Devils' house.

I burst through the door, scanning frantically for my hiding place. I can't run outside. I'm in nothing but tiny shorts and a thin tank top. The cold will ravage me before Luke does.

The girls' communal bathroom. It's nearly one in the morning—there may not be anyone in there to tell him to get the hell out, but that's where I'll have the best odds of hiding from him.

Before he can burst through the door behind me, I take off down the hallway and skid into the restroom.

The toilet and shower stalls don't do much for privacy, but they'll have to be good enough for now.

I dart into one of the shower stalls and lock the door behind me, ducking back to the wall, heart jackhammering and chest heaving.

Ten seconds tick by. Twenty. Thirty. A small bubble of hope begins to rise in my chest. Maybe he lost me. Maybe he really won't catch me in here.

How long should I wait before I head back up to my dorm? He could be waiting to ambush me. I can't leave too soon.

Once my heart has finally slowed and my breathing evened, I step forward, reaching out to flick the lock.

Until the door creaks open.

Heavy footsteps echo in the silent room. Through the crack in the stall door, I spot the reflection in the row of mirrors on the opposite wall.

A masked man.

My stomach drops to my feet. He's going to find me. There's no fucking way I can hide from him now.

An insane part of me doesn't want to. Part of me wants him to find me.

"Sienna." He calls out my name not like a question but a taunt. He knows where I am. He's simply a cat playing with its prey before delivering the final blow.

I squeeze my eyes shut as his footsteps approach and he smacks every stall door open with a clatter as he passes. Soon, he'll reach mine.

I'll do everything you want me to do to you.

There's so much I want him to do to me. Everything.

"This is my new favorite game," he croons. "Can't wait for what we play next."

Do I try to run now? Swing the door open and dart past him? Or do I give in? Let him do what we both want and hope no one walks in on us. My pulse echoes in my ears as his footsteps grow closer.

A squeal of the bathroom door opening.

"Hey!" A sharp, feminine voice calls. An RA. "What are you doing in here?"

Luke's rumbling voice follows. "Just came in to take a piss."

"Out. And take off that silly mask."

To my relief, Luke's footsteps retreat. "Come on, the mask is sexy."

"Uh-huh." The RA's voice tells me she doesn't care to hear his bullshit at one in the morning.

The door clicks shut behind them.

Every tight muscle in my body relaxes at once. Yet my stomach dips with disappointment that the RA on duty intervened. The horny part of my brain wanted to find out what Luke had planned for me in the shower stall.

With weak legs, I leave the stall and peek out of the restroom. No one in sight. No masked man waiting for me in the shadows. I escaped him.

At least for tonight.

This is what I get for hooking up with a stranger at my father's wedding. Of course he would be unhinged. And of course, despite my better judgment, I would be into it.

I head for the stairwell and slowly climb the steps, exhausted. My bed sounds so good right now. The slickness hasn't disappeared from between my legs—if anything, the chase and anticipation only made it worse—but I don't have the energy for an orgasm tonight. I've got early morning classes tomorrow, and I have a bad feeling if I slip that vibrator down my shorts again, I won't be able to stop fantasizing about Luke being the one between my legs.

When I finally reach the top of the stairs, I grab the door handle.

But when I start to pull it open, a huge hand slams it shut.

I gasp as someone grabs me and pins me to the wall, my escape just out of reach.

Drown in You

Luke looms over me in his mask, hands gripping my hips in an unshakable hold.

My breath catches in my lungs as every muscle in my body stills.

He tips his forehead against mine, stormy gray eyes glazed with lust through the hollows of his mask. "I told you what would happen if I caught you."

Before I can react, he presses his mask against my neck, his hot breath hitting my skin through the small cluster of holes. With his body, he keeps me glued to the wall, one hand gripping my hip and the other drifting down my shorts.

I writhe and push at his chest, trying to escape him, but he warned me what would happen if I failed to hide from him.

This can't be happening. Not with him. We can't get caught. We can't do this—

His warm finger slips over my pussy before parting me, dipping in just enough to drag my arousal up to my clit.

A whimper escapes my lips at the sharp contact with that sensitive bundle of nerves.

"Beg me to make you come," he murmurs.

I shake my head. I won't beg him for that. I won't let him make me. I'll stave off the orgasm, push it down so he doesn't get the satisfaction he craves. "No."

"We'll be in this stairwell all night."

"Your finger will fall off before you make me come."

Even though I can't see his face, I can hear his wicked grin. "If you don't come in five minutes, you can go back to your dorm. If you do, you'll stay in my room."

I hesitate. This bet isn't fair. I'm already horny as hell, and we're both well aware of the effect he has on me. "No, you need to get off me. This is *wrong*, Luke."

"It isn't wrong and you know it," he growls. "We're meant to be, Sienna."

I freeze. How can he think that when we barely know each other? One night of mind-blowing sex can't be enough to convince him we're soulmates.

"Either I make you come in five minutes, or I take you back to my room right now." His low threat is clear. He's not budging. I can either let my stepbrother finger me in the stairwell, or I can let him hold me hostage in his room. "Do we have a deal, Sienna?"

I hate the way he says my name. So low and alluring and perfect.

We shouldn't do this. I shouldn't let my stepbrother fingerbang me in public, but it's clear I don't have much of a choice.

Besides, I can suppress an orgasm for five minutes. "Deal."

I can't believe the word actually left my mouth. I'm literally making a deal with the Devil.

"That's my good girl." He's not allowed to say shit like that. That wasn't part of the deal. That has to be against the rules. Against the rules of this new, fucked-up game we're playing.

His finger travels down before slowly sinking into me. I bite back the groan at the delicious stretch. His breath hits my neck before he moans. "*Fuck*, you're so tight. I've missed being inside you."

My heart skips, thighs clenching around his hand as the ache builds between my legs. *No*. I won't come. I won't let him make me. "I haven't missed it."

A blatant lie, but maybe he'll believe it.

Luke keeps his finger inside me as he pulls back so he can glare at me from beneath his mask. "Don't lie to me."

His finger eases back before plunging into me again, sharper and harder this time. Punishing.

I cry out. The pleasure is building dangerously, the threat of my orgasm looming. I try to tamper it back down. Try not to look at the mask that turns me on way more than it should or the stormy gray eyes that make me want to see how they'll change when he watches me come.

A minute must've passed by now. Only four more to go. I can do this. If I hold off, I can go back to my dorm. I can avoid him for another night.

I can't let him take me back to his room. To the seclusion of that house where only the Devils will hear me scream. Because if he does, I won't want to leave.

The hand Luke uses to grip my hip drifts up to my neck. I swallow hard, panic stirring in my belly as his fingers encircle my throat. "Luke, don't—"

"I decide when you breathe." *Damn it.* The same pillow talk I told him makes my knees weak. He's using my kinks against me.

His thumb hits my clit at the same time his hand tightens around my throat.

I gasp, dragging the tiniest current of air down as Luke squeezes hard. He slips another finger inside me, the squish of my arousal obscene. I wince against the stretch until his thumb rubs my clit, pleasure shooting through me and mixing with the adrenaline.

The slowed blood flow from my neck makes my head grow lighter, somehow increasing the pleasure coursing through my veins.

"Such a good fucking girl," he groans. "You're going to come for me, sweetheart."

He's so certain, so cocky. He already knows exactly how to touch me. Knows how to play my body like he's known me forever. His thumb grinds against my clit as he finger-fucks me, and the wave of the orgasm is building to a dangerous height.

His grip on my throat loosens, letting me catch my breath for just a second.

Don't come. Don't come—

"You know what I did while you were sleeping last night?" His voice is breathless, like fucking me with his fingers brings him just as much pleasure as it does me. "I put on a mask, snuck into your room, and jerked off while I watched you sleep."

I freeze, hating the pleasure building between my legs, the flood of arousal that greets his fingers at the thought of him jerking off to me while I was blissfully unaware.

He grinds his hard-on against me. His hips thrust forward like he's inside me, like he's imagining how he would fuck me. It makes me ache for him to fill me. "You were so beautiful. I wanted to eat your pussy while you slept and make you come before you even opened your eyes."

I clutch at his arm as he squeezes my throat again. The pleasure from his fingers inside me, his thumb on my clit, his hand controlling my breathing, his cock grinding against me, becomes too overwhelming. I bite my lip. He's going to make me come, and there's nothing I can do to stop it.

"Then, when I was about to fucking *explode*, I grabbed your dress. I covered it in my cum. Now I wish I'd made you wear it."

My eyes sting. I can't push the orgasm down now. I can only hope the five minutes have passed.

At once, everything stops.

I suck down air as Luke's grip loosens, heart racing and the pinnacle of pleasure ebbing away as his hand stops moving between my legs. But he doesn't pull it back out of my shorts.

What the hell is he doing?

"Beg me to make you come." That same command.

My eyes water. I'm aching to come, need it like I need the air he's allowing to flow down my throat.

But I can't give in to him.

Even as every cell in my body is screaming at me to plead

with him to keep going, to make me come as hard as he made me come in that hotel room, I keep my mouth shut.

At my silence, his eyes narrow.

I brace myself for him to shove his fingers inside me again and fuck me hard until I'm shattering around him.

Instead, he yanks his hand from my shorts and drops his palm from around my throat.

Disappointment rockets through me as the orgasm completely subsides. A sob builds in my chest. I've never wanted to come so badly I could cry before.

This is a far worse punishment than him dragging me back to the Devils' house and tying me to his bed for the night.

He steps back, turning from me and descending the stairs. My heart plummets, even though it's exactly what I wanted.

Convinced myself I should want.

"So is the deal off?" I call, embarrassingly breathless as my heart continues to hammer, still coming down from that mountain of pleasure.

I can't stand that he's walking away. Exactly how he wants me to feel.

On the landing, he pauses and turns back to me. The mask is equal parts eerie and arousing. "Yes."

I expect relief to rush through me, but it doesn't. What the hell is wrong with me?

"Great." I spin on my heel before he notices how much he's flustered me. How disappointed I am watching him walk away.

"You won't spend just one night in my room now. You'll be there all weekend."

Chapter 14

Luke

Back at the hockey house, I hear everything going on. Everything.

On the other side of my bedroom wall, Knox, Finn, and Damien are sharing a girl. Her high squeals are quickly muffled by a cock in her mouth whenever they move her around the room or change positions. The three of them love finding new puck bunnies to share but only for a night or two.

They've yet to find a girl they want to keep, but god bless her when they do.

Upstairs, Wes and Violet are going at it in his room. Sienna and I could be doing the same if she wasn't so fucking stubborn.

After I stole the key card from Juliet's bag, I snuck into their dorm, figuring Sienna would be asleep. But when I inched the door open, a man's voice and the buzzing of a vibrator filled the room.

My stomach dropped to my feet. In a split second, I was convinced that I was walking in on Sienna fucking some other guy. A guy I was about to kill. Didn't matter if he was one of my teammates.

Until she bolted upright in bed and scrambled to turn off the vibrator and the audiobook playing from her phone.

My cock twitches at the memory. Even in the trickle of light from the hallway behind me, I spotted the flush on Sienna's chest and the heaving tits beneath her top. She was close to coming.

A whole night spent with me at home and she didn't try riding my cock once. But the second she gets back to campus, she can't control herself. As if a fucking vibrator could ever replace me. Could ever make her feel what only I can.

Pulling out of her right as she was on the verge of unraveling beneath me was a feat reserved for the gods. Even when she refused to beg, I nearly relinquished my control and plunged my fingers back inside her just to remind her how she screams for me. Even if she uses that vibrator to come tonight, she won't be satisfied. Not until it's me bringing her to that height of ecstasy.

If she knew I was Ten, she'd already be in love. Now I need to make her fall for me all over again.

Upstairs, a shower kicks on. Wes and Violet are finished, but Knox, Finn, and Damien aren't done with their toy yet. I clamp the pillow around my head to muffle Damien's groans and Knox's shouted words of praise. Not that I can sleep anyway. Not with Sienna running through my head.

My phone lights up.

SIENNA

Juliet thinks I should stop texting you.

For a second, I wondered if maybe she was right. Maybe I'm pathetic for continuing to send messages to someone who clearly isn't reading them.

> But I'm not giving up on you. I know how much it hurt when my dad abandoned me. I know how much it hurt you when you lost yours. I won't let you abandon me too, and I won't let you lose me.

Lump in my throat, I type back a response.

> **TEN**
> Fuck, Sienna. I'm sorry. I love you.

Then I delete it. I'm a piece of shit for letting this go on as long as it has. For not coming clean the second she showed up. But it's too late now. If I tell her the truth, I'll lose her forever. She'd never forgive me.

I text her from my real number.

> **LUKE**
> Send me that audiobook.

She needs a distraction from Ten, and I want to know what book she was listening to. What she was getting off to. We can come to it together.

The minutes tick by, the puck bunny in Knox's room getting louder, her moans high and whiny, and my teeth grind together. I know Sienna is up. She's ignoring me.

> **LUKE**
> I'll send the Devils to drag you here if you don't respond.

Seconds later, Sienna sends me a link to the audiobook.

> **LUKE**
> Good girl.

Drown in You

SIENNA

How did you get my number? Don't say light stalking.

LUKE

Asked Mike for it.

I click the link, buy the audiobook, and download it.

LUKE

What chapter?

This time, I don't have to threaten her to get an immediate text back.

SIENNA

Ten.

I grin. Once the audiobook finishes downloading, I slip on my headphones.

I skip right to chapter ten. Plenty of mentions of cocks and pussies and thrusting. Every groan the narrators act out triggers memories of my night with Sienna in the hotel room.

Her moans, her gasps, her little whimpers. Every sound of pleasure she couldn't contain, every clench of her thighs around my head, every spasm of her pussy as she came on my fingers. She's better than I ever could've dreamed.

I pull my cock out of my sweats before they're wet with pre-cum. The vein on the underside of my shaft throbs, and I stroke down. *Fuck.*

With every pump of my fist, it's Sienna riding my cock. Her tight, soaked pussy gliding up and down my shaft, her wetness dripping down to my balls.

She was soaked for me that night in the hotel room. Soaked after I chased her and cornered her on the staircase. It took every ounce of self-control not to shove those flimsy shorts to the side and slide my stiff cock inside her. Bend her leg up and remind her just how much she loves getting fucked by me.

I need to feel that again. Feel her tight walls clench around my shaft as I drive my cock into her relentlessly. Feel her spasms when she comes, watch as her eyes roll until she's screaming my name—

My hand slams onto the bedside table, frantically searching before I snatch a handful of tissues just in time, catching the shot of cum that shoots out of my dick.

Pleasure rockets through me and my heavy breaths drown out the audiobook still playing in my ears.

But it's nothing compared to the real thing. Nothing compared to coming inside Sienna. My need for her isn't quenched in the slightest. With every dry jerk-off, my appetite for her only grows.

I'll never be satisfied until she's mine.

Knox claps me on the shoulder while we wait to climb onto the bus. "Grab a nap on the way, Valentine. You're working yourself too hard. You look like shit."

"Thanks," I grumble.

He's not wrong, though. My arms and legs are weak, hands shaky from the exertion. Normally, I only get like this when I haven't gotten enough protein, but I ate a hearty breakfast, lunch, and dinner and supplemented with protein powder before my workout this afternoon. Yet hitting the weight room after classes wiped me out and we've still got a game against the Wildcats tonight.

But the buzzing in my head is quiet, all thoughts focused on the pain radiating throughout my body. The only way I find peace anymore other than with Sienna.

"Yeah. I'll take it easy tomorrow."

"What's your stepsister up to tonight? I was thinking we could convince her to come to my room with Finn and Damien after the game. We'll rock her fuckin' world."

I punch his shoulder, arms too weak to do any damage. "She's coming to the game."

He lifts a brow. "Yeah? Wearing my jersey, I hope."

"Shut the fuck up, asshole."

Knox laughs his ass off, breath clouding in the air as he heads for the bus. Wes, Finn, and Damien are already in their seats, slipping on their headphones to get into the zone before the game.

"Luke!" From the sidewalk, Sienna waves, long hair flowing behind her as she races for me.

I grab my bag from the ground and swing it over my shoulder, grinning at her. "Ready?"

"What the hell?" She scans me from head to toe. She's so adorable in her puffy winter coat and knit hat, the tip of her scrunched nose tinged pink. "You texted 911!"

"Right."

She gestures to me with a wild hand. "You're completely fine!"

"Yeah, but the bus is here. We're heading to the game."

"What does that have to do with me?"

"You're coming."

She retreats a step, folding her arms. "Um, no. I'm not going anywhere with you."

"Come on, I volunteered you to shadow one of the doctors. I told them you need some hands-on experience." I flash her a grin. I'll fake an injury just to get her hands on me.

"I'm not even going to be a doctor."

I shrug. "Still gotta know the same shit. Come on."

When I reach for her, she leaps away and spins on her heel. "No. Tell them I got sick. I'm leaving."

"I'm trying to help you out." But she keeps striding away. My jaw clenches. I hate watching her leave me. "You're not the reason your parents got divorced."

That stops her. Hesitantly, she turns back to face me, green eyes softening. "What are you talking about?"

"Your dad's got a gambling addiction." My search through Mike's laptop turned up plenty of interesting information. Turns out keeping secrets runs in the family. "Your mother must've found out he had tens of thousands of dollars in gambling debts. He chose his addiction over his family."

That's probably why Ma dumped his ass the first time they dated. His debts have been wiped, but I don't know if it's because of my mother's generosity or her ignorance. Did she give the money to Mike willingly or did he steal it? She won't be able to get it back now, but she deserves to know and she needs to divorce his ass before he steals from her again.

Sienna is silent, chewing her lip as she processes this information. "So you think he's using your mom for her money? To feed his gambling habit?"

I shrug. "Maybe. Probably. I'm going to let her know what I found."

Sienna doesn't try to argue. She nods, still mulling over the revelation that what she always believed to be true—that she's responsible for her parents' divorce—is a lie. "Thanks for telling me."

"What happened between your parents wasn't your fault, Sienna. It wasn't because you weren't good enough or deserved to be abandoned." No one ever should've let her believe that. Her parents should've paid attention to the ways she punished herself for their split. How she takes on every-

Drown in You

one's burdens like they're her own, like everyone's problems are hers to fix.

Maybe that's what got her here.

She bites her lip, and before the tears come, she launches herself at me, throwing her arms around my middle and squeezing. My heart soars.

"Thank you," she murmurs. The sweet, jasmine scent of her shampoo wafts up my nose and I pull her closer, breathing her in until she eases back, neck craning to meet my gaze. "What happened to your dad and Chloe wasn't your fault either. I hope you know that."

My jaw sets. What happened to my pops is nothing like what happened with her parents. She couldn't have saved their marriage, but I could've saved my father's life. I could've saved Chloe's too.

I nod at the bus in front of us. "You can thank me by getting on the bus."

AFTER TEN MINUTES on the road, all the Devils have either slipped on noise-canceling headphones, pulled out their phones to play games, or passed out.

By my side in the back row, Sienna is fully awake. Alert. As focused on avoiding eye contact with me as I am on her every blink, every breath. She's fidgeting with nervous energy, barricaded between me and a locked window. So no one can see what I do to her.

After getting chased and cornered the other night, she's eager for what I'll do next.

"Where's the doctor you allegedly volunteered me to shadow?" Her lip curls with suspicion.

"Relax. They'll have plenty of lessons to teach you at the game." I lean closer, lips brushing against the shell of her ear. "But I've got a few lessons to teach you first."

A delicious blush warms her cheeks. Her coat is draped over her lap, pinned down by her palms. Like that will stop me from getting my hands on her. But this time, I'm not wearing my mask and we'll have to be more discreet.

"Unless they're skating lessons, I don't need them." She keeps staring out the window at the asphalt flying past, unable to meet my eyes.

Her cheek is silky smooth beneath my rough, calloused fingers as I force her to face me. The same fingers I had inside her. Goosebumps spring up my arms at the contact. "Apparently, you do," I murmur. "When I tell you to beg, you beg."

My hand drops from her face and slides beneath the coat on her lap, trailing over the denim covering her thigh.

She yanks away from me, but there's only so far she can go. She's not escaping me. My teeth clench. "Stop trying to run from me."

"Stop trying to grope your stepsister," she hisses. A quick glance around tells her no one hears us, not even Knox's nosy ass in front of us.

I tighten my grip on her thigh, anchoring her in place. "You weren't complaining when you were about to come on my fingers."

"You know how reckless and stupid this is, right?" She gestures around the bus. "There are so many witnesses. You know what will happen if anyone finds out."

My hand finds the button on her jeans. "Then you better keep quiet."

Before she can protest again, I yank her zipper down and slip my hand into her panties.

As soon as my finger makes contact with her clit, her breath hitches and she stops fighting me. She wants this so fucking bad. Almost as bad as I do.

My breath caresses the shell of her ear. "I bet you're already so wet for me."

She can't even deny it. Of course she is.

Her eyes roll as I take her earlobe between my teeth and rub gentle circles over her clit. Her hips buck involuntarily into my hand, needing more. Needing everything I'm eager to give her.

A chuckle rumbles from my throat. "Tell me how wet you are."

"Dry as the Sahara," she bites, even as she grinds against my hand.

I click my tongue and my finger travels lower, parting her and brushing against her entrance, dragging the proof of her arousal up to her clit and swirling.

Sienna bites her lip hard to suppress the moan on the verge of escaping. "*Fu—*"

She stops the curse before it can escape and give me further proof of the effect I have on her.

"Beg me to make you come." In the stairwell, she wouldn't beg for me. Now she will.

My mouth finds her neck, pressing a gentle kiss there before my tongue strokes from the base up to her ear, her sweet taste nearly enough to make me combust. She can't stop the full-body tremble that follows. "Good girl. Show me how much you love my mouth on you."

She shakes her head, unable to form words. I suck on her neck at the same time my finger dips inside her. She clamps a hand over her mouth before the moan escapes.

I wrap my other arm around her shoulders, pushing her hand from her mouth only to cover it with my own, her lips soft and supple beneath my palm.

With Sienna effectively silenced, my hand down her panties works her faster, finger plunging in and out as my thumb circles her clit relentlessly. Her punishment just as much as it is her reward.

She clings to the coat still on her lap, covering the obscene act taking place at the back of the bus.

The only sounds are the ruffle of fabric and my low groans in her ear. "When will you learn that everything I do is for you? I chase you, I pleasure you, I protect you. Be mine, Sienna. Be mine and I can give you everything you want. Make your every fantasy a reality."

Her chest rises and falls faster. If I keep going, she won't be able to stop the orgasm from crashing over her.

I remove the hand from her lips but keep my arm tight around her shoulders. "Beg me, Sienna."

Her eyes are shut, the pleasure overwhelming, but she stays silent.

I spear her pussy with a second finger, plunging them in and out of her harder, deeper, the heel of my hand smacking against her clit over and over, drawing a whimper from deep in her throat. Her arousal soaks my fingers, and my cock twitches, aching to be inside her. "Fucking beg. Or I'll let everyone on this bus hear you come."

Her green eyes fly open as I keep slamming my fingers into her. I'm not bluffing. I'm going to make her come, and it's up to her whether everyone on this bus finds out what we're doing or not.

"*Please.*" The plea leaves her lips on a desperate whisper.

"Please what, sweetheart?"

She digs her nails into the soft, fluffy fabric of her coat. "Please make me come."

Her words alone have me groaning. My hand slaps over her mouth again and I suck her earlobe as my thumb finds her clit.

Drown in You

The slickness between her legs lets me plunge my fingers in and out of her with ease, creating a soppy mess in her panties.

As her walls tighten around my fingers, I don't give a fuck who hears, who sees, or who finds out about us. I don't want to ever stop doing this to her. "Come for me, Sienna."

Her limbs go limp as she shatters in my arms. She cries out against my hand, my heavy palm keeping her quiet. Her walls clench over and over around my fingers, making my eyes roll. I'll be getting off this bus with the worst blue balls of my life.

My hand follows her back down to earth, the thrust of my fingers slowing and the pressure of my thumb on her clit gentling. Beneath my palm, she pants, chest heaving as she desperately tries to catch her breath and compose herself.

Finally, I slip my hand from her jeans and settle back into my seat. "Good fucking girl." I pop the fingers I had inside her into my mouth and suck. Damn, she tastes good.

With narrowed eyes, Sienna tosses her coat onto my lap.

"What are you doing?"

Her hand slips under the coat, sliding over my sweats until she finds my waistband. She tugs down, unsheathing my erection beneath the coat. My balls tighten.

"Sienna." Her name comes out somewhere between a demand and a plea.

"Let's see *you* try to keep quiet this time." She bats her lashes at me while licking her hand in one long stroke. *Jesus.* Then she slides her hand back under the coat and wraps it around my shaft.

My cock jumps in her hand as she squeezes and strokes down. The motion makes my heart thud. Fuck, she's sexy like this. I smirk at her. "Maybe I want an audience."

"You really think they'll let you stay on the team if they find out you were fooling around with your stepsister on the bus?"

Her little smirk tells me she knows exactly what cards she's holding.

But if she thinks jerking me off at the back of the bus isn't going to make me fall more in love with her, she's sorely mistaken. "Thought you didn't want anyone finding out about us."

She keeps stroking, her hand mouth-wateringly small wrapped around my shaft, spreading her saliva over every inch. "You won't let them. Because if you do, I'll get shipped off and you won't get your hands on me again."

My jaw clenches. She's right—I'll never fucking let that happen. It'll be a cold day in hell before I go without her again. How I survived five years without her by my side is a damn miracle. I won't survive it again.

When her hand drops my cock, my stomach falls to my feet. She's going to leave me hanging like I did to her in that stairwell.

But then her fingertips graze my balls before her palm cups them. I hiss through my teeth. *Shit*. There's no way this girl is real. She's too fucking perfect. I've known that since we met. Way too perfect for me. I'll never deserve her.

Her hand drifts back up to my cock, stroking again. This time, she rubs the underside of my tip, and my shaft twitches with every graze of her thumb. I bite my lip to hold back the groan.

She flashes a cocky smirk. "You're going to come in two minutes, aren't you?" She tsks. "Thought you'd last a little bit longer."

I grit my teeth. I'll last until we get to the game if that's how she wants to play this. "Careful, sweetheart."

She leans closer to purr in my ear. "Beg me to make you come."

Drown in You

My fists clench. She's turning this back around on me. "Sienna—"

Suddenly, her head drops to my shoulder and her hand stops moving. I'm about to protest when I spot Knox's eyes on me over the top of the seat and jump.

"Sorry, bud. Didn't mean to scare you." He smiles. "Got any gum?"

On my shoulder, Sienna pretends to be asleep, but her hand still grips my cock.

"Nope." I have a full pack in my bag, but there's no way in hell I'm moving.

Knox glances between me and Sienna. "She's so cute. Tell her she can sleep on my shoulder on the way home."

I flip him off, and he chuckles before dropping back down in his seat.

My heart's still hammering. *Jesus.* That was close.

Sienna withdraws her hand from my sweats, and my balls pinch, aching for release. "What are you doing?"

"Sleeping." She gives me a sickly sweet smile before resting her head on the window and shutting her eyes.

The hell she is. I'm going to be thinking about her hand down my pants the whole game. Thinking about her mouth on my cock while her hand cups my balls.

"Sienna," I warn.

"Better get some rest before the game, sweetheart."

Chapter 15

Sienna

Someone's eyes are on me.

I'm an idiot for leaving the library past dark, especially after staying up late last night following the Devils' game against the Wildcats. To my shock, Luke actually wasn't lying about me shadowing the medical staff. I learned way more than I needed to know about common hockey injuries like shoulder dislocations and groin pulls.

On the bus ride home, Luke was so exhausted, he fell asleep, but I was too paranoid that he was faking it to let my eyes fall shut.

While I was studying, concentrating was nearly impossible with my mind completely distracted by thoughts of Luke, by the memories of our trip on the bus. I still can't believe what we did, and I shouldn't be aching for more of it.

Now, after three hours in the library, I'm exhausted and beyond paranoid.

I should've at least asked Juliet or Violet to go with me. I'm like the lone survivor in a post-apocalyptic movie on this dark campus. A few lamps and security call boxes light my path, but the campus is deserted at this time of night.

Yet I'm certain someone is in the shadows, watching every hurried step I take.

I clutch my arms to my body, shivering in the arctic air despite the winter coat and hood over my head. Maybe I'm wearing enough layers that if I get punched or stabbed, the blows won't do as much damage.

My phone rings and I jump. When I spot the photo of me with my mom, both of us smiling at my high school graduation, I heave a sigh of relief and answer. "Hey, Mom. I'm heading back to the dorm now."

"Oh, good." She's out of breath. "I just got back from book club and now I've got grilled cheese on the stove."

"Book club?"

She's never mentioned book club a day in her life. Her only hobby outside of work and men is rewatching her favorite TV shows.

"Yeah! It's great! The girls and I get along so well. And we've discovered some *amazing* new books this month." She actually sounds really happy. Hopeful.

I wish she could've experienced this revelation while I was still home.

Guilt follows the intrusive thought. I should be happy for her, not making this about me. "That's amazing. I'm glad you're enjoying it."

"How was your day?"

"Fine." I'm tempted to launch into a dull explanation of my classes and schoolwork and what Juliet and I grabbed from the dining hall for dinner, but I haven't been able to get what Luke told me about my father out of my head.

Gambling addiction. If Mom didn't tell me, she probably

doesn't want me to know. But I need confirmation if Luke is right about this.

Normally, I sweep any potential interpersonal conflict under the rug. But I can't this time. "Did you and Dad divorce because he had a gambling addiction?"

"He told you?" Her voice goes up an octave.

The words hit me like a gut punch. Was she just going to let me believe I was to blame for their divorce for the rest of my life? Or maybe she hasn't had any idea about the guilt I've been harboring.

"No, I . . . figured it out." I can't admit Luke found out by snooping. There's a lot about Luke that I can't admit to her. What he did to me in the stairwell, on the bus to the away game, in my hotel room the night we met—"So is it true? Did you ask for a divorce because of his gambling?"

She sighs. "Not exactly. A few years before our divorce, he became more distant. Secretive. When I finally found out what he was doing, I confronted him. I gave him a choice—he could keep gambling, or he could keep his family. He made his choice."

Maybe this revelation should make me feel like shit, knowing my father picked slot machines over me. But instead, relief floods through me.

I didn't drive my father away. He left of his own accord. Their divorce had nothing to do with me. I'm not to blame. I'm not the reason Mom has been nursing a broken heart for the past decade.

In the background of the call, an alarm blares. "Shit!" Mom hisses. "I forgot the grilled cheese. Hey, hon, I have to go. Text me when you get to your dorm. Love you!"

As soon as I hang up, I spot texts from the unknown number. Probably Marcus, but I still have no way of proving it.

UNKNOWN

Found you.

The next message is a photo of me, walking alone on campus.

Heart in my throat, I whip around, nearly dropping my phone.

But there's nothing. No one following me.

My heart pounds, and I'm tempted to sprint all the way back to Nohren Hall.

A closer look at the photo shows I'm wearing a different outfit and the sun is still up. But he knows where I am. Tracked me down somehow.

He's already been here. He knows how to find me, and he could show up again at any time. When I least expect it. When I'm completely alone and vulnerable. Just as he and Stephen and Kade found me that night.

Have I learned nothing? I'm such an idiot.

Tears sting my eyes. I wish I could talk to Ten. Wish I could confide in him as I've always done and he'd comfort me in the way only he knows how. But it's been weeks since I last heard from him. I've been through some of the biggest changes in my life recently, and he's ghosting me. He obviously doesn't care anymore, and I should stop hoping to hear from him again.

But I can't give up on him. And I'm just as pissed at myself for that as I am him.

In a fit of rage, I type out a text.

SIENNA

I could really use a friend right now and it's honestly shitty of you to

A crunch behind me.

In the dimly lit parking lot, I catch a glimpse of red. The same Cadillac that was parked outside of the bar.

Marcus.

I hurry up the sidewalk. I need to get the fuck out of here. Somewhere with other people, where there will be witnesses if he gets his hands on me.

When I round the corner by the Village, a masked man leaps into my path.

A scream rips from my throat.

Four hulking masked men burst out laughing.

"Holy shit!" Knox lifts his mask and wheezes, bending over at the waist. "You should've seen your face!"

I smack his arm. "What the hell is wrong with you?"

Behind him, Wes and Damien reveal their smirks beneath their masks. The only one who leaves his mask in place is Finn, his lean, beautifully sculpted face entirely hidden under the mask with x's over his eyes and mouth.

"You scare easy." Damien's smirk doesn't waver as the low words rumble from his mouth.

"You're four giant men in masks in the dark. Of course I'm going to scream."

"I don't know about four." Damien claps Wes on the shoulder. "But the three of us can make you scream."

Knox's bright eyes dance, and I'll admit the masks are working for me. I'm into plenty of kinky shit, but even I don't think I could handle three massive hockey players at once. The recovery time would take weeks.

Not to mention none of them are the Devil I've been fantasizing about. None of them are the Devil who's made me come harder than I ever have in my life—twice. Except I absolutely, one thousand percent should not be fantasizing about *that* Devil.

"What are you all doing out here anyway?"

"Luke sent us," Wes tells me, and their smiles turn eerie.

What the hell does that mean? It sounds more like a threat than an explanation. "For what?"

A low, quiet voice little more than a hum in my ear. "For you."

Finn. He disappeared behind me without me noticing.

Before I can open my mouth, a hand covers my lips. Another covers my eyes.

Without a word of warning, they grab me.

The Devils drag me kicking and screaming to the house they share. At least, I attempt to kick and scream against their hold.

If Luke knew what really happened to me back in Wakefield, would he allow his teammates to do this to me?

Maybe they were lying. Maybe he has no idea what they're up to. But none of them breathe a word about their plans for me while Wes drives us off campus.

We don't go far. My heart thunders as we stop in front of a house on Lamont Row.

"Come on, beautiful." Knox's hold on my arm turns tender. "Let's get you inside."

"What are you doing?" I demand for the tenth time. "I'll scream."

I hardly fought back when Marcus, Stephen, and Kade got their hands on me. If the Devils want to do the same, I'm going to fight back tooth and nail, with every ounce of strength in me.

A slow, devastating smile creeps over Damien's face on my other side before his hand velcros over my mouth. "Then we'll have to keep you quiet, won't we?"

Even though I thrash in their arms like a feral cat, the four of them manage to pull me inside with little effort.

In the dimly lit house, my heart is about to burst out of my chest. A pair of sneakers is discarded in the middle of the kitchen floor, a jersey tossed onto the counter, a pile of dishes in the sink.

This is their house. The Devils' house.

Damien finally removes his hand from my mouth. They aren't worried about keeping me quiet anymore. "Let me go!"

Knox, Damien, and Finn have made it no secret that they want to share me in bed. But Wes? He's hopelessly devoted to Violet. Why would he be involved in this?

Unless he's planning to have his way with me too. That makes him even more of a scumbag than the rest of them, if that's even possible. Violet is angelic compared to all of them. I bet she has no clue what her boyfriend is up to.

What they're all about to do to me.

"He said you're not allowed to leave until his room is spotless." Wes nods to a hallway, and my stomach twists violently.

"Who?" I force the word out, even though I already know the answer.

"Your stepbrother." Knox grins at me. "He said you owed him one."

I fold my arms. "So what? I'm his servant now?"

Knox shrugs. Finn still hasn't removed his mask, and he's more relaxed with his beautiful face hidden.

I know Luke didn't actually have his teammates kidnap me so I can play maid. *You won't spend just one night in my room now. You'll be there all weekend.*

Luke can't really be planning on keeping me here. The other Devils will know who he has locked up in his room. There's no way they wouldn't be suspicious.

One minute, he's the knight in shining armor, a prince I

don't deserve. The next, he's a Devil, in every sense of the word.

And all four of them are just as bad for going along with it. For doing Luke's dirty work for him.

"You fucking your stepbrother?" Damien folds his arms, enormous biceps bulging.

All three of them look amused, and I'm sure Finn is wearing an identical smirk beneath his mask.

"No!" I bite my lip, hoping the word didn't sound too defensive, even though it's true. I'm not fucking him—it only happened once, and it hasn't happened since. But I can't be sure that it never will again.

"You want to?" Knox's question makes the rest of them laugh.

"*No*." My face must be flaming red now. "You're all gross."

"Then when you're done with his room, come find us." Knox heads for his own room so I know exactly where he'll be waiting for me.

The other Devils don't budge, guarding the door to prevent me from making a run for it.

"Go on." Damien gives me a sharp slap on the ass, spurring me on deeper into the shadows. "Maybe do some topless maid service around the rest of the house while you're at it."

I grind my teeth and leave the kitchen, unsure which Devils I'd rather deal with—the ones at my back, or the one waiting for me in his bedroom.

Even the walls hold their breath while I shuffle through the living room and down the hallway. Far away from the kitchen and the Devils' eavesdropping ears, the door to Luke's bedroom waits, silent on the other side.

I knock. Silence. No shuffling feet or shout of acknowledgment.

Maybe the Devils weren't lying—maybe Luke really did order me here to clean his room. What an asshole.

Gritting my teeth, I turn the knob and shoulder the door open.

Inside, the room is immaculate. Hardly lived in. Dirty clothes tossed in a laundry basket, an organized desk with little more than a laptop, textbooks, notebooks, and a lamp. Hockey gear peeking out of the partly open closet.

What the hell? His room isn't even messy. Not that I should complain there's not actually anything he could force me to clean. Even the bed is made, the corner of the blanket and sheet folded neatly to the side as if ready to welcome me in.

Behind me, the door clicks shut. Then locks.

I whip around. A shirtless Luke is holding up a pair of pink handcuffs. My mouth goes dry. He's wearing those infuriatingly sexy gray sweatpants low on his hips, that deep *V* plunging into the waistband making my breath catch.

Though I wish I was disgusted by him, wish his antics repulsed me, I can't help the way my knees turn to jelly. His giant body looms in the shadows of the dark room, the mouthwatering muscle on his bicep tight as he dangles the handcuffs from a finger.

Even in the minimal light, his gray eyes gleam, honing in on me. I am the ant; he is the microscope. He tracks every slight move, every nervous fidget of my hands, every shallow breath that makes my breasts rise and fall beneath my coat.

Whether I want to admit it or not, my stepbrother owns me. He can order the biggest guys on campus to wear masks and kidnap me in the dark, all to bring me to him.

The worst part is that none of this makes me fear him. It only makes me want him more.

"They think I'm your maid now." I fold my arms. On the

opposite wall is a window. He's on the first floor—I could leap for it, fling it open, and jump out.

But I stay where I am. I don't want to escape him. As insane as it makes me, I want to stay here with him. Want to find out what Luke Valentine has planned for me.

"Better than them thinking you're my girlfriend, right?" He saunters forward. "At least for now."

"I'm *not* your girlfriend." My pulse picks up speed.

"You will be." He cradles my face, and I long to lean in to his touch. To give in and take what I want. "Then you'll be my wife."

My spine stiffens. Yeah, my stepbrother is officially delusional. "You barely know me, and even if that was even remotely something I was interested in, our parents are still married. Pretty sure that's illegal, and if not, at least not socially acceptable."

"Who gives a fuck what anyone else thinks?" His gray eyes turn stormy. "We're right for each other. That's all that matters. Our parents aren't going to stay together anyway."

I've never even bothered entertaining the idea that our parents might break up. They just got married, and they seem perfectly happy together. But I also don't know either of them that well. "How are you so sure?"

"They've already broken up before. Once Ma finds out about his gambling, what he did with her money, she'll come to her senses." The hand cradling my face slides into my hair. "I'll do anything to have you, Sienna. Anything."

A sick bubble of hope rises in my chest at the possibility of a future in which our parents aren't together and Luke and I can be. I shouldn't be hoping for the demise of a marriage. I'm selfish, screwed up in the head. I wish I could blame Luke for making me this way, but I've been fighting my desire for him since we met. And failing miserably.

"Anything? Including letting me go?" That's what I *should* want. But no part of me does.

"You remember our deal. I get you for the whole weekend."

My heart skips. "Your teammates are already suspicious of us."

He shrugs like this is no big deal. "I'll tell them you left late. They won't even know you're in here. Until you scream, anyway."

I freeze. "Luke, no one can—"

"I know." His gray eyes grow cold. "No one can know. I'm your dirty little secret."

Impossibly, my chest squeezes with guilt.

"You want this just as much as I do. Now take off your clothes, Sienna." The rumbling command turns my limbs to liquid. He grabs a shirt off his bed and tosses it to me. "Put that on."

I catch the soft cotton in my hands, examining the black and red stitching. His jersey.

When I hesitate, he barks, "*Now.*"

His voice travels down to my toes. Slowly, I shrug out of my clothes, his gaze burning through me with every article of clothing I discard on the floor.

"Bra and panties too," he commands when my underwear is all that remains to shield me.

I do as he instructs, reaching around to unhook my bra and letting the straps slide down my arms. My breasts fall, and his breaths turn shallow.

When I slide my panties down my legs, his head follows as he tracks every inch of movement.

As soon as I'm fully naked in front of him, I slip his jersey over my head. *Valentine* stitched across my back. Marking me as his.

From another part of the house, a heavy bass thuds.

Drown in You

Someone is blasting music in one of their rooms. The Devils have finally given up their posts in front of the door.

When he sees me eyeing my escape, Luke tosses me onto the bed, knocking the breath out of me. The drumming of my heart is thunderous, and a small smile crawls across my lips.

Luke grabs my hands and cuffs them, cool metal closing around my wrists.

"What the hell are you doing?" I jerk against the metal, but the handcuffs don't budge.

With a thin rope, he binds the cuffs to the headboard. Where the hell did that rope come from? "I told you. You're staying here for the weekend."

"So what—you're going to keep me strapped to your bed for forty-eight hours? You realize I'm going to need to pee at some point."

"Bathroom's right there." He nods to a door. Of course his room would have a bathroom attached. No chance of anyone discovering he's keeping me locked in here.

Once he has more rope, he grabs for my ankle. My heart leaps into my throat and I kick at him, but he catches my ankle in an unyielding grip that only tightens as he plants my foot on the mattress and binds it to the bed with the rope.

"Stop it!" I hiss as he reaches for my other ankle.

My heart shouldn't be pounding in anticipation of what he's going to do to me next. My chest shouldn't be flushed from adrenaline, and my thighs shouldn't be attempting to clamp together to relieve the building ache between my legs.

He literally sent his friends to kidnap me and now he has me tied down to his bed. He's planning to keep me here all weekend and do god knows what to me. And for some insane reason, I'm not at all terrified. I'm not even mad, despite fighting him at every turn. Instead, my entire body is crackling like a live wire in anticipation.

After how hard he's made me come, I can't bring myself to dread his hands on me. No matter how wrong and dangerous it is.

He can't possibly know about my fantasy of getting tied down and fucked. He knows me better than I would've thought possible for anyone, even Ten.

Every muscle in my body tenses when Luke strides from the bed and digs in his bedside drawer. What could he be looking for? Condoms?

"You're going to stop running from me, Sienna." His lethal voice sends ants skittering down my spine. "You're going to stop hiding. You're going to stop giving a fuck about what other people think or want, and you're going to be with me. Because you know we're right together. Because you know we're the best thing to ever happen to each other. And I'm going to remind you about that all night."

When he approaches the bed again, he holds up a pink vibrator. One that looks all too familiar.

"You stole my vibrator?" I really need to find that key card he stole from Juliet and shred it.

"Borrowed it."

"Just like you borrowed my phone and my dress and Juliet's key."

He shrugs. "Ready for our new deal, sweetheart?"

I'm tied up, so I don't exactly have any leverage to argue. "What deal?"

"You tell me you're mine, and you can leave. You let me hold you at night and walk you to your classes and keep you safe. You come to my games and cheer me on and let me show you how much I care about you, every day." He traces the vibrator along my thigh without turning it on. My breath catches. "Or I make you come over and over with this all weekend until you give in."

Somehow, Luke wants more than sex from me. This isn't just about his twisted fantasies of his stepsister. I still don't know why he wants more from me, but I'm starting to want more from him too, no matter how reckless that is. I definitely want more of *this*.

He has no idea how badly I want to give in to him. How an ache settles in my chest every time I try to push him away, try to convince myself that he's forbidden and I shouldn't want him. How terrified I am that if I let him in, he'll hurt me like Dad hurt Mom. Like Ten hurt me. That he'll leave me behind because that's what always happens.

So I keep my mouth shut.

His gaze drops to my body splayed out in front of him, disappointed. "Guess you've made your choice."

Without another word, he yanks the jersey up over my eyes, shielding my view of him.

A dull drone hums from the vibrator as Luke turns it on. My heartbeat turns staccato as he glides the silicone up my body, the pulsing pressure on my bare skin foreign. When the silicone reaches my nipple, I stop breathing as he increases the pressure.

I bite my lip, trying not to give away just how good it feels. My nipple hardens and the space between my legs grows slick.

For a fleeting moment, I wish he would use his hands and mouth on me. Sink his fingers back inside me like he did in my hotel room, in the stairwell, on the bus.

"You ready to say it yet?" he purrs. "Admit it?"

Several seconds of silence tick by before Luke lifts the vibrator from my breast and smacks it down onto my clit.

I yelp, jerking against my restraints. They don't budge—only make my ankles and wrists and shoulders ache deliciously. *Yes, keep doing that. Don't stop.* I bite the words back down before they can escape.

His mouth comes down on my peaked nipple, sucking it into his mouth. I gasp, arching into him.

The shock of his unexpected touch, the anticipation from not knowing where or when the next brush of contact will come, makes it that much sweeter, makes the pleasure pump harder through my veins.

He cranks up the pressure on the vibrator until it's pulsing hard on my clit, electric bursts zapping me down to my toes and up to my scalp.

"Luke!" I mean his name to come out like a warning, but he must take it as encouragement because he presses the silicone harder against that sensitive bundle of nerves. My heels dig into the mattress of their own accord, trying to get away from him.

"Stop trying to escape me, Sienna. You never will." His mouth crashes down onto my nipple, sucking it as deep as he can into his mouth, abusing it far worse than the other. I cry out, writhing beneath him. "Every inch of you belongs to me."

My pussy pulses, arousal pooling and threatening to spill down to the sheet beneath my ass. Overwhelming pleasure makes my eyes sting, and I can't bite back the moans that leave my throat unbidden.

"That's it, sweetheart," he murmurs, barely audible above the depraved drone of the toy. "Come for me."

Against my ribcage, my heart thumps wildly. I can't hold back my orgasm even if I wanted to. That crest of pleasure barrels toward me like a runaway train.

Fireworks explode in my head as my pussy pulses, clit throbbing beneath the unrelenting pressure of the vibrator. I claw at my restraints, struggling to get away from the overwhelming sensation between my legs, but Luke doesn't relent. He keeps the vibrator glued to me, still cranked to one of the highest settings.

Drown in You

"Stop!" I pant, tears pooling. The stimulation is too much. I can't take any more.

His finger dips down to swirl in my arousal, but he doesn't remove the vibrator. "You're the only one who can stop this."

I swallow the lump in my throat. I'm aching to be filled, to feel him stretching me and thrusting into me over and over while he keeps that vibrator on my clit until I'm coming with his cock inside me.

But I can't give in to him. I can't. I may be willing to give him my body, but not my heart.

He tsks at my silence, at the absence of the words he longs to hear but I can't say to him. "We'll have to give you another then. And another. And another."

Anticipation and panic mix. How many orgasms is Luke going to force on me before he lets me leave this room? How many will my body be able to handle before my heart explodes? It already feels like I just swam ten laps.

With a soft click, he cranks the vibrator to the highest setting.

A scream rips from my throat, back arching as my still-sensitive clit gets pulverized by the vibrator. No amount of thrashing against my restraints helps. Luke tugs the jersey down off my face before pinning my hip to the mattress, forcing me to take the pulsing vibrator against my clit with legs spread wide.

I whimper, tears spilling down my face as the second orgasm rockets through me, wringing every remaining ounce of energy from my limbs.

This time, Luke lowers the pressure from the vibrator as I come back down, heart pounding. Relief settles in my bones. Maybe this sweet torment is over.

"You're so fucking beautiful when you come." He dips the

silicone down, pressing it against my entrance. Playing with me.

I try not to preen at the praise.

He positions the vibrator so it rests on me when he lets go and backs away. Panic constricts around every muscle. "Where are you going?"

No response comes as he digs through his drawer again. This time pulling out a mask and covering his face. My heart skips.

Next, he finds a lighter and flicks it with his thumb, a flame springing to life. In the darkness, shadows play across his mask. He lights candles around the room.

"Very romantic." I try to force sarcasm to drip from my words, even as my chest squeezes.

When he's finished, the room fills with a sweet jasmine scent, and goosebumps prick up along my exposed skin. The scent I told Ten was my favorite.

Luke searches through my clothes on the floor until he finds what he's looking for. The disposable camera he gave me.

"What are you doing?"

He holds the camera above me and snaps a photo.

"Luke!" I fight against my restraints. "Delete that!"

I don't have to see his mouth beneath the mask to know he's smirking. "Relax. No one will see it but me."

He ditches the camera on his bedside table and grabs the vibrator again, swirling it in the mess between my legs. I whimper. "Please."

But I'm not sure what I'm begging for anymore. Him to stop and release me, or to keep going and give me release.

"Is this what you imagined with Ten? That he'd still be wearing a mask when you finally met and make you come over and over again?"

"N-no." Every inch of me is wound tight. I don't know what answer he wants to hear—the truth or a lie.

He smacks the vibrator against my clit and I cry out, jerking hard. My muscles are already aching. "Don't lie, Sienna."

"*Yes*," I breathe. "That's what I imagined."

What if my doubts were wrong? What if Luke really is Ten? That would explain the intensity in the way he watches me, his insistence that we're meant to be even though we hardly know each other. Because maybe we actually know each other better than anyone else does.

But why wouldn't he tell me? Why would he allow me to think Ten ghosted me? If he actually is Ten, he's an asshole for not telling me sooner, for letting me think my friend abandoned me.

Yet part of me still hopes he is. That the masked man who's been my friend for years is also the hockey goalie who can't get enough of me.

Luke glides the vibrator up my pussy slowly, and I brace for the impact against my swollen, overly sensitive clit. "Forget about Ten. Forget about every other man before you met me. Because I'm the only one who will ever do this to you. The only man who will ever make you feel this way."

Forget about Ten. Maybe they're not the same person. Because Ten would never want me to forget our friendship. He would know I'd never be able to forget him, and even if our friendship is over, I would never want to.

When I left Wakefield to come here, this isn't at all how I expected things to turn out. I didn't dare hope my new stepfamily would want anything to do with me, let alone . . . this.

This fucked-up, twisted, taboo affair between me and my stepbrother.

My eyelids are heavy, ready to fall shut when the vibrator

finally reaches my clit and every muscle in my body goes rigid as the pleasure radiates through me.

"Ready for another, sweetheart?"

Chapter 16

Luke

Watching Sienna come is like watching the sun rise and shine down on you. Her breaths become increasingly shallow, she bites her bottom lip like she stands any chance at holding it back, and her chest flushes. When the orgasm finally barrels through her, her back arches and she cries out, music to my ears.

By the fifth orgasm, she's a wet, trembling mess. Thighs shaking violently, legs and arms limp, cheeks streaked with makeup, eyes red-rimmed. So fucking beautiful.

She's more resilient than I expected. Even after two a.m., she doesn't give in.

Her silence crushes me. She'd rather take this for hours than be mine. No matter how perfect we are for each other, she doesn't want me.

Would she have already given in if she knew who I really am? But I already know exactly how that confession would go—she'd leave me and never look back.

Finally, I let her up to pee. She waddles into the bathroom, simultaneously pale and flushed, eyelids droopy with exhaustion and hair a tangled mess. *This* is my favorite version of her. Not done up like a doll—fucked up like my own personal plaything.

This is the tip of the iceberg. That night in the hotel room was only the beginning. She'll never know how much better it can be between us if she refuses to ever give us a chance.

When she shuffles back, bleary-eyed, she bends slowly to grab for her jeans.

"Not a chance." I scoop her up and drop her onto the mattress between me and the wall, draping an arm over her. "You're not going anywhere. I get you all weekend."

She stiffens. "Luke," she whines. "I can't take any more."

I smile and flip her onto her side before pulling her against me and tucking the blanket around us. "I know, sweetheart. I'll let you get some sleep." Briefly, she relaxes until I add, "You'll take it in the morning."

She's too drained to protest, and even though my balls are aching to come after watching her writhe and cry out in ecstasy for hours, we both fall asleep in minutes.

When I wake up, she's still sound asleep beside me. A huge grin stretches across my face. I slept like a damn baby, and so did she. I want her in my arms every night. My perfect girl.

Silently, I climb out of bed. Just in case, I toss her clothes in the closet where she won't find them and head for the kitchen. She'll need sustenance.

By the time the eggs are fried and the bacon is burning, a door squeaks open and Knox shuffles out of his room, rubbing his eyes. He gives a groggy chuckle when he spots me. "Who's the girl you had screaming in your room last night? *Please* tell me it was your stepsister."

Shit. I figured with the music blasting, none of them would overhear us. "Don't know. Forgot her name."

He gives me a wry smile. "But you're making her breakfast?"

"Gotta keep her energy up."

That makes him laugh. "My favorite kind of puck bunny. What happened to Sienna?"

"Went back to her dorm last night after she cleaned up my room."

"Tell her she can come clean my room next. I'll keep her busy all night long."

"No-sister rule," I remind him and toss him a few strips of burnt bacon to buy his silence. He scarfs them before digging in the cupboard for cereal.

Even if he knew it was Sienna in my room, he wouldn't tell anyone. Until she showed up and he opened his big mouth to tease her for it. Then she'd murder me.

Sienna stirs once I open the door and lock it behind me. I hand her the plate and fork, and she sits up to take it with a sweet smile. God, I love being the one to put that smile on her face. "Thanks."

She's still in my jersey, her messy brown hair falling over the fabric. This is how I want her in my room always. In my jersey or naked whenever we're alone.

She yawns. "I didn't have any nightmares last night."

"Do you usually have nightmares?"

Her eyes drop to her plate, realizing she's confessed too much. She pops a piece of bacon in her mouth. "Usually. It's not a big deal."

She's never told me about nightmares, not even as Ten. Her silence is pissing me off. Doesn't she realize how much I love her? That I would do anything for her? She doesn't have to hide shit from me.

Whatever horrors plague her mind each night, I guarantee

they have something to do with whatever asshole she ran from to come here. The same asshole who sent her that text.

I sit beside her on the bed, needing to be close to her warmth again. "I didn't have any either."

For the first time in a long time, I slept peacefully through the night. I don't remember a single dream. All I remember is the soft warmth of Sienna in my arms.

She lifts a brow, her nose nearly brushing my skin as she turns to face me. "What do you have nightmares about?"

What the hell have I already told her? As Ten, I admitted to nightmares about Pop's death. The air around us grows heavy with her suspicion. I rest a hand on her bare thigh and rub my thumb along her soft skin. "Losing you."

Not the whole truth, but not a lie. Losing Sienna is my biggest fear.

Her eyes soften. "Because you lost your dad. And Chloe."

I nod. "I don't want to lose you too."

She bites her lip and silence falls between us as she returns her full attention to her plate. Because she can't promise that I won't.

IN THE LIBRARY, Wes flirts with Violet behind the circulation desk. Sienna sits at a table with Juliet while a few puck bunnies swarm our table. One on Knox's lap, two fighting over a seat on Damien's, and one perched on the table in front of Finn with her legs practically spread open for his viewing pleasure. I already pushed away the blonde fawning over my lap, hence the fight over Damien.

Even though I know she wouldn't dare, I want to leave the spot open for Sienna.

Drown in You

I've tried to give her space since the Devils kidnapped her. From the shadows, anyway. Lurking where she won't see me, my eyes never leaving her. Give her the chance to miss me, to miss my hands on her and cock inside her, to miss the praise I murmur in her ear and the way my attention sets her on fire, until she finally comes to her senses.

At Sienna's table, Juliet rises from her seat. My stomach twists when she sets her sights on me with a grin.

Sienna must've encouraged her to come over here to talk to me.

Except an ember of jealousy flickers to life in Sienna's eyes when Juliet rests a hand on my shoulder. Her tight black skirt rides up so high, I can nearly see the curve of her ass.

Sienna may think she wants me to shift my focus to Juliet, wants me to find another girl who can fit into that spot in my heart reserved for her, but the jealousy is already eating her alive.

I rest a hand on the small of Juliet's back and tug her closer. Sienna's jaw clenches, and she forces her eyes back on her textbook, but she's not reading.

When Juliet claims the space on the table in front of me, I don't protest.

She drops her boot in the spot between my spread legs and leans forward, cleavage on full display. Her overwhelming perfume floods my nose. Too strong. Sienna's scent is more subtle, softer. Like her.

"You want her, don't you?" Juliet murmurs, so quiet no one else at the table can hear. "I can tell."

Her smirk tells me she knows the bulge in my pants isn't for her—it's for my stepsister. The stepsister I can't drag my gaze away from. The stepsister who watches from the corner of her eye as her best friend perches in front of me.

"Sienna's a rule-follower and a people-pleaser. I've spent

our whole friendship trying to corrupt her, but she's tougher than she looks. If you want to get her, you'll have to keep things between the two of you quiet. I can keep a secret, but these?" She points at my eyes. "They're telling the whole world how badly you want to fuck your stepsister. I support it. She wants you too, even if she won't admit it. But you need to get better about pretending you don't so no one suspects anything. Otherwise, she won't bother with you. She won't risk it."

I don't know how long they've been best friends, but as much as I hate to admit it, Juliet knows Sienna better than I do and she's probably right about this. I've done a shit job of bottling up my feelings for my stepsister. Anyone on this campus could take one look at my face while she's in the room and know how much I want to fuck her. How much I care about her. I'd rip every inch of this world apart for her.

Luckily, no one suspects anything is going on between us when she goes out of her way to ignore and avoid me. Everyone assumes the attraction is one-sided. The only person who doesn't is the one who knows Sienna most—her best friend.

I've been selfish, wanting her to be public with me when she isn't ready. But I'd rather have her in the shadows than not at all.

Juliet's breath hits my ear. "And you better treat her right, Valentine. Or you'll have me to deal with."

"I'll take good care of her. I'm a great big brother."

"Careful." Juliet smirks. "You might actually turn me on."

I cock a brow, knowing how much Sienna is seething with jealousy at our little performance. "What does turn you on?"

She shrugs. "A masked man chasing me in the dark. Knife play. Somnophilia. A little bit of pain with a lot of pleasure."

I snort. "So unhinged psychopaths."

Too bad for Juliet, Trey Lamont was kicked off campus last semester. She just missed her dream man.

Drown in You

We know it won't last, though. Trey's father is the Head of Athletics. Daddy's money and influence will buy his way back onto campus and the Diamond Devils team. Just a matter of time.

"I'm going back to my table now. Pretend to stare at my ass while I walk away."

"Why are you helping me?"

"It's not for you," she says simply. "It's for her. Sienna is the best friend I've ever had. She's been through a lot, and she deserves to be happy."

I can't keep my eyes off Sienna anymore. Her cheeks are pink as she flips through pages of her textbook. Hard proof of her jealousy. "Why is she really here? What's she running from?"

Juliet stiffens. "She'll tell you when she's ready." She hops down from the table, blue eyes softening with concern for her friend. "Just look out for her, okay? Protect her."

"I will. From anything."

Chapter 17

Sienna

Sigma Chi knows how to get a girl drunk. Give me some fruit juice with vodka I can't taste and I'm the happiest girl in the frat house.

In the dimly lit living room packed with sweaty bodies, Juliet, Violet, and I are the only ones dancing. At least, dancing in a way that doesn't involve grinding on someone.

I'm in the new black dress Luke bought me. On my bed, he left the box with a note on top. *Wear this to the Sigma Chi party.*

Buying me a new dress was the least he could do after he ruined the last one, but I still grinned like an idiot when I pulled it from the box.

Juliet brays a laugh at my outrageous, spindly dance moves, bending at the waist. "You are *sooo* drunk!" she slurs.

Violet giggles. "You both are."

"You're not?" I hiccup.

"Wes only likes to fuck me when I'm sober." Even through his mask, she can tell he's watching her from across the room. She waggles her fingers at him and he nods his chin up at her.

Drown in You

"I'm so jealous that you're getting laid by a masked man tonight!" I shout over the music.

"You can too." Violet grins, and I panic that she means Luke until she gestures at the crowd. "You have plenty of options."

All of the Devils are here tonight wearing masks. Ghostfaces, Punishers, Jasons. Skull masks, purge masks, gas masks. All of the Devils except one. Luke is a no-show.

I'm pretty sure, anyway. I'm starting to not be able to tell them apart, and I'm not certain if it's because of the masks or the alcohol. Who knew college hockey teams had *twenty-five* players.

Juliet points at a guy with a five o'clock shadow on the couch. "I'm going to make out with that guy. Bye, bitches." Without another word, she stumbles away. I'm surprised she's not waiting for Luke to show up.

I'm not allowed to be jealous when I encouraged the two of them to get together. I just didn't think they'd take me up on the suggestion so readily. Or right in front of my face.

In a fucking *library*, for god's sake. Is no place sacred anymore?

Seeing my best friend flirting with Luke confirmed my biggest fear—I don't want him to be with anybody else. I want him to be mine.

Violet bursts into a fit of giggles when Juliet climbs onto the guy's lap and his eyes pop open. But when Juliet kisses him, he doesn't protest and his hands land on her hips.

Wes appears behind Violet, wrapping his arms around her waist. She spins in his arms, looping her hands behind his neck. I'm forgotten, and I can't blame either of them. I would definitely rather be grinding with a hot masked man right now than dancing among a bunch of sweaty strangers.

Now that I'm dancing by myself, I drain the rest of my

drink. I can't remember the last time I was this drunk. My head is starting to swim, but my legs still manage to keep me upright.

A man in a gas mask stops in front of me.

I freeze when I spot the cold, vacant hazel eyes beneath the mask. My heart drops to the floor.

Marcus.

I take a step back, bumping into sweaty, gyrating bodies. He finally found me again.

A pair of massive arms wraps around my middle from behind. The thumping bass of the music turns to a buzz.

"Hey, gorgeous." His murmur in my ear is muffled by the mask covering his mouth.

In front of me, the guy in the gas mask disappears into the crowd.

I spin around, the twin holes in his Jason mask displaying the green eyes and betraying his identity. "Knox, hey." My racing heart slows. "Wow. I'm *really* happy to see you."

Through the holes in his mask, I spot his grin. "I like your moves." He steps closer and I'm forced to lift my chin to maintain eye contact. "Want me to show you a few more?"

The innuendo is obvious. I guess he's following through on Damien's offer to make me scream.

He must not know Luke had me in his room all weekend. Otherwise, he wouldn't dare touch me.

Another warm body presses against my back. The two of them pin me, sandwiching me between them. My pulse jumps to my throat.

"We both can." The edge of Damien's punisher mask brushes against my neck as his hands land on my hips.

I shiver, imagining it's Luke beneath the mask. Luke's hands on me. Luke staring down at me with lust glazing his gray eyes.

But the eyes eating me up are green, not gray.

I shake my head. "Actually, I better go."

Luke will burn the whole frat house down if he finds me sandwiched between his teammates. Worse, he'll be hurt. I can't do that to him.

I'm almost positive he's Ten. After he lit those jasmine-scented candles and told me about his nightmares, I thought of Ten, who's had nightmares about his father's death since I've known him.

I can't decide whether the possibility of Luke and Ten being the same person is heartbreaking or heartening. I've missed my friend so, so much, and part of me is comforted by the possibility that he's been right in front of me all along.

But another part is gutted at the possibility that he's been pretending this whole time. That he's been keeping this huge secret and not caring about how much it's hurting me.

If Luke is Ten, he must've known who I was when we hooked up at the hotel. Not just his friend—his stepsister. The whole thing is so fucked up that I don't even want to think about it for too long. Because then I might realize there's no way I can forgive him if it's true.

Knox's hands drift down to the hem of my dress, tugging me closer. In a split second, Damien follows, pressing into me even harder than before. Damien's long erection rubs against my ass through his jeans while Knox's stabs into my stomach.

Knox brushes my hair over my shoulder. "He wants you upstairs."

Luke.

They must know something is going on between us now. Maybe Luke is right—maybe they'll keep our secret. "You won't tell anybody?"

Behind me, Damien chuckles. "We won't have to."

My cheeks warm. They definitely heard me in Luke's bedroom.

But I can't bring myself to care. I want them to take me to him. The alcohol is turning my brain to mush. Making me forget my inhibitions.

"We won't tell anyone. Come with us," Knox murmurs. Part order, part plea.

They already know. They won't tell anyone, and I'm done fighting it. Besides, when they see me leaving with Knox and Damien, everyone at this party will assume I hooked up with them, not my stepbrother.

"Yes," I breathe.

Without another word, Damien grabs my hand and pulls me through the crowd, parting the sweaty bodies with ease. Knox is right on our heels, and my heart pounds.

My vision wavers as they lead me upstairs, and I stumble over a step. Knox laughs a little too hard, as drunk or drunker than I am. Damien hardly notices, his focus honed in on reaching the door at the end of the hallway.

In the dim lighting, he turns the doorknob and Knox grabs my ass, making me jump. "What the hell—"

Damien guides me into the dark bedroom, the only illumination trickling in from the streetlamp outside and the flickering traffic light at the nearby intersection, casting the rest of the room in an eerie glow.

Someone is already sitting at the end of the bed. Another masked Devil.

But it's not Luke.

My stomach twists.

"Sienna wants to have some fun with us, Finn." With a hand on the small of my back, Knox nudges me further into the dark room.

Finn stands slowly, and my stomach flips. All three of them.

"Wait—" Before I can retreat, Damien shoves me up

Drown in You

against the wall, knocking the air out of my lungs. I gasp as my head smacks against the plaster. The whole room spins.

Damien steps aside, keeping me pinned to the wall with a hand on my shoulder.

Knox grabs my other shoulder, rubbing soothing circles over my exposed skin. "You ready for our hands and mouths all over you, beautiful?"

Before meeting Luke, Knox's words of praise would've made my knees weak. But my body doesn't react to the sweet words because they aren't coming from my stepbrother's mouth.

"I better go." My tipsy words come out shaky.

"You're not going anywhere." Damien's voice is brusque, sharp.

Finn moves like a shadow until he's directly in front of me. With my gaze finally glued to him, he hooks a finger under my chin, lifting it to meet the eyes I can't see beneath his purge mask. But he sees everything.

A lump forms in my throat, and I stop breathing when Finn sinks to his knees before me.

Oh my god. "What are you—"

Finn's calloused hands land on my thighs, gradually drifting up, goosebumps budding in their wake. I can't form the words to stop him.

My heart beats wildly. Finn's hands are shockingly, achingly tender as they brush along my thighs and up, inch by inch, until they're sliding beneath the hem of my dress.

When he catches the edge of my panties between his fingers, my heart stops. "I'm not—"

"We're going to have so much fun with you," Knox promises.

In a blink, Finn tugs my panties to my feet.

The cool air kisses between my legs, and before I can stop

them, a pair of lips brush against my neck. "You're going to love having all three of us inside you."

The door bangs open, knob smacking against the wall. Light from the hallway spills into the room, a bucket of ice water jolting us awake from a sound sleep.

Another masked man rounds on us. The pair of holes in his mask display his fiery gray eyes.

Luke's gaze spears through me like I'm about to suggest he join the fun.

He wrenches me from their grasps, his fingers digging into my arm. "She's my stepsister, assholes. *Drunk* stepsister."

Knox hiccups. "We're all drunk."

"No-sisters rule," he snaps.

"Don't break up the party, Valentine," Damien protests. "Your sister was finally about to have some fun."

Wordlessly, Luke hauls me out of the room.

"Where are you taking her?" Knox calls.

"To sober up."

At least, I'm pretty sure that's what he said. Sights and sounds are swirling around me, words distorted as they reach me as if they were spoken through water.

He pulls me into a tiny bathroom, flicking on the bright fluorescent light. I shield my eyes against it like a vampire burning under the sun and smack the light back off.

Luke whirls on me, picking me up and slamming me down onto the sink so fast, I yelp. The sink is icy against my ass, covered only by the thin fabric of my dress.

"What the hell are you doing?" I squeal.

"What the hell are *you* doing with those three?" His growl is distorted by the mask covering his face. I hate the way it makes my stomach knot.

"Knox said, *he wants you upstairs*. I assumed he meant you."

With a rough hand, Luke grabs the back of my neck. "You were coming upstairs for me?"

I bite my lip. I've lied and kept so many secrets from him. I need to finally be honest. "Yes."

Luke tears the mask off and yanks me to him, our mouths colliding.

I don't breathe, don't move, as his lips press against mine.

When his tongue slips past my lips, I moan into his mouth. He grabs me by the hip and drags me closer, my pussy smacking against him.

I whimper, and he groans into my mouth. The sound makes my limbs go weak.

My heart pounds as Luke sinks his teeth into my bottom lip and I gasp. Of their own accord, my hands drift from his chest to the collar of his shirt and tug him closer.

He unleashes himself on me. He sucks on my tongue, my thighs shaking around his hips. My high moans mix with his throaty groans to create an obscene echo in the tiny bathroom.

When he grinds his zipper between my legs, he makes contact with the sensitive bundle of nerves and I cry out.

He swallows down the cry, pulling me even closer so I'm flush against him. Until he breaks the kiss and sinks to his knees in front of me.

Luke's finger swipes up my slit to my clit, drawing a low moan from my throat. "Did any of them touch you here?" he growls.

I shake my head quickly. Even if any of them had touched me, admitting that to Luke right now seems incredibly dangerous. He might not hurt me, but he would end all three Devils in that bedroom. "I didn't want them to touch me. Only you."

He slides a finger inside me and curls it. I gasp, thighs clenching together. "You're mine, Sienna." He adds a second finger, and I whimper at the stretch. "Don't ever forget that."

I couldn't even if I wanted to.

The questions I'm dying to ask him are on the tip of my tongue. *Are you the man behind the mask? The man who's been my friend for years? Why are you still hiding?*

But what if he's not Ten? He'll be insulted and hurt that I'm hoping they're the same person. No, I need more evidence before I confront him about it. Something more concrete than a hunch.

A small creak. My gaze flashes to the door. Is it shut? I can't tell in the dark.

Luke's lips find my clit and suck. My hips buck into him, the pleasure excruciating. No one compares to the man on his knees before me. No one compares to Luke Valentine.

I squeeze my eyes shut. My stepbrother has his mouth and fingers between my legs. And I'm letting him.

My clit throbs as he sucks that bundle of nerves and his fingers grow slippery, sliding in and out of me with ease. He hums in satisfaction at the arousal pooling in his hand.

No matter how wrong it is, I've never wanted anyone more. He makes me crave him, in every way.

"You're going to drown." The words fly out of my mouth in tipsy ecstasy.

"I would happily drown in you," he murmurs.

My pussy tightens around his fingers as the first wave of my orgasm pulses through my clit.

I clap a hand over my mouth to suppress the cry, gripping the edge of the sink for dear life.

Luke pumps his fingers inside me while his mouth keeps devouring me, sending shockwaves of pleasure through my whole body. My eyes water, the pleasure too much for me to handle until he drops my clit from his mouth and his fingers slow.

He grabs his mask and slips it over his head as he straightens. With one hand, he grips my hip while the other reaches into his gray sweatpants.

Any second now, he'll pull out his cock, sink into me, and fuck me right here.

And I won't stop him.

No. *Fuck.* I have to.

"Stop!" I shove my hands against Luke's chest, so unexpectedly it surprises both of us and he stumbles backward. "Stop. We can't do this. Not here."

Through his mask, his gray eyes darken. "I need to fuck you, Sienna."

God, those six words alone are enough to make me want to spread my legs and let him. "You will, just . . . not here. We're at a fucking party. This was so stupid."

I jump down from the sink and smack the door. To my horror, it swings open.

I whirl on him and hiss, "You didn't close the door?"

"You see anyone out there watching us?" he drawls. Somehow, he's completely calm.

The hallway is empty. We're alone. My thundering heart slows. We would've heard someone if they had seen us. There's no way they wouldn't have shouted something about the stepsiblings hooking up in the bathroom.

I leave the room on unsteady legs. "We need to be more careful."

He squeezes my ass as he joins me. "Don't worry, sweetheart. I'm not letting anyone take you from me."

Chapter 18

Luke

I can still taste my stepsister on my tongue.

I'll kill my teammates for daring to put their hands on her. The three of them had her pinned to the wall, her dress unzipped. Her panties off.

We never did double back to get them. One of those assholes is probably jerking off with her panties right now.

Sienna is just another puck bunny to them. Just another girl. But she's way more than that.

I don't have any games this weekend, so Ma called us home now that they're back from their honeymoon.

At the dinner table beside me, Sienna fidgets with the napkin on her lap as she answers Ma's and Mike's barrage of questions about classes and friends.

"Are you dating anyone, Sienna?" Ma smiles as she carves into a stalk of asparagus.

I bite back my grin.

"I'm not interested in anybody," Sienna squeaks, and heat crawls up the back of my neck. The hell she isn't. "Or looking for a relationship right now."

"What about you, Luke?" Ma asks.

I flash a cocky grin. I'm going to have fun with this. "There's a girl. She seems pretty into me."

Ma gasps, eyes lighting up while Sienna goes rigid beside me. I don't have to read her mind to know exactly what she's thinking. *You better not.*

"Who is it?" Ma beams at the same time Mike asks, "What's she like?"

I fix my grin on my stepsister. "She's Sienna's friend."

Her eyes narrow.

"Well, tell me about her, honey! I want to hear everything about this girl."

"She's gorgeous." If looks could kill, Sienna would be burning me alive. "Brown hair, green eyes—"

She pinches my thigh in warning. Did she really think I was going to sit here and make up some story about how hot her best friend is when I only have eyes for her?

"She can be pretty ruthless." I jerk my leg away from her. "But she's a badass too. She's been through a lot of shit, but she's still somehow really sweet. Cares about people. Even when they don't deserve it."

Mike points his fork at me. "Sounds like a keeper."

Ma grabs a slice of pie and drops it onto her plate. "She sounds wonderful, honey. If things get serious, I want to meet her."

Before I can tell her she already has, Sienna jumps up from her seat, thanking Ma for the meal and announcing she's grabbing a shower before heading to bed.

Part of me aches to follow and join her in that shower, but I've got to tell Ma what I discovered about her new husband first. Once she learns the truth about the man she married, she can get an annulment, and Sienna and I won't have to sneak around anymore. We can fuck each other's brains out and it won't matter who knows.

As soon as Sienna's out of the room, Mike scoops up our empty plates and heads for the kitchen to dump them in the dishwasher. "I'm going to grab my wallet!"

"Grab my purse too, please!" Ma calls.

"Where are you two going?"

"We have a double date with some friends."

I suppress my grin. Sienna and I will have the house all to ourselves. "Before you go, I need to talk to you about something."

A crease forms between my mother's brows. "Is something wrong?"

"I dug up some stuff on Mike while you were away."

Her eyes spring open. "Luke! Why would you—"

"He's a gambler, Ma. Before you got married, he had a lot of debt. A *lot*. I think he stole money from you to clear it. He's after your money. You can still get an annulment without losing half your shit."

Instead of gasping in horror or jumping to Mike's defense, Ma does the last thing I expect—she bursts into a fit of giggles.

She squeezes my arm and tries to take a sip of her water, but she sputters into her glass, unable to stop laughing.

"I don't see what's funny about any of this."

"Oh, honey. I appreciate you trying to look out for me, but I already know about all that."

"You knew?"

More giggles. "Honey, we reunited at my therapist's office. I told you that."

"Yeah, you told me you were going to therapy, but you didn't tell me why Mike was there. I just assumed it was about his divorce."

She shrugs. "It was. And his addiction. But it wasn't my business to tell."

"So what about all his debts? You don't think there's any chance he tried getting in your pants for your money?"

She swats my shoulder. "No son of mine will talk like that. And no, Mike never asked me to help him with his debts. He's never asked me for a dime—I offered. *After* we got serious. And he's already paid me back."

"Ready to go, dear?" Mike calls, stuffing his wallet in his pocket and holding Ma's purse out to her.

She smiles up at him before standing and kissing the top of my head. "Have a good night, honey. Don't wait up."

Disappointment knots in my chest. The news of Mike's gambling addiction was supposed to tear them apart. Break them up so I could finally have Sienna the way I want.

Mike doesn't even love her like I love Sienna. He doesn't track her every move, doesn't spend every second she's in front of him memorizing each inch of her face, doesn't reach for her every time she's in front of him because he can't stand not touching her when she's near.

And Ma doesn't look at him the way Sienna looks at me.

Yet they get to be together. They get to have everything I want with Sienna, and we only get to have each other in the shadows.

Chapter 19

Sienna

I can't sleep. Not when Luke is in a bedroom mere feet away. Not when my door doesn't have a lock.

I'm filled with the same feeling I had that night when he snuck into my dorm—a restless need for him.

If Luke really is Ten, then he's right that this thing between us is way more than sex. I've fantasized for years about the face beneath the mask, and Luke is even more gorgeous than I could've imagined. Ten is the best friend I've ever had, the person I trust most in this world, and I've always hoped that someday we'd meet and fall in love. I just assumed it was some silly fantasy, not something that could ever really happen.

Even though it'll take me time to forgive him and he'll need a great explanation for why he's been ghosting me, he's not the only one who's been keeping secrets. We're both guilty of that, and I can't hold that against him without being the biggest hypocrite.

Maybe if I tell him my secret, he'll tell me his.

Heart in my throat, I yank open my bedroom door and

hurry down the hall to his room. I have to do this quickly, now, before I chicken out.

His door is shut when I reach it. I lift my fist to knock and hesitate. If I tell him what happened, I can't take it back. This could change everything. He'll know everything about me, and he might reveal the true identity of the man beneath the mask.

Sharing our secrets could bring us closer together. Or tear us apart.

I'm not sure which one I'm more afraid of.

I swallow, heart thumping, and knock. The whole house is silent. Beyond the door, no movement follows. I wait a few beats before knocking again. Still nothing.

I try the knob. He's snuck into my room before—more than once—and it's about time I return the favor.

But the knob doesn't turn. He's locked it. Locked me out.

The small bubble of hope in my chest deflates. What if Luke is Ten and he shuts me out again? What if I lose them both?

I'm not sure I'll be able to recover from the loss.

Get a grip. I'm pathetic if I can't get over an internet friend ghosting me and my stepbrother losing interest in me. I'm just like Mom—searching for a man to fill that hole in my heart.

I turn around and head back to my room.

UNDER THE CLOAK OF DARKNESS, I sprint through the park, passing benches and rows of trees. Parents and children watch me race past, but none of them help me.

None of them stop the men from chasing me.

Their footsteps thunder behind me, getting closer and closer.

I'm panting, running as hard as I can with every muscle in my body on fire. Until my steps slow. I'm running through quicksand.

Their heavy breaths hit my ears. They've caught up to me.

Marcus's voice rattles in my head. *Found you.*

I blink into the darkness of the dimly lit room. Sunlight trickles past the blackout curtains covering the windows.

At first, I'm certain the nightmare is what stirred me from sleep. Until something wet and soft strokes between my legs.

I attempt to clamp my thighs together, but there's something hard and round between them.

Consciousness comes to me slowly. My shorts and panties are gone. Someone is hidden under the blanket, tongue sliding in my pussy as he groans at my taste. How long has he been doing this to me? Judging by the mess between my legs, he's been eating me for a while.

His mouth latches onto my clit and sucks hard. Before I fully realize what's happening, my pussy pulses and back arches, the orgasm hitting me.

I can't help the broken moan that escapes, heart hammering in my chest. Pleasure pulses through me, bringing me to full consciousness.

What the fuck just happened?

He shifts under the blanket before emerging. I blink, trying to identify him, but a mask covers his face. The same one he wore the night he chased me in Nohren Hall—gray with scowling eyes and red devil horns.

"We're in our parents' house," I whisper. "We could get caught."

Luke shakes his head, trailing his fingers over my jaw. "They went out."

We have the house to ourselves. I give him a sleepy smile. I don't care if we're step-siblings—I want him. I want him in my

Drown in You

bed like this every night, and I'm tired of fighting it. We can keep this thing between us a secret.

We're both great at keeping secrets.

I grip the hard muscles on his arms as he braces himself over me. "I knocked on your door earlier. You didn't answer."

His voice drops, intense and gravelly, as he threads a hand in my hair. "I'm here now. I'm not going anywhere."

He always knows exactly what to say. Just like Ten.

"Good." I squeeze his arms, tears pricking my eyes. "This is exactly where I want you."

His throat bobs. "Do you want *me*, Sienna?"

This is what he's been waiting for. For his feelings for me to be reciprocated. I care about him, I know that. And I want him. Every inch. "Yes. I want you, Luke. I don't care about the rest of it. Our parents or anybody else. I just know . . . I want you."

He comes down on me, the nose of his mask brushing against my neck, and a whimper builds in my throat. The adrenaline and desire mix as wetness pools between my legs.

"I've wanted you for so fucking long." Through the few pinprick holes in front of his mouth, Luke's hot breath hits my bare skin. I'm already burning beneath his warmth. Then he murmurs, so low I almost can't hear, "You have no idea how long."

He trails his mask along my collarbone and across my chest, softly blowing the entire way. Goosebumps prick up along my skin. I've fantasized about sharing a bed with a masked man for a long time, but it's a thousand times better knowing it's Luke beneath the mask.

When he suddenly straightens, taking his warmth with him and leaving me in the cold, I nearly whine in protest. But before I get a chance, he lifts me up until I'm sitting, pulling my tank top over my head as tenderly as he did that first night.

My breasts fall in front of him, and through the mask, his

eyes are glued to them. Eating me up. "Tell me how long, Luke."

"How long what?"

"How long you've wanted me."

He stiffens briefly before murmuring, "Since the moment I met you."

Does he mean at the hotel bar or online? Why can't he just admit to the truth? Why can't I?

I push the thought aside. Neither of us is ready to bare our souls entirely. But we are ready for this.

"Can you blame me?" He pushes me back down and grabs my breasts with both hands, squeezing to the edge of pain. I gasp, wanting him more than I ever have. "Every inch of you is incredible."

The tip of his masked nose glides down between my breasts and to my navel. He sweeps the mask from one hipbone to the other. All of my nerve endings collect where he touches me, making every brush of contact set me on fire.

I grab for the hair spilling out behind his mask. "Every inch of you is mouthwatering."

He growls as I tug and wriggle beneath him. "Waiting to take you again has been agony."

My heart is about to burst, and I gasp, "So stop waiting."

His chuckle reverberates down my spine, and my god, I've missed that sound. "You've made me wait way too long, Sienna. Now I'm going to torture you the same way."

Oh fuck. This is going to be a long night.

"Take your clothes off," I breathe. I'm fully exposed in front of him while he's completely covered. Even his face. I miss his hard, devastating body. I want to eat him up exactly like he's doing to me.

He shakes his head. "Not yet. You're going to have to suffer a lot longer than this."

Goddamnit. The wait is already excruciating. My protest comes out in a whine. "*No.*"

Luke slides off the bed. Onto his knees.

My heart stops.

Until he jolts it back to life by tugging me to the edge of the bed. He tucks my legs over his shoulders, spreading them wide. My bare pussy glistening in front of him.

Yet he still doesn't remove his mask. Instead, he leans down, his mask brushing against my clit as he blows on my pussy.

I jerk beneath him. He tightens his grip on my legs, clamping them against his hot neck.

We're both burning up. Both of us on the edge of exploding.

When he blows on my wet pussy again, I clutch at the bedsheet. I can't help writhing beneath him. But his hold on me is so strong, I hardly move in his grasp.

He keeps blowing softly, his mask barely brushing against my clit. The overwhelming sensations are driving me insane. Enough to keep me aching, needing more, but nowhere near enough to drive me over the edge.

If this is anything like the agony I've inflicted on him, I'm a monster. I'm not going another day without letting this man get his hands on me.

Finally, he tosses the mask off his head. His intense, seductive, stormy eyes bore into my skull. No man has ever looked at me the way Luke Valentine does. "Keep your eyes on me, sweetheart."

I do as I'm told just as Luke's tongue sweeps up my slit.

When his tongue strikes that tense bundle of nerves, I cry out. Thank god our parents went out. There's no way one of them wouldn't already be storming up here to ask what all the noise is.

Only to find Luke kneeling between his stepsister's legs.

When his tongue sweeps up me again, his throaty groan alone makes the muscles in my thighs wind tight. *Jesus.* I'm already on the verge of coming again.

The effect Luke Valentine has on me is beyond dangerous. It's cataclysmic.

"You taste so fucking good, sweetheart." His tongue swirls over my clit, sending shockwaves pulsing through my veins before he laps up the flood of arousal that trickles down to the bedsheet.

When he slides a finger in, I involuntarily clench around him. "You feel so fucking good."

The groan that slips past his lips is obscene. "Fuck, Sienna. You're so tight. I can't wait to squeeze my cock inside you."

An unexpected dose of panic zips up my spine. I've made a grave oversight. Luke's cock barely fit inside me the last time we did this.

He must sense my uneasiness because he slides a second finger in, stretching me for him. We groan in unison. A man's groan shouldn't be enough to make me want to burst, but it is. My god, it is.

"You're coming on my cock this time. And when I'm finally inside you, I'm not going easy on you. You're getting fucked hard and fast."

He went easy on me last time? There's no way in hell—

Luke's tongue returns to my clit, stealing my breath. When his lips wrap around that sensitive nub and suck, my back arches and I tear at the bedsheet, pulling it up from the mattress. My cries echo in the room.

"God, that sound is so sexy," he murmurs.

How have I gone so long without allowing this man to do whatever he wants to me? I must've had an iron will. That's completely disintegrated now.

Just as the orgasm begins building, Luke drops my clit from his mouth and pops his fingers out of my pussy. Being brought to the edge of pleasure and suddenly having it stolen away makes the corners of my eyes sting. "No. Please don't stop. I need more."

I yelp when Luke abruptly stands and flips me onto my stomach. He doesn't give me a chance to orient myself to the new position before he's hauling my hips up.

His hands leave my skin only briefly as he yanks his shirt and pants off. I ogle him as he strips, admiring the ripple of hard muscle beneath taut skin. He is perfect. A specimen to be admired, studied.

When he catches me watching him in the dark, a grin blooms across his face. He grabs his throbbing cock and gives it one long, slow stroke. "Watch me while I fuck you, Sienna."

My name is filthy leaving his lips. A four-letter word. R-rated. Not suitable for virgin ears. Hell, he's making me blush.

But I do as he instructs, leaning down on my elbows and never taking my eyes off him as he presses the tip of his cock at my entrance.

Despite his promise to fuck me fast and hard, he sheaths his cock inside me slowly, deliberately.

I hiss at the stretch. The burn of his cock inside me makes me claw at the mattress again. I don't know how much more I can take.

His hand slips around to rub my clit, mixing the pain with overwhelming pleasure and building that orgasm back up. "That's my good fucking girl."

His growl makes me shiver. My cheek falls to the mattress, neck weak, and my eyes flutter shut.

A sharp slap on my ass makes me gasp and eyes fly open to find him glaring at me. "What did I tell you? Eyes on me."

What the fuck have I gotten myself into? I should've

known the moment I met Luke Valentine that my life was changed forever.

I force my eyes to stay open and glued on him as he slowly rocks his hips back. Once the tip is all that remains inside me, he slams in to the hilt.

A scream rips from my throat, and the bed rocks with every movement as Luke buries his cock inside me over and over. The intensity makes my head grow lighter. I've never passed out from sex before, but I wouldn't be surprised if Luke fucks me back to unconsciousness.

My nails bite into the mattress, and he holds me firmly in place with one hand on my hip while the other frantically circles my clit, driving pleasure through me to unprecedented levels.

"You feel so fucking good," he pants, barely audible over the frantic smack of skin on skin. "I'm going to paint you with my cum."

I expect him to yank out of me, but he keeps up the delicious torment, pounding into me relentlessly. No matter how badly he aches to come, he's going to make sure I finish first. That his cock slamming inside me is what makes me scream this time.

When he presses down harder on my clit, the familiar crescendo of an orgasm climbs steadily to the crest. My legs and arms tighten as I brace for the impact.

Luke's stormy gray gaze boars into mine as he splits me in two. My name leaving his lips on a mix of a groan and a plea is my undoing. "*Sienna.*"

Release barrels through me and I can't keep my eyes on him anymore as they cross through the overwhelming waves of pleasure.

My throat grows hoarse as I scream around the gag, and

Drown in You

Luke hisses a string of curses and praise as his thrusts turn shallow and staccato.

I jerk, yelping and collapsing onto the bed as he suddenly pulls out of me. Hot cum hits my ass and then my back. Was that my neck? *Jesus Christ*. He meant it when he said he'd paint me in his cum.

I'm still panting and weak, nowhere near recovered, when Luke returns and cleans the cum off me with a towel. "At least you're a gentleman afterward," I mumble.

He smirks. "Next time, I'll make sure to come where you can lick it off." When I part my lips, he adds, "Or maybe I'll just come in your mouth. No mess to clean up then."

I wouldn't say I've ever been eager to swallow somebody's cum before, but Luke Valentine is a totally different beast. A Devil.

Luke climbs onto my bed and throws the blanket over us.

"What the hell are you doing?" Spinning to face him, I try to push him out, but he tosses an arm around my waist, pinning me against him.

"Going to bed. Big day tomorrow." He's so beautiful this close. I want to memorize every inch of his face so I see it in my dreams.

"What's tomorrow?"

"I plan on waking you up with a slow, tender fuck before our parents come looking for us."

Panic thrums through my veins at the possibility of our parents waltzing in here and catching us. "They can't know."

He squeezes me. "They won't."

"Do you still think they'll split up?"

When he hesitates, my heart drops. "I don't know," he admits.

"What happens if they don't?" I whisper.

His hand drifts up to my hair, tucking it behind my ear.

"You'll always be mine, Sienna. No matter what. Nobody will come between us."

"But what if they do?" I blink back the tears that threaten to spill out. "They don't have to let me stay here. If they find out—"

"They won't." His voice is hard, sure. "We won't tell anyone. Not until we graduate. Then we can go anywhere, and I'll keep you safe."

"You're okay with keeping us a secret?"

He gives me a small smile. "Your crazy friend talked sense into me."

Juliet. So they weren't flirting after all. More like conspiring. I grin. God, I love her.

"I'll do anything to keep you. Anything. Even if that means I can't hold your hand in public. Even if that means I can't kiss you when someone else is in the room, no matter how much it kills me. As long as you're mine, the rest doesn't matter."

My heart soars. He's willing to make that sacrifice. For me. To keep me, and to keep me safe.

But to keep me safe, he needs to know what happened with Marcus. He deserves to know the truth. "I need to tell you something."

His arm around me stiffens. "What?"

I take a shaky breath. "I've been getting these threatening texts and . . . I think they're from someone back home."

I could mention the times I've spotted the red Cadillac and the hazel eyes beneath the mask at the party that I thought belonged to Marcus, but I'm still not sure if that was actually him or someone else. Or drunken paranoia.

Just by saying the words out loud, a small weight lifts off my chest. It's not my burden alone to bear anymore.

Luke pulls back from me so he can peer into my eyes, brows scrunched low. "Who?"

My heart pounds with the terror that after I tell him the truth, he won't look at me the same anymore. But I can't keep this secret bottled up any longer.

"His name is Marcus." I sit up and take a deep breath, attempting to calm my racing heart. "Last summer, I thought I saw something. Something bad. Really, *really* bad." A lump lodges in my throat at the memory, flashing through my mind again like a movie I've watched a hundred times. "A crime."

Luke doesn't interrupt as I keep going, silent and motionless other than his hand brushing up and down my arm. Comforting. Encouraging. Nowhere feels safer to me than when I'm in Luke Valentine's arms.

So I finally tell him everything.

That night, Juliet wasn't responding to my texts. We had plans to hang out, but she mentioned earlier that she might want to meet up with Marcus first. When she didn't answer my calls either, I knew where to find her.

Her parents built a giant treehouse for her when we were in middle school. Truly *giant*. Like one of those treehouses you see built on reality TV shows. That became our fortress, our castle. Where we'd go when we wanted a place that was just for us. On warm summer nights, we'd even sleep out there.

That's the first place I went. Maybe she was waiting for me and her phone died. Juliet wasn't the most reliable texter, but she almost always followed through on plans. If nothing else, Juliet is dependable, even if she's rarely predictable.

I snuck past the gate onto Juliet's huge family property. A few lights from the first floor of her massive house trickled onto the pristine, manicured front lawn. A trail of calf-high lamps bordered either side of the stone walkway that led to their front door. Visiting Juliet was like entering a castle. If I didn't love her so much, I'd envy her for her fantasy life.

But I knew what Juliet had been through, and it wasn't anything to envy.

Her parents' Mercedes wasn't in the driveway, but Juliet's Audi was. So was Marcus's Cadillac.

I should've turned around then. Waited for Juliet to text me after he left. But I waltzed up to the front door and tried the knob. Locked. I knocked, rang the doorbell. Silence.

So I slunk around the house and into the backyard like a burglar until I was standing at the foot of the ladder that led up to the towering treehouse. I didn't hear anything, no voices. Probably another dead-end. Juliet and Marcus were likely up in her room fucking, so she'd want to meet me out here anyway. I'd just wait for her.

I climbed the ladder, each rung groaning slightly under my weight. The treehouse was years old now, the ladder aged and better at withstanding the weight of the two twelve-year-olds we were than the nineteen-year-olds we'd become.

This was our safe place. Our sanctuary. It was supposed to stay that way.

Once I reached the top of the ladder, I could make out a person hunched over in the darkness.

Wait. Not one. Two. One of them was bracing on all fours, the other prone on the wooden floor beneath them.

Juliet's parents had lights built into the treehouse. We always turned them on when we were out here in the dark.

But Marcus kept them off.

His grunts were the first thing my senses registered. Then it was the thrusts of his hips.

My face burned and I was about to climb back down before they noticed me until I spotted the rope he tightened around her neck.

Beneath him, Juliet was silent. I'd overheard her having sex with guys often enough that I knew she wasn't quiet in bed.

Certainly never silent.

Worse, she wasn't moving. She was limp beneath him, her head lolled to the side and eyes shut.

My best friend was unconscious. While Marcus—

After that, there were no thoughts in my head. My body went into panic mode, acting of its own accord like I was watching myself move but my mind wasn't in control of any of it. "What the *hell?*"

Marcus dropped the rope and stopped the second he saw me. He scrambled off Juliet, tugging his pants back on with a jangle of his belt.

Her face was red from lack of oxygen. From how hard he'd been choking her with the rope.

"What the fuck are you doing to her?" The scream ripped from my throat so violently, I wondered if the vibration of your vocal chords could scar you.

He held up his hands. "It's not what it looks like. She wanted it."

She wanted it. How many fucking times has that been used as a defense for men who take what they want without permission?

No. Not Juliet. Not my best friend. She'd already been through enough. I wouldn't let this monster get away with it.

Hot tears stung my eyes, but I blinked them away. I'd break down later. Right now, I needed to get this motherfucker far away from her.

Trembling, I moved between them, pointing to the ladder. "Leave."

He hesitated, and my heart dropped. I came up here without a weapon. I didn't have anything to defend myself or my best friend. He was a football player. He could hurt both of us.

"No. I'm telling you, she wanted this. Just wait for her to wake up—"

"Get the *fuck* out!" Fury blinded me. All I saw was black as I lunged at him and shoved.

"Sienna!" A small, husky voice called out in the dark. "No! Don't!"

But it was too late. His foot caught on the ladder, and my lungs froze as his arms windmilled and he tumbled back, plummeting into the darkness.

He didn't scream as he fell.

The next second, a sickening thud as his body hit the ground.

Juliet climbed onto wobbly legs, scrambling for the exit. "What did you do? He wasn't doing anything wrong!"

"He had you unconscious!" The tears spilled down my cheeks, my heart breaking that I had to be the one to tell her what Marcus was doing to her. "He was . . ."

She shook her head adamantly. "He wasn't! I wanted it like that. *Fuck!*"

Juliet scrambled down the ladder and screamed his name, shaking him. Marcus's leg was bent at the wrong angle. My stomach turned and I heaved.

Now, my hands shake as I relive that night with Luke. "Juliet wanted to try breath play. He'd choke her until she was unconscious and stop until she came to. Then he'd do it again, if she told him to. She explained that to the police, so they didn't press charges. She forgave me right away; she knew why I did what I did. But Marcus . . ." I squeeze my eyes shut, and Luke sits up, pulling me close. "The injuries he sustained to his leg and back were permanent. Physical therapy might help him, but he'll never play football again. He had to give up his scholarship. He had to give up his team and his future. All because of me."

Drown in You

Luke hooks his hand under my chin, forcing my gaze up to his. "You didn't do anything wrong, Sienna. You did what any good person would've done in that situation. You thought you were witnessing a crime, and you stopped it. The fact that it was happening to your best friend made it that much worse."

I shake my head. "I should've waited until she woke up. I should've waited ten more seconds. Then she could've explained and Marcus wouldn't have gotten hurt—"

"It's *not* your fault." His conviction breaks me, and I bury my head against his chest as a sob wracks through me. He wraps his arms around me tight, squeezing like he'll never let me go. "If I'd walked in on anything like that happening to you . . ." He pauses, collecting himself as he swallows audibly. "I would've killed him."

I cry harder. Too hard to speak. Luke Valentine would kill for me. Somehow, I didn't need him to make the promise out loud to know he would.

"He's the one who attacked you." Luke's voice is gentler now, even as a current of rage underlies his words. "You moved here to get away from him."

I sniffle, managing to pull myself together enough to form watery words. "Yeah. Him and two of his friends. They attacked me in the park. But I left because they turned the whole town against me. Everyone saw him as the golden boy, the star athlete, and I was a nobody. I was just Juliet's best friend, the poor girl with a single mom glomming onto the rich kids. Mom and I knew they wouldn't get punished for what they did to me. They have family in law enforcement. Everyone in Wakefield sided with Marcus, and I became their villain."

"Who gives a fuck what you are to them," Luke says simply. "You're a hero to Juliet. That's what matters."

"I'm not a hero to her." I choke on the sob building up

again. "I ruined her life. I ruined her chance with Marcus, and now she's uprooted her whole life to come here with me. I'm a burden."

A burden to Juliet, to my mother, to my father, to Deb, to Luke. To everyone.

Luke sits up, pulling me close until I'm straddling him. Our noses are inches apart as he holds my face with both hands. "You are *not* a burden, Sienna. Juliet moved here with you because she loves you. She's your best friend, and I guarantee if the roles were reversed, she would've done the same thing. That's why she followed you here—because you're her best friend. And you proved it that night."

My nose stings as I try to blink back the tears.

"I'm glad you're here. Because if you didn't leave Wakefield, I never would've met you." His hand caresses my jaw, and his crystal-lined eyes trace my face. "And meeting you is the best thing that ever happened to me."

I throw my arms around him, burying my face in his shoulder and losing myself again. I can't remember the last time I cried this much, but a catharsis washes over me. Like I've been bottling up these tears for a lifetime and it feels so fucking good to finally let them out.

Meeting you is the best thing that ever happened to me. I think it might be the best thing that ever happened to me too. Luke makes me feel safer, sexier, happier than anyone else ever has. He makes me feel loved unconditionally.

And I think I'm starting to fall for him too.

"Morning, gorgeous." The rumble of Luke's morning voice

blended with that tinge of a Southern accent makes my toes curl.

I've barely blinked awake before his hand caresses my jaw and he brings his lips down onto mine. Sunlight peeks around the edges of the blackout curtain. I wish we could stay here all day. Stay in this blissful bubble, where nothing and no one else exists.

His tongue slides past my lips and he flips me onto my back, sliding his hand down my stomach—

A knock makes me yelp. "Sienna? Are you up?"

Shit. My fucking *dad.*

Before I can shove Luke out of bed, he grabs my chin. "Confront him."

"What?" I hiss. "No! Go hide."

His eyes narrow. "Not about us. About him abandoning you. Tell him how it really made you feel."

"Fine." I push him toward the edge of the mattress. "Just *go!*"

His bare ass is mouthwatering as he snatches his clothes and ducks into the closet, silently shutting the doors behind him.

"Just a second!" I call, scrambling to slip back into my shirt and shorts. "Come in!"

Even with my permission, Dad eases the door open slowly. "Good morning, kiddo. Sorry, I didn't mean to wake you. I wasn't sure what time you usually get up."

I offer him a smile. "It's okay. I was up. Just on my phone."

"Oh, good." He shuffles into my room like he's uncertain of every step before perching on the edge of my mattress. "Now that we're home, I wanted to check in. Make sure you're adjusting to school, that you're comfortable here."

Thank god. He doesn't know about me and Luke. Every

tight muscle in my body relaxes. "It's great, actually. I'm definitely comfortable here. Deb is really nice."

He smiles. "She is very nice," he agrees. "I'm glad you like her. And Luke?"

I stiffen, bracing for his throaty chuckle from the closet, but he keeps quiet.

He's right, though. I need to finally confront my dad. About everything. "He's nice too. I feel really welcome." I clear my throat, not sure which subject I want to discuss with my father less—my new stepbrother or my parental abandonment. "I actually wanted to talk to you."

He straightens, pressing his lips together like he knew this conversation was coming. "Of course. What's on your mind?"

"Why did you pick gambling over us?" Just saying the words out loud brings fresh tears to my eyes. I thought I'd buried down the pain, compartmentalized it, but now that the question is out, a new wave of hurt crashes over me.

My dad drops his gaze to his lap, where his hands are clasped together. He shakes his head. "I'm so sorry, Sienna. There's no excuse. I can only tell you what I've learned in therapy—that addiction is a sickness. A sickness that sometimes leads us to make the worst decisions of our lives. That makes us hurt the people we love the most." He pauses, taking a moment to compose himself. Seeing him get choked up only brings more tears to my eyes. "My greatest regret is leaving you and your mother. Your mother made the right call, asking me to leave when I couldn't stop." He rubs the back of his neck, letting out a brief, self-deprecating laugh. "I've spent the years since trying to become better for her, to deserve her. But it wasn't until I found therapy last year that I was able to really . . . start trying to be the man I've always wanted to be. By then, I knew it was already too late to fix my broken marriage. But with you." His hand lands on my knee and he squeezes. "I hoped you'd still let me be your father, even if it's a second chance I don't deserve."

I already want to throw my arms around him and let him hug me while I cry, but I restrain myself and bite my trembling lip. "It really hurt. You only sent me cards on holidays. I got one awkward phone call on my birthday. I thought you left because of me." My hands and voice tremble, but I have to get this out. I have to tell him everything. "It made me feel like shit. Like I wasn't lovable. Like I couldn't ever make someone mad or upset with me because then they'd leave for good, and I'd never see them again. Just like you."

He scoots closer, the hand on my knee squeezing. "I'm *so* sorry—"

"And Mom." I gasp as the tears spill down my cheeks now. My chest aches, from all the years of keeping the hurt bottled up. "You know how many times I came home to find her crying on the couch? You broke us. But I could get over you breaking me—I couldn't get over you breaking her. Not my mom."

The sob racks through me as my father finally wraps me in a hug, pulling me close and enveloping me in his woodsy scent. The hug I've been needing for years. For what feels like a lifetime.

"I'm so sorry, Sienna," he repeats, his voice cracking. He's trying to stay strong for both of us. He knows only one of us deserves to cry, to be comforted. "I'm sorry I hurt you, and your mom. I didn't know how to be a dad. Or a husband. I could barely be a person." He clears his throat. "But that's no excuse. I'll never make excuses for my behavior. I was wrong, and I understand if you can't forgive me. I don't expect it. But I'll spend the rest of my life trying to be the father you deserve, even if I never succeed."

I nod against his chest. I don't know if I'll ever be able to fully forgive him, if the pain of his abandonment will ever truly go away. But I want him in my life. I want us both to try to repair the father-daughter relationship we once had.

When we've both finally composed ourselves, he pulls back and swipes at a tear on my cheek. "I'm sorry you blamed yourself, Sienna. I'm sorry you lived with that feeling for so long. But you did absolutely nothing wrong. Please don't ever think that. Not for another second."

I nod, unable to speak, and let him hug me again. The familiar, heavy weight that's been resting on my shoulders for so long has been lifted.

Luke did that for me. If not for him, I never would've confronted my father. Never would've gotten the closure I so desperately needed.

No matter what we are to each other, no matter what happens, I'll always be grateful to him for that.

Chapter 20

Sienna

IN THE LIBRARY, Juliet hunches over her phone, bored with her assignment since we sat down. I can't believe I've been managing to keep my secret relationship with Luke from her. I've been attending classes, cheering for the Devils at hockey games, and grabbing dinner with our friends like everything is normal. I guess this is our new normal. At least until a time comes that Luke and I can be public about our relationship. If that time ever comes.

Juliet's screen displays an article featuring a photo of a devastatingly handsome man with brown hair and serious green eyes in a red-and-black Devils jersey.

I nudge her. "What are you doing?"

"Reading an article about Trey Lamont."

"That guy who got kicked off campus for trying to kill Wes?"

She nods, her curtain of red-streaked black hair nearly covering her face. "That's the one."

"Tell me you're not developing some morbid fascination with him. He hurt Violet, remember?" I cringe. I don't even want to think about the hell Trey Lamont put our friend through. And Wes.

"I know that. What he did is awful. But . . . I don't know. I think there's more to the story."

I roll my eyes. "What's that paraphilia for people who are sexually attracted to criminals?"

"Hybristophilia. And yes, I know I have it."

"At least you're self-aware."

While Juliet continues reading about the new object of her obsession, I check my phone.

No notifications. Guilt hits me like a wave as I realize I've forgotten to text Ten for a few days. *Forgotten.* I haven't forgotten about him since I got here. Since we met online all those years ago.

Luke told me to forget about Ten, and I'm starting to.

Maybe he wants me to forget, to move on so he doesn't have to come clean if he really is the man behind the mask. But I told Ten I wouldn't give up on him. My dad didn't give up on me when his texts went unanswered for months, and now our relationship is better than ever. I won't give up on Ten.

Instead of scrolling to our texts, I open the email browser on my laptop. I haven't sent Ten an email in forever. We reserved those for the lengthy messages we sent each other, the long-winded updates and incoherent two a.m. ramblings that were too much for a text. The emails were special. We texted everyone, but we only ever sent those letters to each other.

I chew on my lip, trying to figure out what the hell to say. If Luke and Ten are the same person, I need to convince him to finally open up to me.

Dear Ten,

Apparently, I attend hockey games now. Can you believe it? The girl who hates sports, sitting in a hockey jersey at a

Drown in You

college game and cheering for the team. I can send you a picture if you need proof.

Did I ever tell you how I imagined cheering for you at your games? I'd be the loudest person in the bleachers. I hoped that even if your dad couldn't cheer for you, it would help, knowing someone out there is cheering for you so loud, their throat is raw after. I probably wouldn't even be able to talk, but it would be worth it if it helped you play. If it made you happy.

Even more news: my dad and I talked. About how he left after the divorce. I know. Shocker, right? I thought you'd want to know, since you helped me through all of that. I feel better about our relationship now. A lot better. He's really trying, and he feels bad for what he put me and my mom through. I'm still trying to figure out how to fully forgive him and fix our relationship. Maybe it'll always be a challenge, but that doesn't mean it's not worth trying.

I told you about Luke, right? My new stepbrother. He actually helped me gain the courage to be honest. To confront people when I need to. I'm still learning, but I'm getting better. I think you two would really get along. You're actually a lot alike. You both like hockey, you both lost your dads, and you have the same sense of humor. He's kind of been my rock lately, like you always have been.

I hope you're doing okay. Whatever you're going through right now, I'm here for you when you're ready.

Love,
Sienna

With a deep breath, I hit Send. Maybe this will be what finally gets a response from Ten. What finally gets Luke to confess to the truth, especially after I confided in him the other night. I don't want there to be any more secrets between us, and

I won't be fully convinced he and Ten are the same person until I get confirmation. After Luke explains himself and I forgive him for ghosting me and opening up old wounds, we can be closer than ever. Closer than I ever thought possible before it occurred to me that he could be one of my favorite people in the world.

I snap my laptop shut. "I'm going to drop my stuff off at the dorm, and then I'll meet you at the Village."

Juliet nods, but her eyes are glued to the image of Trey Lamont on her phone screen. I swear she's already infatuated.

Outside, spring is finally blooming. Tufts of grass pop up among the barren ground and small buds of leaves bloom on this quiet, abandoned side of campus.

As I pass the sparse end of the parking lot, a horn beeps. I jump, and I'm about to flip off the driver until I spot the lone car.

A red Cadillac.

The windows are too dark to see inside, but I don't need to. The driver creaks the door open and emerges.

Marcus.

Chapter 21

Luke

THE DEVILS DART across the ice, shouting to each other. They're all brimming with energy, but I'm already drained, barely keeping myself upright in front of the net. I pushed too hard in the gym earlier. Should've known better than working myself to the bone before practice, but all I could think about as I curled weight after weight was how long Sienna and I will have to hide our relationship.

If I come clean to Ma about what's going on between me and my stepsister, she'll only drive us apart. She wouldn't send Sienna back home like Sienna fears, but she'd separate us. Maybe send Sienna to some private university on the other side of the country. Maybe ship my ass off to Canada. Or maybe she'd play the money card again—either I stay away from my stepsister, or she'll quit paying my tuition.

When Sienna showed up, I was convinced nothing would come between me and hockey. Between me and my future. Me and Pop's dream.

But for Sienna, I'd give it all up. I'd pack up and move to

Europe if it meant she was safe. If it meant I got to keep her. Pop would send me off with a smile.

She finally trusted me enough to tell me the truth about what happened back in Wakefield, but now my own secret claws at me. It's too late to confess the truth. If she ever finds out I catfished her, if she ever learns Ten's true identity, she'll never forgive me. And I wouldn't blame her.

In my peripheral vision, a flash of black and red darts toward me, but I don't react in time.

Damien slams into me, knocking me off my feet and sending me onto the unforgiving ice, pain shooting through my limbs.

Beneath my helmet, my brain spins.

The other Devils are on him in seconds. Finn pummels Damien first, shortly followed by Knox who shouts, "Don't fuck with my goalie!"

Back flat against the wall as the Devils pin him, Damien shouts, "He would've stayed on his feet if he'd been paying attention!"

"Off the ice, Valentine!" It takes a second to register that Coach's order is directed at me.

I climb back to my feet, knees ready to give out, but my aching spine manages to keep me upright. "I'm good, Coach."

He closes the distance between us in seconds, planting a hand on my back and guiding me off the ice. "Your sister said you've been overdoing it with your workouts. You need to chill out so you have enough strength for practice and games, got me?" He nudges me to the exit. "Break your body when you're in the NHL, not now."

"But Coach—"

"I don't want to hear it, Valentine." He's already got his back to me. "You're done for the night."

Coach doesn't budge when he's made up his mind. I head

for the bench, and even though I'm pissed at Coach for kicking me off the ice, a smile breaks across my face. Sienna told Coach about her concerns for me. She isn't hiding how much she cares about me anymore.

In the locker room, I check my phone before hitting the showers. She sent Ten an email. My chest squeezes as I read it, hating myself more with every word.

She has no idea how long I've fantasized about seeing her in those bleachers cheering for me. How it makes me feel like the luckiest guy on the planet when I spot her in the crowd in my jersey with that gorgeous smile on her face.

She's happy she confronted her dad, and she credited me with helping her. Finally mentioned my name to her friend of five years. She misses him. Misses our friendship just as much as I do.

I hope you're doing okay. Whatever you're going through right now, I'm here for you when you're ready.

The guilt is eating me alive, and I'm not sure how much fucking longer I can take it.

But I might not need to come clean. She's already getting suspicious.

I think you two would really get along. You're actually a lot alike.

I'm doing a shit job of keeping my hidden identity a secret. I keep slipping. Knowing things only Ten would know. She said she wants me, but that would change the instant she found out the truth.

After I hit the showers and change, someone nudges me. Droplets from Finn's jet-black hair drip down to his chin. He holds out his phone to me, brows drawn together.

"What?" I glance at his phone screen displaying a map. Takes a minute to process what I'm looking at until it dawns on me.

Finn managed to track the number of the asshole who's been harassing Sienna.

But according to the map, he's not in Wakefield.

I fumble with my phone and call Sienna's number. *Fuck, fuck, fuck.* The phone rings. And rings.

"*Shit.* She's not fucking answering." I jam my phone in my pocket, snatch my bag, and race for the door. "We need to go."

The bastard is in Diamond. He's fucking on campus.

Chapter 22

Sienna

My heart plummets to my feet. Marcus isn't in a mask to conceal his identity this time. The sun is still setting—he wouldn't attack me in broad daylight in a deserted parking lot on campus. Would he?

How the hell did he find me? He's been following me since I spotted his red Cadillac, waiting for his moment to pounce. Those hazel eyes beneath the mask at the Sigma Chi party really did belong to him.

What would've happened to me if Knox and Damien hadn't appeared to lure me upstairs?

What will happen to me now?

With every step he takes toward me, the knot in my stomach twists tighter and tighter.

Marcus doesn't have anything to lose. I've already taken away his shot at the NFL and his shot with Juliet. His spot on his college football team, his ability to walk without a limp. I ruined his life.

Just like that night in the treehouse, I don't have a single weapon on me. Nothing I can use as self-defense beyond a backpack full of borrowed textbooks and an ancient laptop.

He let me get the upper hand then. He won't let that happen again.

Flashes of that night in the park come racing back. Marcus landing a punch to my stomach, shoving me to the frozen ground and straddling me, yanking down the zipper on my jeans.

You think you can accuse me of some sick shit I didn't do? You think you can get away with ruining my life? If you're going to accuse me, I might as well be guilty.

"Get in the car." The serpentine voice slithers down my spine. The voice I hear in my nightmares, as clear as if he's whispering the words in my ear.

I retreat a step, heart jackhammering wildly against my ribcage. Even with a limp, he'll catch me if I run. But I have to try. "No."

A deep scowl transforms his face to the monster I remember. "You think you can just run away? Hide out like nothing happened? Nah, you don't deserve to get away with what you did."

I back up another step. Another. Panic bubbles up and stings my eyes. "I'm sorry. I'm so sorry, Marcus. I didn't—"

"You didn't mean it," he snarls. Even with his casual, staggering pace, he's closing the distance between us too quickly. "But you did. You shoved me out of that fucking treehouse. You're lucky you didn't get an attempted murder charge."

"If I could take it back . . ." Tears stream down my face, but I can't finish the sentence.

You didn't do anything wrong, Sienna. You did what any good person would've done in that situation. You thought you were witnessing a crime, and you stopped it. It's not your fault.

Luke is right—what happened to Marcus wasn't my fault. I

Drown in You

acted how anyone would in that situation. And I wouldn't take it back. In fact, if this is the kind of person Juliet was sleeping with, I'm glad I shoved him. I only wish he'd stopped breathing too.

"You can't." Marcus's voice echoes off the library wall behind me. "So now I've got to do something about it. You ruined my life. Now I'm ruining yours."

I've never been this afraid in my life. Not in the treehouse, and not even that night in the park. Now I know what Marcus is capable of. "Was it you? Sending me those messages?"

His laugh is mirthless. "You never responded. Not very nice of you."

Running me out of town wasn't enough for Marcus. Beating me in the dark with his friends wasn't enough to satisfy him. I don't know what will be, and I don't want to find out.

I retreat another step only for my back to collide with the rough brick. *Fuck.* He has me cornered. "How did you find me?"

His grin is eerie. "So you haven't found it yet."

"Found what?" My heart thunders so hard I can barely hear the words leave my mouth.

"Give me your phone." He holds out his hand. He's mere feet away now. This is my last chance. I have to run—"Give me your *fucking* phone."

I toss him my backpack, where it lands on the concrete with a thud. My phone isn't in there, but his search might buy me some time. He upends the bag, spilling the contents onto the sidewalk. I cringe as my laptop hits the concrete with a clatter, along with my notebooks and pens and disposable camera.

Without a second thought, Marcus stomps on my laptop with a sickening crunch.

Then the camera.

My heart shatters with it. *No.* The camera Luke gave me

the night we met. The camera with all the photos I've taken this semester.

"Where is it?" he barks, spreading the mess with his foot.

He wants my phone so he can stop me from calling for help. With his attention on my belongings at his feet, I spin and dart down the sidewalk.

My breath heaves out of my lungs as Marcus smacks me against the brick wall of the library, crushing me. My whole body aches, lungs desperate for air as his heavy weight pins me, unmoving. "You're not running from me again."

His hazel eyes don't blaze—they're lifeless. Vacant. He has only one objective, one final mission in life.

To destroy me.

A sick smile distorts his features. "How do you like getting railed by your stepbrother?"

My heart stops.

He knows. He knows about me and Luke. How the hell did he find out?

"I'm going to make sure everyone knows that you're a little cum slut for your stepbrother." He jerks me forward only to slam me back against the brick wall.

A pained cry bursts past my lips. "Marcus, *please—*"

Behind him, tires charge up the parking lot. Marcus turns as the high beams blind him and the horn blares, deafening us.

The first car skids to a stop, followed by another. Four Devils pop out. Knox, Damien, Finn, and Luke.

Marcus releases his hold on me to face the four giant hockey players.

Relief like I've never felt before nearly makes me collapse to my knees. I clutch at my heart in a weak attempt to stop it from exploding in my chest and scramble away from him, keeping a hand braced against the brick wall.

"Get the *fuck* away from her!" Luke puts himself between me and Marcus while Damien, Knox, and Finn surround him.

Miraculously, Marcus holds up his hands in surrender. Even he's smart enough to know he wouldn't stand a chance against them.

"Four-on-one doesn't exactly seem fair, does it?" he drawls.

"He obviously doesn't know us." For the first time, Knox's cocky smirk has a sinister edge.

"We don't give a fuck about fair," Damien snarls. "Get off our campus, poodle."

Marcus's cheeks flush a deep shade of red, rage darkening his eyes. "We're the Bulldogs."

"*You're* nothing." Luke's protective arm wrapped around me tugs me close.

When Finn steps closer, arms folded, Marcus retreats. "Relax. I'm going."

He heads for his car, flashing one final glare at me. A threat and a promise rolled into one.

Luke pushes me behind him, out of Marcus's line of sight. "Don't come back here again if you know what's good for you. It'll be the last thing you do."

Marcus peels out of the parking lot, and my shoulders don't relax until the bumper of his red Cadillac is out of sight.

I fling my arms around Luke, sniffling into his chest. "Thank you!" To the other Devils, I add, "All of you."

They nod, looking more morose than victorious.

"How the hell did he know where to find you?" Luke's brows rest low over his eyes.

"I don't know. I asked him, and he said, *So you haven't found it yet*. I don't know what the hell that means. How did you know he was here?" It's a miracle they showed up when they did. Marcus already thinks his life is over—what's a little prison time?

"Finn." Luke nods to his teammate. "He managed to track the asshole's number."

Thank god for Finn. Thank god for all of them. Especially Luke. "How did you get his number?"

I don't remember ever showing it to him.

He stiffens for a second before admitting, "Your phone."

Just admit it, Luke. Admit you're Ten. Why are you still hiding it from me? You know I love you—both versions. The masked man and the stepbrother.

I do. I love him. As terrifying as it is to admit to myself. When I'll be able to admit it to him out loud, to risk my heart, I have no idea.

But I'm too exhausted to argue with him about the secret he may or may not be keeping from me right now. All I want to do is go somewhere quiet with him and forget any of this ever happened.

Finn kneels and collects the belongings Marcus dropped on the ground, handing my bag and the smashed camera back to me.

"Thanks," I manage, but I can't bring myself to smile at him. This camera meant more to me than I thought. I didn't realize how much until it was destroyed.

Luke must spot the obvious distress on my face. "We'll get you another."

Stupid tears spring to my eyes, and I have to turn away so the other Devils don't see me cry over a fucking camera. "It's okay."

"We'll see you back at the house?" Knox asks Luke.

Luke gives a single nod before his hand shifts to my lower back and he guides me to his car. The three Devils climb back into the other and take off. Luke grabs my bag and tosses it on the passenger seat before taking the camera from me and examining it.

He smiles as he pulls out a small piece. "The film is still intact. You might not be able to take any more photos, but you can get the ones you already took developed."

I throw my arms around him again, relief washing over me.

Luke presses me against the door before returning the hug. This one is tight and warm. The kind of hug I never want to end. "I don't want you walking around campus by yourself anymore. If you need to get somewhere, you call me for a ride."

"You're too busy to drive me everywhere. You have class and practice and—"

"I'm never too busy for you. I'll make it work." His tone is as soft and soothing as the arms wrapped around me. "If I really can't be there, I'll send one of the Devils."

I roll my eyes. "Right. Because it's not like they've kidnapped me before or anything."

"They won't try anything with you now. They know."

"Know what?"

"That you're off-limits." His gray eyes bore into me, and my heart stutters.

"Marcus knows about us, Luke."

His brows pull down low over his eyes as his spine goes rigid. "That's not possible."

"He asked how I enjoy getting railed by my stepbrother, so yeah, apparently it is." I bite my trembling lip. "He said he's going to make sure everyone knows."

Luke pulls me close again. "He has no proof. He was just saying that to scare you. I don't know how the fuck that asshole found out, but no one else will, okay?"

I nod, even though I'm not totally convinced he's right. If Marcus found out, surely anyone else can. Someone on campus probably fed him the information.

Luke opens my door, and when he slides in behind the steering wheel, he turns the car on. "If you're ever on campus alone and you can't get ahold of me, you need to call campus security to escort you. That's what they're here for."

Before I can open my mouth to reluctantly agree with his order, the radio blares.

To my horror, my phone connects to the Bluetooth speaker, blasting the audiobook I was listening to on my walk to the library.

I squeeze her supple tits—

"Oh my god!" I spin the dial on the radio, turning the volume all the way down as my heart hammers in my throat.

"Fuck that." With a sly grin, Luke turns the dial back up to even louder than it was.

I pull her soft nipple between my lips.

My face is on fire. "Luke, don't—"

"Take your clothes off."

"What?" I squawk.

"You heard me." He nods to the backseat. "Climb back there and take your clothes off. We're acting out these audiobooks you love to come listening to."

I beam. Exactly the distraction I need right now. Except— "We literally just discussed someone finding out about us. We need to be more discreet."

He gestures around the deserted parking lot. "You see anyone else around here?"

He's right. We're completely alone. So I do as he says, climbing in the backseat as he joins me.

Once he's in front of me, he cradles my cheeks delicately, making my heart squeeze. "I thought I almost lost you, Sienna. You know how much that would've ripped me apart?"

I nearly start crying all over again. I slide my hands over his, gliding a thumb up and down over his soft skin. "You didn't. You won't."

His eyes fall shut just before he brings my mouth to his,

tasting and cherishing me with a new reverence. Seeing me cornered by Marcus shook him more than I realized.

If this is what he needs too, to get as close to me as he possibly can, I'll happily give it to him.

He yanks my shirt above my head, desperation leaking from every pore as he undresses me as quickly as he can, the audiobook still narrating the steamy scene.

She gasps when I suck her nipple into my mouth as hard as I can, my hand slipping between her legs so I can feel how wet she gets for me when I go at her rough.

As if the audiobook is commanding him, Luke sucks on my nipples so hard, I'm sure they'll be covered in hickeys tomorrow. I gasp, clawing at his soft hair and arching into him.

Luke's hand lands between my legs, his finger gliding up the slickness waiting for him there. I hiss, the sultry words from the narrator and the warmth of Luke on top of me already making me ache. Maybe each time will always be the best time as long as it's with him.

His mouth comes down on mine and he plunges a finger inside me. I whimper against his lips and his tongue slips in to devour me, his finger pumping gently to stretch me and prepare me for everything he has planned.

I flip her onto her back, diving right into her pussy with my tongue.

"I've wanted to do this to you since that night I walked in on you listening to that audiobook with your vibrator."

My words come out breathless. "I wish you'd done it sooner."

"Careful what you wish for. I'll make up for lost time." He shoves me along the backseat until my head smacks against the door and his tongue dives into my pussy, just as the audiobook narrator instructed.

Oh my god. I cling to his hair, thighs clenching around his head as he eats me like a man starved. The wet, squishy sounds of his tongue parting me and licking up my arousal are obscene, and my tits shake as he pushes his head against me harder.

Pleasure zips up through my clit as he grinds his tongue against it. "Holy fuck!" I gasp. "That's amazing. Don't stop."

My heart thunders and then explodes when his tongue rubbing against my clit finally drives me over the edge. My pussy pulses and he slams a finger inside me to feel my orgasm. His groan nearly drowns out my moans, my pleasure nearly as tangible to him as his own.

When I finally start to come down from the crest of pleasure, the audiobook narrator's voice fills my ears again.

I don't give her a chance to recover before I'm flipping her on her stomach and sliding inside her, wanting to feel her pussy throbbing through the throes of her orgasm.

Luke flips me onto my stomach and wrenches my thighs apart. He nudges his tip at my entrance, and I brace myself, still panting from the orgasm.

He pushes my face into the leather seat and slams into me. I cry out, legs involuntarily trying to close but unable to with him in between them.

Luke plants both hands on my back, keeping me pinned beneath him as he pounds me into the leather. I cry out, the stretch intense and borderline painful as his thrusts turn relentless.

But this animalistic side of him and the friction against my clit drives pleasure through me again.

Her screams grow hoarse when I thrust into her again and again. She's so beautiful when she's getting fucked.

Luke leans down to purr in my ear, "I love fucking you, Sienna."

"Good," I breathe. "Don't ever stop."

"I won't." His vow is low and sincere.

He straightens, his thrusts growing harder and faster. Punishing. I scream into the leather, grasping for anything to clutch onto as the pleasure barrels through me and the orgasm crests.

"Fuck, Sienna!" Luke's groan is sharp, and he slams into me one last time as my pussy pulses around his cock, spilling every last drop into me.

I wait until we've both stopped panting and he unsticks himself from me, slowly pulling out, before I sink to my knees on the floor.

His head tilts to the side, confusion adorable on him. "What are you—"

I grab his still-hard cock and stroke down his length. His breath catches. "You've made my fantasies a reality," I purr. "Now I want to do the same for yours."

"*Sienna.*" My name comes out strangled.

He's done so much for me since we met. Everything he possibly could. It's long past time that I return the favor, that I show him just how much I'm willing to do for him too.

"You already made my biggest fantasy a reality." His hand threads in my hair when I wrap my lips around his tip, and he groans. "When I saw you in that hotel, and you smiled at me."

I squeeze my eyes shut before his words can make me cry again. No matter how much it terrifies me to be in love with him, I can't deny anymore that I am.

I swirl my tongue around his tip while continuing to stroke down. With my other hand, I cup his balls. "What are your other fantasies?"

A wolfish grin spreads as he peers down at me. When he bites his bottom lip, I nearly combust. "It's gonna be a long night, sweetheart."

I haven't gotten any texts from Marcus or seen his red Cadillac since the Devils chased him off campus. I can finally breathe again.

Luke located a tracker on my car, which explains how Marcus found me. He smashed it, so even if I drive somewhere alone, Marcus won't be able to follow me again. Maybe I'll finally be safe.

Violet invites me to another Sigma Chi party, and this time, I don't hesitate to slip into my favorite dress. One I know will make Luke drool.

We find Wes, Damien, and Knox first. Violet immediately goes to Wes's side, and he tips her chin up for a kiss. My chest squeezes. I wish Luke and I could do that. But we can't take our relationship public anytime soon. I'll deal with the scrutiny and weird looks after we graduate, but for now, we have to keep our secret from everyone.

"Where's Finn?" I shout over the music.

Damien nods to the corner, where Finn is nursing a drink and watching two girls grind on each other in front of him. Somehow, his features don't indicate any sign of interest, despite his gaze not drifting elsewhere.

To my friends, I call, "I'll be right back."

Finn hardly glances at me when I stop inches from his side. Luke really did warn them to keep their hands off.

"How did you trace that number for Luke?"

He takes another gulp before returning his gaze to the girls. His mouth remains shut. What's up with this guy? He may be gorgeous, but the whole silent, mysterious type doesn't exactly work for me. My type is an obsessed, golden retriever man with an alpha side.

"Can you trace a number for me?" I hold out my phone to show him Ten's number.

He gives a single nod, pulling out his phone to snap a photo of the number.

"Thanks."

Finn doesn't say a word, attention already focused on tracking the number. My chest squeezes with hope. If he can somehow link the number back to Luke or Deb, I'll know for sure who Ten really is.

When I rejoin my friends, two hours tick by while we dance our asses off and grab refills without Luke showing up.

I should've confided in him earlier about Marcus. I'm certain Marcus showing up on campus and cornering me really fucked with his head. He's already lost his dad and Chloe. If the Devils hadn't shown up on time, he could've lost me too.

"I need a break!" I shout before finding a vacant spot on a couch and collapsing onto it.

No texts from Luke promising he'll be here or ordering me to wear what he wants. I fire off a text to him. When it's ignored, I send another.

SIENNA

Are you coming to the Sigma Chi party?

Where are you?

No response. Maybe he passed out at the Devils' house. More likely, he's probably working out in the gym.

Still, dread prickles up the back of my neck. I'm not used to Luke ignoring me, and it's starting to remind me entirely too much of Ten. He can't pull the same shit on me twice.

Violet pushes her way through the crowd to me. Behind

her, Juliet is dancing with some random guy with brown hair and green eyes who looks entirely too much like Trey Lamont.

Next to me, Violet plops onto the couch. "What's wrong?"

I plaster on a fake smile. "Nothing."

Violet narrows her eyes at me, but the kindness never leaves her face. "You're drop-dead gorgeous at the best party of the semester and you look like somebody kicked your puppy. I'm not leaving until you tell me what's wrong."

There's so much I want to tell her. Marcus knowing about me and Luke, my fear that he'll somehow expose our relationship, the secret identity Luke might be hiding, and worst of all, whether I'm actually making Luke's life better or worse.

Behind us, a low voice booms, "Where the hell is Luke?"

Wes towers over the couch, Finn a silent shadow at his side.

"I don't know." Violet's gaze darts around the party. "I haven't seen him."

Finn sits on the arm of the couch beside me and shows me his phone screen displaying a texting app.

"What's this?"

He points to my phone. The number I asked him to find.

"You think he's texting me from an app?"

Finn nods, stuffing his phone back in his pocket.

"So what does that mean? Is he texting from California?" My pulse echoes in my ears. If Ten really is in California, then I've been wrong about Luke for weeks.

I'm not sure which outcome will be more disappointing—the masked man being a total stranger or being my stepbrother.

Finn shrugs, finally opening his mouth to speak. "Could be anywhere."

Ten could've been texting me from anywhere in the world. Maybe he's never lived in California at all.

I stand from the couch. I know the man beneath the mask. His laugh, his voice, his face, his name. The way his jaw clenches when he's pissed, the way he groans when he comes, the way his gray eyes instantly find mine in a crowded room.

Not Ten. Luke.

This whole time, Luke has been the masked man. He's lied to me, hidden his identity, and ghosted me . . . for what?

I need to know why.

"We need to find Luke."

Chapter 23

Luke

I'm finally starting to understand Mike's gambling addiction. Pretty sure whatever hit he got from it is the same I get when I'm in the gym or on the ice.

I'm hurting Sienna. Her dad caused her the worst pain of her life by abandoning her, and now I'm doing the same. I've been the friend she's relied on for years, her rock, and I abandoned her just like he did, knowing exactly the kind of pain it would cause. All because I can't take the agony of losing her.

Seeing her with Marcus was a gut punch. The possibility of losing her hit me like a train. I won't get that lucky again, and I won't risk losing her. Even if it hurts now, she'll forget about Ten eventually. I'm the one she can't live without.

The double doors to the gym swing open. Knox, Damien, and Juliet are all stumbling drunk. Even Violet is giggly-drunk and Finn's typical sure, steady gait is colored by the occasional misstep.

Wes and Sienna are the only two completely sober. As hockey captain, Wes is strict about avoiding alcohol during the

Drown in You

season. And Sienna was no doubt sitting at the party worrying about me. That's why they're all here.

The gym is almost entirely vacant except for me and the metallic clatter of my weights. Sweat pours down my face as I drop the dumbbells. "What the hell are you doing here?"

"What the hell are *you* doing here?" Wes snipes back.

"You're working too hard, Luke." Violet jumps in because she knows I won't pick a fight with her. "You need to go to a party once in a while and have some fun. Rest."

I ignore them, gaze burning right through Sienna as if the words left her lips. Without shifting my gaze from her, I tell the rest of them, "Get your drunk asses home. I need to talk to my stepsister."

Violet gives Sienna a sympathetic smile and Juliet mouths, *Good luck*, but none of them object as Wes guides them all out.

Sienna gulps as I stand and saunter toward her slowly. Sweat drips down from my temple and neck, soaking through my shirt.

"I'm worried about you." Her voice is shaky. "You're going to get hurt if you keep pushing yourself like this, and you've already been hurt enough."

I close the space between us and reach for her, caressing her soft cheek. God, I'll never stop being grateful for how much she cares about me. Almost as much as I care about her.

"You need to stop destroying your body like you're punishing it. There's nothing wrong with you. Nothing that's ever happened to your dad or Chloe or Violet or me has been your fault." Her hand caresses my cheek, sending chills down my spine and bringing me warm comfort all at once. "You saved me. You're so good, Luke. Way better than you believe."

My lips crash against hers. Sienna is way better than I deserve.

Her lips mold to mine. She latches onto my shirt and tugs

me closer, sinking her teeth into my bottom lip before sucking. I sweep my tongue past her lips, dancing with hers until she moans. I suck on her tongue until she's putty in my hands.

"You saved *me*, Sienna. There were so many times I didn't know how I'd keep going. Then I thought of you."

Tears glisten in those gorgeous green eyes that captured my heart that first night in the hotel. "If you get hurt, you might not be able to play hockey anymore. You might not get drafted."

I nod, thumb brushing over her cheek. Her eyes nearly flutter shut. "If that's what you want, I'll ease up. Okay?"

She nods, opening her mouth, but I don't give her a chance to respond before I'm scooping her up and kissing her, carrying her to the showers in the locker room.

When I set her on her feet, I caress her face before pulling off her shirt while she smiles at me.

Memories of that first night with Sienna in her hotel room come flooding back. The way she batted her lashes at me as she asked if I wanted to follow her to her room, the way she stood on her toes to slip the jacket off my shoulders, the way she tried to keep me from seeing her bruises, the way her every touch set me on fire.

Her fingers brush my cheek, ignoring the sweat. "I'm really, really happy I met you, Luke."

I grab her face with both hands. I love staring at her body, but I'd rather stare into her soul. "I'm so fucking happy I met you, Sienna. If you asked me to, I'd rip the whole world apart for you."

Her little smile melts me. "I know."

I carry her into the shower and turn on the water while we strip off the rest of our clothes. She steps under the water, and I revel in her as her eyes fall shut, head tipping back as the water soaks her bare skin, rivulets streaming down her perfect body.

When Sienna's eyes open, she saunters toward me with a

smile. The same one she wore that night at the hotel bar. "Let me clean you up."

She grabs the shampoo and instructs me to bend lower, hands braced against the wall behind her as she squirts shampoo into my hair before massaging my scalp. I can't help the groan that escapes.

Once the suds are rinsed from my hair, running down my shoulders, she scrubs me with the soap, admiring every inch as she washes my face, shoulders, back, chest, abs. Then she pushes me against the wall before dropping to her knees.

I nearly groan. "I'll never get tired of that sight."

She smiles at the praise before fisting my cock and swirling her tongue around the tip. I drop my head back against the shower wall, clutching at her head and groaning her name.

Her mouth follows her hand as she glides it down to the base, gagging softly when my tip hits the back of her throat. I bite back my chuckle so she doesn't change her mind about sucking me off. I'll never know how I got this fucking lucky. "You're doing so well, sweetheart."

Sienna reaches with her other hand to cup my balls, and I hiss through my teeth. "How's this?"

From the sultry way the words pass through her lips, she knows exactly how incredible it feels. "Don't fucking stop."

"Not until you come down my throat," she promises. "Every drop."

Jesus. I thread my fingers through her hair, needing something to grip onto. "You're making another one of my fantasies a reality."

She smiles around my cock in her mouth before swirling her tongue around the tip. My balls tighten, and I'm not sure how much longer I'll be able to stave off the load primed to explode into her mouth.

Her hand on my balls squeezes gently as she sucks down

my shaft, tip hitting her throat over and over. With every gag, I get closer and closer to spilling into her mouth.

"You sure you want every drop?" I pant.

She nods, her mouth bobbing up and down my slick cock faster and faster. I fist her hair, keeping her from standing or scrambling away when she realizes *every drop* means swallowing every . . . fucking . . . drop.

Sienna tightens her grip on my balls just enough to drive me wild and I don't get the chance to warn her before my cock is spurting into her mouth, hot cum hitting the back of her throat. She gags, lurching and eyes widening with surprise, but she takes it like a good fucking girl, swallowing every fucking drop I spill down her throat.

My chest heaves, heart pounding as I come down from the height of my orgasm. She rises slowly with a smug smile, and I'm like a pathetic, horny teenage boy panting in front of her. "What other fantasies of yours can I make come true?"

Just hearing the words from her mouth makes blood pump to my cock again. I grab her ass and tug her to me so our naked bodies are pressed flush together, her pointed nipples against my torso. "Let me take you here."

I give her slick ass cheek an echoing smack in emphasis.

Her eyes round, and I expect her to reject the idea immediately, but she chews her lip. "I've never done that before."

"I know, sweetheart. That's why I want to do it. I want to make you feel good everywhere."

She spins, pressing her palms against the opposite wall as her soaked hair falls down her back. "So make me feel good."

I push off the wall and grab her hip, reaching around to work her clit and prepare her for me. She moans at the contact. Music to my fucking ears.

Fisting my cock, I slide nearly every inch into her pussy,

Drown in You

taking my time and letting her acclimate. "*Oh my god,*" she breathes.

Her walls clench around my shaft and I rub her clit harder until her muscles relax. We moan together as I thrust into her, slow and deliberate. When her walls start to clamp around me again, I slide out of her. She whimpers.

"I know, sweetheart. But you're going to love this next part."

I drag the arousal from her pussy up, swirling and dipping a finger in. She immediately tightens around me, bracing herself.

"Relax." I taunt her ass, fingering her gently while I rub her clit with my other hand, driving pleasure through her every limb again.

Finally, she starts leaning back into my thrusts. "Please don't stop."

"I'll never stop fucking you." I pull my finger out and nudge the tip of my cock at her entrance, still working her clit. "I'm going to take your ass now, sweetheart."

"*Yes.*"

I slide my tip in, her ass heaven around that sensitive underside, and groan. Her sharp moan echoes off the shower walls. "You okay?"

"I . . . I think so." Her uncertainty has me ready to back off until she adds, "Keep going."

"That's my girl. You can take it." My cock pushes deeper into her ass, and her moans turn shrill. I rub her clit hard and keep my thrusts slow until she's pushing back against me again. "Tell me you love this."

"I love this," she moans.

"Tell me you love me."

She freezes. "What?"

My heart thunders, and not just from fucking her. I turn

her head so she's peering over her shoulder to face me. "Tell me you love me, Sienna. Just like I love you."

I need to know. Need to hear it from her lips. That it's not just me who's fallen head over fucking heels.

Sienna reaches back to stroke my cheek, her eyes tender. "I love you, Luke. Just like you love me."

My chest squeezes so hard it hurts. I tighten my grip on her. "You have no idea how long I've been waiting to hear you say that."

Feels like a fucking lifetime.

"Me too." A seductive little smirk plays at her lips. "Honestly, I expected you to say it a while ago."

I thrust hard into her, making her gasp. "You're going to hear it all the time now, sweetheart."

My breaths turn ragged as I fuck her slow and hard. She turns back to face the wall, bracing her palms flat against it until they curl into fists as her muscles tighten and the pleasure approaches the summit. "Oh god. Luke—"

That's my only warning before Sienna unravels in front of me, screaming as her clit pulses beneath my fingers and I pump hard and fast into her ass, needing to come with her.

The orgasm sweeps over me to the symphony of her moans, the pleasure making my eyes sting. I keep driving my cock inside her until I collapse against her and groan in her ear, her soft, wet body writhing with pleasure beneath me.

When we've both come back down, trying to catch our breaths, she pants, "Holy shit. We have to do that again."

I laugh and finally unstick myself from her, heart still hammering. "We will, sweetheart. We'll do whatever you want every day, for the rest of our lives."

Her legs shake as she turns around, leaning back against the wall to keep herself upright. Concern lines her green eyes.

I smirk. "Need me to carry you home?"

"Yes. But let me get dressed first."

"Obviously. No one gets to see you naked but me." I follow her out of the shower, both of us drying off and dressing.

She's mysteriously gone silent, chewing her lip.

"Ready?"

She only nods and follows me toward the door until stopping in her tracks. "Are you him?"

Her question throws me. "Who?"

"Ten."

My stomach drops.

From her pocket, Sienna pulls out the camera film and examines it. "The night we met, you gave me that disposable camera. After I had just told Ten that I wanted one. You knew about my dad only sending me cards and calling me on my birthday. You had my phone number without asking me for it. You and Ten both play hockey and wear masks and lost your dads. You even chose the same major. You both told me it wasn't my fault that my parents split up. When we first started talking, Ten randomly messaged me out of the blue—around the time our parents dated the first time. In that hotel room, you kissed my bruises like you already cared about me." Her eyes start to glisten as the words choke her up. "You kissed me and touched me like you'd already known me for a long time. You said *I knew this is how it would be with you.* You were obsessed with me, when I thought we'd only just met. But I wasn't sure how you'd been texting me from a California area code until Finn told me the number is from an app."

My fists clench. Fucking Finn. The guy who never fucking talks had to pick this as the one time he opens his fucking mouth?

"The only thing I'm not sure about is why you lied. Why did you lie about your name? About living in California? And why did you keep lying to my face? Why did you abandon me too?" Her lip wobbles, and my heart breaks with hers.

I'll fucking lose her if I tell her the truth now, that much is clear. But I can't lose her. She finally loves me. She's finally mine, and I can't stomach the loss, even if that means lying to her forever.

I close the space between us, lifting her chin to force her shiny eyes to meet mine. "I told you to forget about Ten. He's an asshole for ghosting you, and he doesn't deserve you. You don't need him anymore, Sienna. You have me."

"I know you're him, Luke," she whispers. "Why can't you just admit it?"

I shake my head, hating myself even though I know this is what's best for us. This lie will keep us together. The truth is what would tear us apart. "I'm not. I know you miss your friend, but you love *me*. I'll treat you better than he ever has. Than he ever could. Forget him, okay? You're better off without him."

Silence falls between us, Sienna's uncertain gaze never leaving mine. My pulse hammers. She doesn't believe me. She knows I'm lying through my teeth, and now I'm not sure what will piss her off more—that I lied in the first place or that I still am.

Finally, she nods. Every taut muscle in my body relaxes when she wraps her arms around me. She believes me. This stupid secret isn't going to drive us apart.

I squeeze her back. "I love you, Sienna. So fucking much."

My heartbeat echoes in my ears with every second that ticks by in silence.

At last, she murmurs, "I love you too."

Thank fuck. I squeeze her tighter. I'll never let her go again.

Drown in You

Outside the rink, the crowd is going nuts. This is the worst game we've played all season, and I'm only partially to blame. Sienna was right—I've been pushing too hard. My head is light, vertigo tilting the whole world on its side.

Cheers and jeers echo from the stands while Wes and Coach bark orders. Knox shouts to Damien who yells to Finn. But the blue and white jerseys of our opponents dart across the ice too fast, taking control of the puck.

Damien's face is tomato-red beneath his helmet. Ready to kill to win. Wes is pissed, shouting about our failures. Even Knox wants to crack his stick over somebody's head.

What the hell is wrong with me? I shouldn't have gone so hard in the gym before the game. Should've reserved my energy for the ice when it really mattered. I've let our opponents sail the puck into my net four times already. I'm letting my team down.

My pulse drums in my ears, throat parched. I need water. Need to sit. Need to shut my eyes—

Skates roar across the ice as our opponents race toward my net, our defense failing to stop them.

The Devils shout my name. They're counting on me. I can't let them down again.

I try to track the puck darting between our opponents, but my head is swimming.

When I drop to my knees to protect the net, my vision goes dark.

Chapter 24

Sienna

Medical staff get Luke off the ice after he comes to. My heart pounds against my ribcage, and I long to run down to him, but I wait for the staff to check his vitals and monitor him while he sips electrolyte water on the bench.

Violet pats my hand. "I'm sure he's okay."

"I don't know," Juliet says. "That fall probably rattled his brain."

Judging by the staff's demeanor, it's not too serious. Hopefully nothing more than dehydration or hyperthermia or low blood pressure. As soon as they seem satisfied that he's okay and leave him to recover, I stand and rush down the bleachers.

Even though I know he's still lying to me about being Ten, I can't stop caring about him. Worrying about him. I wish I could close my heart off to him, have some standards and stop loving the man who keeps lying to me. If he's willing to lie about something as major as this, who knows what else he's willing to lie about. How will I ever be able to trust him when he refuses to tell me the truth?

At this point, I don't even care about him putting on a mask and lying about his name and location. We were fifteen—he made a dumb, impulsive decision to get me to talk to him. If he'd talked to me as Luke, I could've easily traced his social media back to his mother and then found out about her relationship with my father. If I'd known that, I might not have been willing to open up to Luke at all. We might've never become friends.

I could forgive that. I could probably even forgive him for keeping up the lie for years. But not coming clean when we met at the hotel? Leading me to believe we were strangers and fucking me when he knew exactly who I was? Lying to my face when I finally had the guts to confront him about it, even after I've divulged all my secrets to him?

I'm not sure how I'll be able to forgive him for that. For now, I'll let him think I'm still in the dark. Let him think I bought the lie until I find solid proof that Luke and Ten really are the same person. He won't be able to lie to me again when I have evidence he can't deny. Then I'll finally, *finally* get the truth.

After that . . . I'll have to decide whether his reason for lying to me for so long is forgivable.

When I finally reach the bench, Luke's gray eyes light up. "Hey, sweetheart."

"Are you okay?"

"I'm okay. A lot better with you here." His radiant smile turns my knees to jelly, and I'm not sure whether I love it or hate it now. He casts his gaze at the audience behind me. "Not worried what people will think about you running to check on your stepbrother?"

"I don't care." The honesty surprises even me. For the first time, I really don't give a shit what anyone thinks. Not about me and Luke. Not about me loving him.

"Hey!" Juliet runs up to us, white gold jewelry jangling

with every frantic step. It isn't fear written across her face—it's horror. She holds out her phone. "Someone posted a video of you two on the Devils' social media page."

My heart leaps into my throat. "What video?"

"Everyone's seeing it. You need to get it taken down. *Now*."

Luke grabs the phone from Juliet's outstretched hand before muttering, "*Shit*."

I peer over his shoulder to watch the video. My stomach plummets to my feet.

The video was filmed in the small space of a partially open door. In the bathroom, Luke kneels before me while I writhe on the sink in front of him with my legs spread. There's no mistaking Luke's face when he grabs his mask and straightens.

Someone took that video while we were at the party. While he was eating me in the bathroom with the door still open.

My cheeks are on fire. Anyone could see this video. It's posted to the Devils' public social media page. Everyone can watch me come on my stepbrother's tongue.

Luke tosses the phone back to Juliet before taking off. "I'm finding the equipment manager. We're getting that shit taken down *now*."

I cover my mouth. "Marcus."

Juliet's blue eyes widen. "You think Marcus did this?"

I nod, tears brimming. "He knew about me and Luke. I didn't know how, but . . . he was there at the party. I thought I recognized his eyes beneath the mask, but I never thought . . ."

Juliet throws her arms around me, pulling me close as I break down, crying into her shoulder. "He won't get away with this," she promises, but it's too late.

He already has.

Marcus found me and Luke in the bathroom together. He filmed us and waited for the perfect opportunity to get his revenge.

Drown in You

To destroy my life, just like he promised.

Chapter 25

Luke

The equipment manager got the video taken down as soon as I reported it to him, but the damage was already done. Ma called me and Sienna home after three hockey moms asked her if she knew about the sex tape featuring her son and his new stepsister.

Bud is blissfully unaware of the tension in the family room as our parents sit facing us on the opposite couch. He drools on our hands and his tail wags hard enough to knock over an empty mug on the coffee table.

Sienna's mom has already driven up from Wakefield so we can all figure out how the hell we're going to handle this situation. Videos like that don't get posted to social media for even five minutes without getting uploaded to porn sites. Who knows where that video is floating around the internet by now.

On the couch beside me, Sienna is stiff as a board. This is her worst nightmare—our secret being revealed. Now everyone knows what we've been doing behind closed doors. And right out in the fucking open, apparently.

What the fuck is wrong with me? Why didn't I think to

lock the fucking door? I screwed up. Even if Marcus was the asshole who filmed that video and hacked the Devils' social media page to share it for all to see, I'm the one who failed Sienna. I failed to protect her.

All I do is hurt her.

Ma is nursing a dark liquid in her hard liquor mug. Mike is perched on the edge of the opposite couch, dragging his hands over his face. Sienna's mom paces in the room between all of us. Not exactly how I was hoping to meet her for the first time. Definitely not the first impression I wanted to make. She'll never think I'm good enough for her daughter now.

Her brown hair is the same shade as Sienna's but cropped just past her shoulders. Sienna got her willowy build from her mom, but her green eyes came from her dad. As she paces, her mom tucks her hair behind her ears over and over like a compulsion.

"You two are very, very lucky I have connections in law enforcement." Ma sets her mug down on the coffee table. "We'll make sure that video is wiped from the internet. We might be able to find out who posted it, but that will be difficult. Best-case scenario: We may be able to charge them for distributing revenge porn, but it's hard to get justice in these types of cases."

Sienna shifts uncomfortably at *revenge porn*. I can't believe I've gotten her roped into this fucking mess.

"What the hell were you two thinking?" Sienna's mom bursts out. Beside me, her daughter flinches. "This might actually be the stupidest thing I could imagine you doing. Hooking up drunk at a party? You grew up in the age of social media. Even I knew not to do that shit at your age, and we didn't all have cameras in our pockets."

"I'm sorry," Sienna murmurs, gaze glued to the hands clasped tight in her lap.

Harmony West

God, I can't fucking stand to see her like this. I squeeze her leg, even as she stiffens. "It's my fault. It was all me."

Her mom lets out a frustrated sigh. "It doesn't really matter whose fault it is at this point. You both were there; you both screwed up. What we need to focus on now is getting that video taken down."

"We'll get it taken care of, Sarah," Mike assures her, voice warm and soothing.

He's practically entranced by her. Now that he's not dragging his hands over his face, his eyes don't move from Sarah.

She nods at him, managing a weak smile. Pain lingers in her gaze when she meets his.

Mike looks at Sarah the way my father looked at my mother. The way I look at Sienna.

I still wasn't really over Sienna's mom. I wasn't ready to love again. That's what he told us when I asked why he and Ma broke up all those years ago.

I've spent the years since trying to become better for her, to deserve her. But it wasn't until I found therapy last year that I was able to really start trying to be the man I've always wanted to be. By then, I knew it was already too late.

My hunch was right. Mike doesn't love Ma the way I love Sienna.

Because he's still in love with his ex-wife.

And by the looks of it, the feeling is mutual.

"What about these two?" Ma points between me and Sienna. All three of them fix their gazes on us.

Sienna's leg stiffens beneath my palm, but I don't move. I'm not letting her go. I'm not letting them rip us apart. This isn't some fling. We love each other, way more than the married couple in the room.

"I'm in love with Sienna." I glance at her, but she refuses to look at me. Refuses to look anywhere other than her lap. "I know we screwed up. What we did was stupid, what *I* did was stupid, and I'm sorry for the mess I made. But you'll have to pry her out of my cold, dead hands if you want to keep us apart."

Ma covers her mouth, eyes shimmering.

Mike glances at Sarah, deferring to her to make the call. She frowns at us. My confession doesn't seem to have warmed her to me. That's fine. I'll spend the rest of my life trying to win her approval if that's what it takes to keep Sienna.

"For now, let's focus on getting that video removed from the internet. After that, we'll discuss your relationship." She folds her arms. "You two will stay here until we can get this sorted out. In *separate* rooms."

Chapter 26

Sienna

When my phone lights up on my bed beside me, I expect it to be Luke asking me to sneak over to his room. Not a chance. We've already made enough of a mess today.

But the text isn't from Luke. It's from Deb.

DEB
Hey, honey. Can you come downstairs?

My heart is in my throat the entire way. Is sweet Deb finally going to chew me out for getting her son embroiled in a revenge porn case? Accuse me of being the succubus who lured her son off the right path? He was a well-behaved hockey goalie until he met me.

As much as he loves me, I'm not sure I've actually made his life better since I showed up. All I've done is brought the dark shadows of my past to his doorstep. Now I've gotten him wrapped up in this nightmare with me. That sex tape could jeopardize his spot on the Diamond Devils team. It could ruin his chances at the NHL.

The dream he and his dad shared. Lost because of me.

Mom, Dad, and Deb are probably all waiting for me so they can come up with some secret plot to get me out of town overnight. Send me somewhere before Luke can find out and follow me. Or Marcus.

In the kitchen, Deb sits at the table with Bud snoring softly at her feet. I halt in my tracks. I didn't expect to find her alone.

From the family room, the grandfather clock ticks. A bouquet of the flowers Luke got me wilts in its vase on the counter. Deb has traded her mug for a wine glass and dark red liquid that stains her lips when she smiles at me.

Relief floods through my veins. She can still bring herself to smile at me, even after all I've put them through. All I'm still putting them through.

"Have a seat, honey." She pours wine into the glass waiting for me.

I do as she requests, swirling the wine in my glass before taking a sip just for something to do. "I'm really sorry, Deb. For everything."

The gentle smile never leaves her face. "When did you know you were in love with my son?"

"Um." My brain scrambles. Is this some reverse psychology? She can't actually want to know about her son's relationship with his stepsister.

She swirls the wine in her glass. Maybe she's drunk and she'll forget this entire conversation in the morning. "It's okay. Your parents might not condone it, and though I might not be thrilled about the circumstances either, I know that true love is an unstoppable force. No amount of reason or logic will talk you out of it. I've noticed the way my son looks at you for a while. He's never looked at anyone that way."

I swallow around the lump in my throat. "When I felt like I could finally tell him about the incident with Marcus . . . that's when I knew I was falling for him. But when he protected me when Marcus showed up on campus . . . that's when I knew I'd already fallen." I grip the wine glass tight, trying to hold back the tears. "Except when I look back, I'm pretty sure I've been falling for him since he gave me that disposable camera."

When he knelt and kissed my bruises in my hotel room. When he told me, *I knew this is how it would be with you.* When he insisted it wasn't my fault my parents split up. When he bought me ten dozen flowers, simply because I told him it would make me feel better.

I've been falling for him for a long time. As long as he's been falling for me. It just took me longer to realize it. To admit it.

"Did Luke ever tell you how I met his father?" Deb's voice is tender, full of nostalgia.

I shake my head, eager for a story I hadn't even thought to ask for. "Luke doesn't really talk about his dad much."

She sighs, gaze drifting up to the ceiling like she can see the memories playing out on a screen. "We were at the grocery store, and we both reached for the same bag of chips. The last bag. We spent the next ten minutes insisting that the other could take it until he finally bought the chips and split them with me." A soft laugh passes through her lips. "We sat in that parking lot for two hours after we finished those chips, just talking and laughing. That man could make me laugh like nobody else. It wasn't love at first sight or anything; I didn't believe in that. But I had a gut feeling that he was special, and I was right."

I can't help but smile with her, even as a small twinge settles in my chest that I'll never meet the man she and Luke loved so much. "I saw a picture. They looked so much alike."

She beams. "Oh, *exact* replicas. If they'd been the same age, you'd guess they were twins."

Silence falls between us as I debate when I should ask

about the giant elephant in the room. I clutch the wine glass in front of me. Deb might be opening up to me and she may have welcomed me into her home with open arms, but we also don't know each other that well and I don't want to step on any toes. Except I also didn't ask Dad the questions I wanted to for years and that didn't do either of us any good.

Luke would tell me to ask. To be his brave girl.

"Deb?"

"Yeah, honey?"

"Do you love my father?"

The question falls between us. Deb hesitates for a beat too long. "I care about him."

That's not how I would answer that question about Luke. "I know. But . . . do you love him?"

She didn't want to tell me the story about how she met my father—she wanted to tell me the story about how she met Luke's.

Deb takes a gulp from her wine, draining the glass before sighing. "I think Mike still loves your mother."

I shake my head quickly. "No, he loves you—"

"Sarah's always been the one for him. He always wished he could win her back, but he never felt like he deserved her."

I can't deny it anymore because that's almost exactly what my father told me when I confronted him about leaving us behind.

"Loneliness brought us together. But I'm not sure it's enough glue to keep us that way." She turns to me. "Do you think your mom still loves Mike?"

"She hasn't said anything to me." But even though my mom might not have ever admitted anything out loud, I know her.

I know the pain she's suffered in the years since the divorce. How poorly she's coped with the demise of their relationship. I could lie to spare Deb's feelings, but I know what Luke's lies have done to me and mine to him.

Deb deserves to hear the truth. We all do. "But I do think she's always been searching for his replacement, and she's never found one."

In the family room earlier, she'd looked at Dad with longing in her eyes. For a love they once shared. For a life they once lived together. The same way I'm sure my friends have caught me looking at Luke. For a future we'll never get while our parents are married.

"If I had to guess . . . I'd bet she's still in love with him."

After a stressful day of phone calls, hushed conversations, and outbursts, Deb has managed to get her lawyer and team on the case so they can figure out who did this and expunge the video from the internet.

But I already know exactly who's behind this. "It was Marcus."

All three of them turn to face me from where they're hunched over computers and phones at the kitchen table, Deb with folders and a fan of printouts at her side.

Dad sits across from her while Mom stands nearby with her palms flat on the table. She frowns at me. "How would Marcus have gotten that video?"

"He filmed it himself." I bite my lip. I never told her about the run-ins with Marcus on campus because I didn't want to worry her after she'd sent me away to escape him. And after the Devils confronted him, I mistakenly thought Marcus wouldn't dare to mess with me again. "I thought I saw him at that party,

Drown in You

but he was wearing a mask and I was drinking, so . . . I convinced myself I was imagining it."

Mom fixes her glare on Dad. "Did you know about this?"

He shakes his head, morose. "This is all news to me."

Mom's eyes fall shut. I've never disappointed her more than I have in the past two days. "How did he find you?"

"Luke found a tracker on my car. He attached it to the undercarriage where I wouldn't see it."

"Why didn't you tell any of us, kiddo?" The words leave Dad's mouth defeated. Like he's somehow the one who screwed up, not me.

I bite my lip. "I didn't want to worry you."

"The only thing I need to do is worry about you, Sienna."

Mom's features soften at his words. Until Luke enters the room behind me, carrying his laptop to add to the cause. His empty hand brushes against the small of my back and I flinch, even though everyone already knows about us. Our parents are doing damage control after our sex tape hit our team's official social media page. We shouldn't exactly be reminding them of how we created this shitstorm.

"Now that we're getting all of this settled, we need to talk about the two of you." Mom folds her arms.

The thick knot in my stomach tightens. This is the moment I've been dreading—the moment our parents tell us we need to split up. That I'm being sent back home, or at the very least, far away from Luke. That it's wrong for us to be together, even though nothing has ever felt more right.

When Luke flattens his hand against my back, I let him. I need his comfort right now more than ever. This may be the last time I ever get it. "Mom, please—"

"I love Sienna. We're adults—"

"You can stay together."

Everyone turns to Deb, her hands folded together on the table. A few beats of silence pass as her words register.

Mom's head tilts in confusion. "Deb, what are you—?"

"I want an annulment."

Luke's hand on my back slides around to my waist to tug me to him. Behind his glasses, Dad's eyes widen. But he doesn't jump up and protest.

What the fuck is happening?

"Deb—what?" Mom stutters. "What's going on?"

Deb manages a small smile at my parents. "I see the love between the two of you. If I could have a second chance with my late husband, I'd jump on it. I care about you, Mike, and I want you both to be with the one you really love."

Mom shakes her head adamantly. "Mike loves *you*, Deb. He married you." She turns to Dad, but when he stays silent, she prompts, "Right?"

But Dad's mouth remains shut. He can't meet either of their gazes.

Oh my god. Luke was right. Something has been off about their relationship this whole time.

Dad and Deb aren't in love. They may care about each other, enough to convince themselves that they could settle for each other and escape the loneliness, but neither of them has felt for the other what they felt for their former spouses.

My parents are still in love. All these years later, even after a broken marriage, they've never stopped loving each other.

"It's really okay." Deb's smile is impossibly warm. "I want what the two of you had. What me and my husband had." Her smile grows when she turns to me and Luke. "What you two have."

Luke squeezes me closer, and maybe now, he'll never have to let me go. Deb obviously took what I said to her last night to heart. I never expected it would lead to *this*.

Drown in You

"I'm not going to be responsible for ruining another marriage." Mom's voice wobbles, eyes glistening.

"I hope you don't actually believe that." For the first time since Deb dropped the annulment bomb, Dad finds his voice. But it's not to comfort Deb or convince her to stay with him—it's to comfort my mom. "You're not responsible for ruining this marriage, and you certainly weren't responsible for ruining ours."

Mom can't say anything as his words choke her up more.

Dad nods to me and Luke. "Could you two give us a moment?"

Luke takes my hand and leads me out of the room, my mind still spinning. Still catching up on the sharp detour my life has just taken. All of our lives.

Behind us, Deb murmurs, "I've already filled out the paperwork."

Chapter 27

Sienna

Luke and I rush upstairs, my heart thundering as Luke shuts his bedroom door behind us. "Holy shit! Did that really just happen?"

Deb wants an annulment. Our parents are splitting up. Because my parents still love each other.

"Yeah, it did." Luke is just as shocked as I am.

"I feel awful. I told Deb last night that my mom still loves my dad. I shouldn't have said anything." If I'm the reason they're breaking up, I'll be crushed. I've already lived years of my life believing I was responsible for destroying one marriage. I don't want to live with the knowledge that I broke up another.

"Don't feel bad. It's good you did. They're not right for each other." Luke rubs my arms in comforting strokes. "Do you think your parents will get back together?"

"I can't even wrap my mind around that possibility." A bubble of hope rises in my chest. "But I think maybe they would both be happier. I'm sorry if your mom is hurt, though."

My heart aches for Deb. I hope she's not just putting on a

brave face for all of us while she's actually harboring more love for my father than any of us realize.

"I'd rather Ma find someone like Pop again. I'd rather all of them be as happy as I am with you." He steps closer, threading his hand into my hair. "I love you, Sienna."

"I love you too." The words fly out of my mouth without a second's hesitation. Even if I'm not sure how many lies he's still keeping from me. "So after the annulment is finalized . . . that means we won't be step-siblings anymore."

"Exactly." He grins. "And when the semester ends, we can spend the break together. Coach will probably keep us coming to practice for another week or two, but we should get some time off for the summer."

"We can finally be together." Deb's announcement changes everything. Soon enough, we won't be family. We'll be free to treat each other in public exactly like we do in private. Well, some things should still be kept behind closed doors. We've learned our lesson there. "Unless you don't want to be with me after all this stuff with Marcus—"

"Fuck Marcus." Luke's gray eyes are stormy. "Fuck that video. He better hope he doesn't give me a chance to put my hands on him again. Ma will take care of it. Tomorrow, it'll be like that fucking video never existed."

"But what about the team? What about the NHL? That's your *dream*, Luke. What if all this shit screws that up?" I blink away the tears. I don't want to be the reason he can't fulfill his dream. I don't want him to resent me.

Luke cradles my jaw. "*You* are my dream, Sienna. Being with you is a dream come true. Nothing else compares to you. I don't give a fuck if I don't get drafted as long as I have you by my side."

I throw my arms around him, and without another word,

Luke picks me up and presses me against the door, lips colliding with mine.

The space between my legs burns with a fiery need. I ache for him. Want him more desperately than I ever have. He must sense it because he locks the door.

"What if they hear us?" I gasp as he sucks on my neck. Tingles race up to my scalp at the delicious sensation of his mouth on me.

"I'll keep you quiet." His promise sends a delicious shiver down my spine.

A few months ago, I thought the worst thing that could happen to me was getting chased out of Wakefield. Being forced to leave my home behind to start over with a new family I didn't know.

But the worst thing that ever happened to me somehow also became the best. Marcus sent me running into the arms of Luke Valentine. And there's nowhere else in the world I'd rather be.

"Take your shirt off." His command is urgent as he drops me to the floor and rips my jeans down.

I scramble to yank my shirt over my head. To my surprise, he leaves my panties on, kneeling between my legs and kissing up my thighs. Blood pumps through my veins, and part of me wants to beg him to hurry up and fuck me because I need him *now*, but another part knows the tortuous buildup will have the best possible payoff.

His tongue glides up my inner thigh in a slow, luxuriating stroke until I quiver beneath him. I can't take my eyes off him. Can't stop admiring the way he devours me.

When his mouth suctions onto my skin, inching up the same trail as his tongue, I whimper.

"I can't wait to taste you," he murmurs.

"No one's making you wait."

He chuckles against my skin and it vibrates all the way to my clit. "But making you wait, making you squirm and whimper while you ache to come, is the best part."

I gulp. "That's evil."

"Then call me the Devil."

If he's the Devil, send me to hell. That's where I belong.

No matter how many times I've been with him, he always leaves me aching for more. Needing him like water, like air.

Luke pushes my panties to the side, exposing me to him before his tongue dives inside me. He claps a hand over my mouth just as the moan escapes.

He shoves me back against the door with a clatter. I try to remind him to hush, but he ignores me, completely absorbed in tasting me. My thighs start to shake as his tongue pumps in me and my panties grind against my clit.

I'm about to burst when he stands. "No," I whine. "Please don't stop."

Luke peels off his shirt, then drops his sweats and boxers. Revealing the hard cock already glistening with pre-cum. Ready for me. "Do I look like I'm stopping?"

I grab his shaft and grind his tip against my clit. He lets out an animalistic groan before he flattens me against the door. I can't move, can't escape even if I wanted to, as he pins me and nudges his cock at my entrance.

"You're mine forever, Sienna." With a swift thrust of his hips, he buries himself inside me.

My mind spins as his cock stretches me. The cotton of my panties rubs against my clit with every slow thrust of his hips. He catches my mouth with his before I can cry out and let everyone in this house know exactly what we're up to.

His tongue dances with mine, coated with my arousal as his cock splits me open. The pleasure is so overwhelming, I can almost ignore the clatter of the door as we fuck against it.

Almost.

Even though our relationship soon won't be forbidden in the eyes of the law, our parents won't exactly appreciate overhearing us fuck in Luke's bedroom. Especially considering the circumstances.

Once he registers the tension in my muscles, he lifts me and smacks me against the wall, the angle even deeper.

"Agh!" I bite his shoulder to muffle my sounds.

He fucks me even harder now, the only sounds in the room our muffled groans and the slap of skin on skin. A forbidden, salacious symphony. Without any leverage, I can't move. I'm forced to take every inch he gives me.

"Luke," I gasp, digging into his shoulders while my eyes roll.

He moves us again, this time laying me on the floor before he flips us so I'm straddling him. "Ride me."

I oblige him, planting my hands on his broad chest while I rock my hips. His thumb circles my clit while he bites his lip, unable to tear his eyes away from me.

Luke may own me, but I own him too. His body, his mind, his heart.

"You're incredible, Sienna." His grip tightens on my hips. "I love every fucking part of you. Those beautiful eyes that betray your every emotion. That cute nose that scrunches every time you're pissed at me. Those soft lips when they wrap around my cock." With that, my lips twist into a smirk. But he's not done. "That contagious, musical laugh that makes it impossible not to laugh with you. That huge, sweet smile that reminds me how to be happy. I don't know what I'd be without you. I don't want to live another day if I can't spend it with you."

My chest squeezes. I don't want to live another day without him either. "Don't break my heart. I won't recover."

Drown in You

There. My greatest fear, laid bare with my soul.

His hand wraps around my throat, squeezing gently with the promise. "Never."

"I want you to fuck me now."

I don't need to make the request twice. In one swift movement, he sits up, sweeping an arm behind my back and flipping us so I'm on the floor beneath him.

The carpet scratches my bare skin, but I don't care once Luke rocks his hips into me.

Pleasure mounts between my legs, through my whole body, as the squishing sounds of Luke's cock driving into me reaches my ears. Arousal drips down between my ass cheeks to the floor.

He pounds me into the carpet, and thank god we chose the floor because the violent squeak of the mattress would undoubtedly give us away.

That familiar pleasure mounts in my limbs, thrumming through my veins, until the orgasm crests. I cry out at the burst of pleasure as Luke continues fucking me through every wave until he collapses against me and lets out a groan into my ear that curls my toes.

Hearts hammering together, we do nothing but pant. As much as I'd love to stay in this room and fuck all night, I know we can't do that here. "We should get dressed. Our parents might know what's happening between us, but they're not going to condone it happening right under their noses."

Luke groans but kisses me and pulls out, leaving me empty and aching for him. He helps me onto shaky legs and grabs our clothes, tossing them onto the bed. Our phones slip out of our pockets, and when he disappears into the bathroom to splash water on his face, my heart leaps into my throat.

His phone is right fucking there. I could try the passcode. Try to unlock it while he's in the other room and search through his texts. But that would be a huge invasion of his trust, his privacy, and we've both been through enough of that lately.

Instead, I grab my phone and type out a text to Ten. If Luke and Ten are the same person, this is how I'll find out for sure. And if they somehow aren't, I'll close the chapter on our friendship for good.

SIENNA

> I just want to let you know that I'm so grateful for our friendship over the years. You helped me get through so much without even realizing it. I'm glad I met you, and I want you to know that I'm happy. I hope you are too. Goodbye, Ten.

I wait for the chime of the notification from Luke's phone. But it doesn't come.

A confusing mixture of horror and relief floods through me. How is that possible? How are Luke and Ten not the same person?

He wasn't lying. All along, Ten really has been someone else.

On the bed, Luke's phone lights up. A silent notification. A text. He must've turned the sound off.

The name on the screen is—

"Sienna? What are you doing?"

I hold his phone up. He tries to snatch it from me, but my grip is stronger than iron.

When he spots the text on the screen, he pales. His voice is so small, broken, when he murmurs, "I'm sorry, Sienna."

"Why the hell did you keep lying to me?" My voice quakes, but not with sorrow. Rage. "I gave you a fucking chance to come clean, Luke. But you kept *lying*."

He sits on the bed in front of me, and I'm not totally sure I want him this close. When he sighs, my stomach twists. Finally,

I'll get the truth. But even after wanting it all this time, I'm not sure I'm ready to hear it. "When our parents dated the first time, I knew you'd basically lost your dad. He barely ever talked to you; you never came around. I'd lost my dad. I knew how much that fucking gutted me. So I found you online. I put on a mask and told you to call me Ten because I didn't want you to know who I was. And I . . . I wanted to make sure you were okay. I didn't think you'd open up to me if you knew who I really was."

My hands ball into fists, nails biting my palms. I could forgive fifteen-year-old Luke for catfishing a girl because he felt bad for her. But he's had literal years to come clean. He could've come clean the day we met. But he didn't. He could've come clean when I confronted him about it. But he *didn't*.

He'd rather let me think Ten was ghosting me, that the friend I'd had since I was fifteen suddenly didn't give a shit about me anymore. That I was being abandoned by one of the most important people in my life, all over again.

Luke lost a friend last summer, and he let me believe I lost one of mine. He ghosted me, even after knowing how much my father's abandonment hurt me.

He let me kiss him, fuck him, fall in fucking love with him while he's been harboring this secret the whole time. He had sex with me, even when he knew our parents had just gotten married. He knew who I was that night in the hotel room. He knew I was his new stepsister, and he still let me believe we were strangers. And even when I figured it all out, he refused to tell me the truth.

Everything has been a lie.

I shake my head. "The sad part is I could've forgiven you if you'd given me the chance."

Pain softens his gray eyes. "I couldn't bring myself to tell you the truth. I was too terrified of losing you."

"But you were willing to let me lose Ten? Lose you?" My hands are shaking. "How am I supposed to trust you when you lie to my face? About something like this?"

Silence falls between us. He doesn't have an answer. I head for the door.

"Sienna!" Luke's voice sounds more broken than I've ever heard it. "Wait!"

I whirl on him, heart beating to the verge of explosion. "No, Luke, you've been lying to me. This *whole time*. You badgered me for keeping secrets from you about what happened to me back in Wakefield, when you've been lying about your fucking *identity*. I thought my friend was *dead*. Or just hated me. You know how much that hurt me?"

His own face contorts in pain. Good. He deserves it. He deserves to feel a fraction of the pain he's caused me.

"I'm sorry." He tries to close the space between us, but I back up. "I didn't know how to tell you. Didn't want you to hate me. To look at me like you are right now. Or to walk out of my life for good. After Pop and Chloe . . . I couldn't bear to lose you too."

"Then you should've fucking said something when we met. *Hey, Sienna, I've been catfishing you since we were fifteen. My bad.* Or when I fucking gave you the chance to tell the truth. When I told you I knew you'd been Ten all along. You could've come clean. You could've said *something*. But you didn't." I point at his phone. "If that text hadn't exposed you, you never would've told me the truth. Would you?"

He can't answer. He doesn't need to.

I have my answer.

"I knew this would happen. I knew I should've stayed away from you, but I didn't, and now look at the mess we've made." I bite my lip to stop it from shaking. "There's fucking *revenge porn* of us on the internet. Our parents are splitting up. You could lose your spot on the team. Your shot at the NHL. Sneaking around has done nothing but make our lives worse."

I should've listened to my brain reminding me over and over to stay away from Luke. That hooking up with my stepbrother would only end badly. Now here we are.

Since the incident with Marcus, I've been letting other people clean up my mess for me. Send me away, protect me, fight my battles. Now it's time I finally clean up my own mess.

Luke's brows dip. "No, it hasn't. Marcus posted that video. Our parents make their own decisions. And I already told you I don't care about the team or the NHL. We're meant to be together. You know that."

I shake my head, retreating. "Goodbye, Luke."

He grabs my hand. His beautiful gray eyes are crinkled around the edges, brows drawn together in a frown and lips pursed. Hurt like I've never seen is etched into his features. "Don't say that. Don't ever say goodbye to me."

How can I still love him even if I can't trust him? When this love between us has done nothing but hurt us and everyone we care about?

"I said goodbye to Ten." Tears sting my eyes, but I won't let him see how much this is breaking me. "Now I'm saying goodbye to you. Don't text me. Either version of you."

Chapter 28

Luke

Mike jumps to his feet in alarm when Sienna flees out the front door in tears, slamming it behind her. "What's going on?"

"Is she upset about the divorce?" Sarah is already slipping her shoes on to follow her daughter.

"No, this has nothing to do with the three of you and the fucking mess you made." Sarcasm drips from my voice.

If Mike and Sarah had figured their shit out years ago, we wouldn't be here. Mike and Ma never would've gotten back together, sure as shit wouldn't have gotten married, and Sienna never would've become my stepsister. None of this would've fucking happened, and I wouldn't have lost her.

Agony has an iron grip on my chest. I told her I couldn't lose her. I've already lost too many people I love. But she ran out the door anyway.

"Watch it." Ma points at me. "You made a bigger mess than any of us, and we're all here to clean up after you."

Sarah and Mike race out the door to follow Sienna, but they're back in minutes with their tails between their legs. "She needs some alone time," Sarah explains. "She's heading back to the dorm."

I plop onto the couch, hands clasped together between my knees. I fucked up. Sienna is the best thing that ever happened to me, and she doesn't want anything to do with me anymore. And I can't fucking blame her.

Ma perches on the couch next to me and shakes my leg. "What happened, Luke?"

"I screwed up." What does it matter now if they all know what I did? If they know I'm not good enough for their daughter when she doesn't want anything to do with me anyway. So I tell them about Ten and about lying to her. About making her life worse, not better, even though that's all I ever wanted.

When I'm done, I brace for Sarah to lay into me, but she doesn't. We fall silent until Mike says, "Give it some time. She'll come around. If she could forgive me, she'll forgive you. My daughter loves you."

His words shouldn't give me hope. Mike might be finally putting in an effort with his daughter, but that doesn't mean he actually knows shit about what Sienna thinks or feels. He doesn't know her like I do. Or like her mother.

I dare a glance at Sarah, who's standing with arms crossed. She and Mike mirror each other, still in sync after all these years. Reluctantly, she nods. "He's right. I've never seen my daughter in love before, but . . ." She trails off, not ready to admit that the little punk who broke her daughter's heart is also the love of her life. "Don't make it a habit of making my daughter cry."

"He won't." Ma's promise is resolute. She squeezes my leg in warning.

Except I already know I won't get the chance. They might believe Sienna can forgive me, but I know how long it took her to forgive Mike. He's her father, and they had a good relationship before the divorce. My entire relationship with Sienna is based on a lie.

I told her to forget about Ten, and now she knows we're the same person. Now she'll forget about me.

I'll never see her again, which means I'll never see Sarah or Mike again after today. The least I can do for Sienna now is what I should've done years ago.

"Sienna blamed herself for your divorce." Her parents' faces fall, concern lining Sarah's and shame lining Mike's. He already knows, but Sarah doesn't. "For years, it ate at her. She thought she was the reason her dad left. The reason her mom couldn't get out of bed. She didn't have anyone taking care of her. She was the one reminding her mom to eat and go to work to keep the lights on. She was the one dealing with all your heartbreak, while you left her to deal with hers all on her own."

Hurt colors Sarah's eyes, but she doesn't say anything. Neither of them can defend themselves because they know they failed her.

"That's why she takes care of everyone else, even when it means she's not taking care of herself. That's why she was so afraid of loving me—because she saw how shitty it turned out for her parents. Because she didn't want to deal with the heartbreak, and who would take care of her when she was the one crying on the couch, inconsolable? Not her parents."

Sarah covers her mouth, tears shining. Ma's eyes are round with horror. "Luke, enough—"

"Let him finish." Mike nods at me.

I shake off Ma's grip and stand. "I'm only telling you because I know she'll never tell you herself. She doesn't want to hurt anyone, even if they hurt her. That's why she blamed herself for what happened to Marcus. That's why she never told you how much she wished her mom would take care of her. But if she doesn't want me around, then she needs somebody else who will, and it needs to be you two."

I'll fight for her. I won't give up on her, just like she didn't give up on Ten.

But someday, I might have to accept that like Pop, like Chloe, Sienna is gone, and I'll never get her back.

Chapter 29

Sienna

"The offer to kill him is still on the table." On her bed in our dorm, Juliet sharpens her pocket knife with a literal sharpening kit. Like a serial killer.

"No murder necessary," I remind her. "Where the hell did you get a knife sharpening kit, and more importantly, why?"

She rolls her eyes. "Knives get dull, Sienna."

In the three days since I last saw him, a literal ache has grown in my chest, but I won't let my broken heart send me back into Luke Valentine's arms. I've never gone through a breakup before. This is simply what breaking up with somebody feels like. Wallowing over how much you still want to be with them, even when you know you're not right for each other.

Juliet's blade scrapes along the sharpener. "If you're not going to kill him, then you should forgive him."

"What?" The word practically leaves my mouth in a screech. Juliet is the last person I'd ever expect to tell me to forgive Luke. "He lied to me for years. He literally fucked me while leading me to believe we didn't already know each other. When he knew our parents were already married. Then he ghosted me, even though he knew how much that would hurt me."

Juliet shrugs. "If you can forgive your dad for abandoning you, you can forgive Luke. After you make him grovel, of course."

I shake my head. "No, you were right before. I'm a people-pleaser. I forgive too easily. That's what got me into this whole mess."

I'm done playing nice girl. Done being the people-pleaser. Where the hell has that gotten me? Broken-hearted with the sex tape of me and my stepbrother broadcasted online for anyone to see. Whispered and gossiped about on campus, the lingering gazes and snickers following me everywhere I go.

I should've pressed charges after Marcus and his cronies attacked me. If the police hadn't been willing to listen to me or take me seriously, I could've gone over their heads. I could've reported the assault to another law enforcement agency or gotten an attorney. I could've fought back.

But I didn't. I didn't want to make things worse for anybody else, even if that meant making things worse for me. I was willing to accept every shitty hand the world dealt me.

If I'd fought back, I wouldn't have ended up here. Luke never would've ghosted me, and I wouldn't have lost my friend or my dignity.

I need to be more like Juliet. I need a tougher shell. I need to stop forgiving people who hurt me.

Juliet slips her sharpened knife into her pocket. "Again, killing him is still on the table. So where are you staying for the summer now that his mom is divorcing your dad?"

"I don't know, actually."

Marcus is still free, but Deb said they should be able to make an arrest soon now that we have a case against him. He could be locked up awaiting trial by the time my finals are over. I could go home.

A knock at the door makes my heart leap into my throat.

Since I broke things off, Luke has been sending texts and voice messages asking to talk. Now I'm the one ghosting him.

I'm honestly shocked he hasn't broken my door down to get to me again. But that must be him now.

I'm not ready to face him. Maybe I never will be. But I won't let him know that. With a long, deep breath, I open the door.

"Hey, kiddo." Dad smiles at me, hand-in-hand with Mom.

My parents are *holding hands*. What kind of parallel universe have I teleported to in the past few days?

"Can we talk to you?" Mom asks.

Juliet hops down from her bed and slips on her boots. "Sounds like awkward family shit. I'm out."

When the door swings shut behind her, my parents hover in the middle of the room while I sit cross-legged on my bed. "What's up?"

They exchange a smile before turning back to me. It's like they didn't spend any time apart, let alone ten years.

"We're going to try to make our relationship work again." The grin crinkling Mom's eyes is the most genuine I've seen on her face in a long time. "We were thinking you could move back home with us after your finals. Unless you want to continue attending Diamond."

A tornado spins in my head. Not only are my parents back together, they're already planning to live together. And they want me to go home with them. "You want me to transfer again?"

"It's fine if you want to finish out your degree here. But now that we have a case against Marcus, you can move back home. You'll be safe. We can be a family again."

Drown in You

"New and improved." Dad's eyes are lit up behind his glasses.

I should be happy. This is what I've wanted—my parents happy and together, getting to live safely in my hometown again, Marcus facing legal consequences for the hell he's put me through.

But it's not happiness squeezing my chest. "Okay. I'll move back."

There's nothing left for me in Diamond, anyway.

Mom's soft footsteps fall across the thin carpet before she sinks onto my mattress. Her hand rests on my knee. "Hon, would you grab us some lunch?" she asks Dad. "I haven't eaten yet today."

Dad nods enthusiastically, all too happy to be useful as he notes our orders on his phone.

Once he's gone, Mom squeezes my knee. "Are you sure you're okay with your father and I getting back together? I want you to be honest with me. It's not your job to spare everyone else's feelings, okay?"

I nod, her words creating a twinge in my chest. That's something Luke would say. "It's a little strange, but I really am okay with it." For the first time since the breakup, a real smile pulls at my lips. "You two seem happy."

She beams. "We are. Really happy." Then she forces her smile away. "I just feel awful for Deb. And for all the drama this has been for you and Luke."

"Don't worry about me. I'm just glad you're happy."

She shifts uncomfortably on the mattress beside me, dragging her hair behind her ears. "Actually, that's something I wanted to talk to you about. I'm sorry you felt like you had to take care of me after the divorce. I didn't do my job as a mother. I let you take care of me instead of the other way around, but that's not how it should be. At least not until I'm really, really old."

A shocked laugh bursts out of my chest, despite the stinging tears. My knee-jerk reaction is to deny it, but I'm done with the secrets and lies. "I didn't think you knew."

Mom gives me a weak smile. "Luke told me."

I straighten. "Luke told you? When?"

"After you left Deb's house. He also said you blamed yourself for the divorce. For what happened to Marcus." Tears brim in Mom's brown eyes. "I'm so sorry you've been carrying those burdens for so long. I hope you know none of that was your fault. None of it. Our divorce had absolutely nothing to do with you. And what happened with Marcus was an accident. You were only trying to protect your friend." Her mouth sours. "I can't wait until that little shit is in jail."

I manage another laugh even as my chest squeezes. "Luke told you all of that?"

She nods. "He did. He wanted me to know because he didn't think you'd ever tell me yourself. Because you wouldn't want to hurt me."

Those words choke me up and a full body ache washes over me. He told my mom the truth because he knew I couldn't, but he wanted her to know my pain. He wanted to heal this wound.

Despite everything, no one has ever loved me like Luke Valentine does.

"If you want to stay here to be close to him, I understand." Her brows pull together. "But no more public hookups, hear me?"

My face is actually on fire. "We're not together anymore."

She pats my knee with a sigh. "It's okay, honey. We can't control who we fall in love with. He told me why you ended things. I had no idea you'd already been friends for so many years."

"Neither did I," I grumble. I never told my mom about Ten, convinced she'd be horrified that I was chatting privately with a stranger I met online who, for all I knew, could be a ninety-year-old creep.

"Do you think Luke might've kept that secret from you out of fear?"

I frown at her. First Juliet, now my mom? "You're taking his side?"

She shakes her head. "I'm always on your side. But I think you've both been afraid of what getting close to each other could mean. I set a bad example for you of what love and relationships can look like." She squeezes my hand. "But they can work with the right person."

"You think Luke is the right person?" She can't possibly know that. But for some reason, I still want to hear her say yes.

Mom shrugs. "You're the only one who can answer that. I just want to make sure that you don't miss out on happiness out of fear. Like your father and I did for so many years."

When her phone rings with a call from my father, she answers it with a megawatt smile.

I pick up my phone and call Deb.

Deb welcomes me into her home with open arms, just like she welcomed me into her family all those months ago. I still can't believe how much has changed since the wedding.

"Come sit down." She leads me out to the deck, sun reflecting off the black spa cover on the hot tub. An iced tea already waits for me beside one of the patio chairs.

When we settle into our chairs, I sip at the cold liquid, the ice clinking against my teeth. "Are you feeling okay? Since the separation?"

She smiles warmly at me and pats my hand. "You've always been so sweet. I'm doing just fine. Actually, I'm a lot happier now that Mike and I aren't pretending to be in a happy marriage. I felt like I was putting on a show for everyone. Slapping on a fake smile to make everyone else happy, even though I wasn't."

For so long, I had no idea that Deb was putting on an act. We're more alike than I thought.

"I'll always care about your father as a friend." Deb sips at her iced tea. "But I know we've never truly been in love. To be honest, I miss your mom more." We both laugh at that. "She's a firecracker. But we've already made plans to form a virtual book club. She recommended a thriller to me, and I couldn't stop reading it last night. I was up until four in the morning! I can't remember the last time I did that."

"I'm glad you're doing okay." I twist the iced tea in my hands, condensation dripping onto my skin. "Can I ask . . . when did you realize my dad wasn't the right person for you?"

My pulse picks up speed. I need to know when she finally came to her senses. When I'll finally come to mine about Luke.

"Honestly?" She mulls the question over while she examines the bright, blue sky. "I had a gut feeling when he moved in. But I didn't listen to my gut—I listened to my head, which was telling me that I'm a mother to a college kid and I had a nice man who cared about me and maybe I shouldn't be picky. Maybe I should stop waiting for someone like my first husband and commit to a man who's good to me. But my heart never got on board."

I have the opposite problem. My heart wants Luke, but my head is telling me to stay away.

"How are you doing?" she asks.

"Okay. Still kind of surreal how much has changed in such a short amount of time. I'm still getting used to it."

"Do you miss him?"

I chug my iced tea. I don't just miss Luke—I ache for him. I see his face every time I close my eyes, I long for his arms around me when I'm asleep, I dream of the masked man chasing me through the woods and catching me and holding me while I profess my love to him. "Yeah, I miss him. But I'm not sure I can forgive him yet. It might not matter, anyway. I'm moving back home."

Deb nods, even though her brows soften with disappointment. "If you change your mind, you always have a place to stay with us. Just because your father and I aren't together anymore doesn't mean you're not family. You became my family that first day I met you."

Tears burn my eyes until I blink them away. Luke told my mom everything I couldn't. Even if I never talk to him again, even if this is the end for us, I want to do the same for him. "Luke told my mom some of the secrets I was keeping from her." Deb nods. "But he was keeping one from you too."

Her brow lifts and she leans closer, clutching her iced tea in both hands.

"Luke has been feeling guilty about his dad's death. He blames himself for not being able to save him. And he blames himself for not being able to save Chloe." I can't blink the tears away fast enough this time. I swipe at one that escapes down my cheek. "I think he needs someone to help him through it. He shouldn't feel guilty. About any of it."

Deb presses a hand to her chest. "I had no idea." Her voice is hushed now. "That explains why he didn't want to tell you the truth—he didn't want to lose you too. You've always been so important to him."

I sniff, trying unsuccessfully to blink the tears away. "He told me to stop being a people-pleaser. That I shouldn't let people treat me however they want."

That includes him.

"No, you shouldn't. I know he's my son, but I can admit when he's made a mistake. I'll be the first to tell him when he's screwed up." Deb's voice is sure, and I don't doubt her for a second. "But I know my son. And he would never hurt you intentionally. Your pain hurts him more than his own."

Another crack in my heart. That's the part that hurts most —not that he hurt me, but that I'm hurting him. "So you think I should give him another chance?"

"You should listen to your heart." Deb sets her iced tea down and stands, pulling me to my feet and in for a warm hug. I bury my face into her shoulder and finally let myself shed the tears desperate to escape. "But I will say, regardless of whether you have a relationship with my son or not, you'll always be a daughter to me."

Chapter 30

Luke

ON THE COUCH, I mindlessly play a video game. Bursting a zombie's head open with a single bullet has never made me feel less.

Bud's head is on my leg, drool pooling on my stained sweats. He hasn't left my side since I came home. We've got one more practice left tomorrow and then Coach is giving us a couple months off for summer break until next semester.

I don't know what the fuck I'm going to do for the next couple of months without hockey, without Sienna. Obsess over what she's doing, where she is, if she's safe.

She's gone. I fucking lost her. Just like I knew I would. Like I should. I've never been good enough for Sienna. I don't deserve her.

She's right—I should've come clean about Ten's true identity years ago. Maybe she would've forgiven me for catfishing her if I'd told her the truth sooner.

Now she knows the truth, she knows how long I kept lying about it, and she wants nothing to do with me.

First Pop. Then Chloe. Now Sienna. I lost them all.

Being with me cost Sienna her reputation. Way too many fucking creeps know what she looks and sounds like when she comes. From her stepbrother's mouth.

I kept lying. Kept secrets from her, even after she finally opened up to me. Still too afraid of putting my heart fully on the line to be honest with her.

I dug my own grave.

Bud lifts his head off my leg when Ma's heels click into the room. She's somehow bouncier and happier than she was while Mike was here. "Well. I sent in the annulment papers."

"You doing okay?"

"Great, actually. I feel like a weight has been lifted off my shoulders." She flings her hands in the air in emphasis. "I can tell he feels the same way. This is what's best for all of us. I'm just sorry we had to drag you and Sienna through it."

I stiffen at Sienna's name. "Don't be. We're both happy for you."

"Speaking of Sienna, she stopped by to see me."

I hit Pause on the video game and toss the controller. "She came by?"

She must've made sure to visit when I wasn't here. The reality makes my gut twist.

"You know, I never talked to you about how guilty I felt over your father's death."

The change in subject throws me. "Why would you feel guilty? He had a heart attack. Nothing you could've done."

Ma wasn't even there. I was the one who was with him when it happened. The one who held his hand while he took his final breath. I'm the only one who should feel guilty.

She bites her lip when it starts to quiver, wringing her hands. "He asked me to go with you two to practice." She clears her throat, the memory still painful. "I didn't want to go because I was stressed with work and the house was a mess. I wanted some time alone, so I stayed home. I spent so much time after that feeling guilty. Like I could've done something to save him if I'd been there."

I knew Ma mourned my pops for a long time after his death. She still does. But I had no idea she was harboring the same guilt that I've been hanging onto for years. "You couldn't have done anything."

She manages a small smile. "I know. And you need to learn that too. With your father, and with Chloe."

I swing my feet onto the floor, ducking my head in my hands. She and Sienna have both been trying to knock sense into me for a long time. I might've been with Pop when he died, but that doesn't mean there was anything I could've done for him. I might've been at that party with Chloe, but I didn't give her that drink or push her in the pool.

Even if I wish things could be different, this is how they are. Now I have to pick up the pieces and deal with it. Figure out a way to be okay without them. What I can't figure out is how to be okay without Sienna. Not while she's still within reach.

"I don't know what to do about Sienna." I swallow around the lump in my throat. "I couldn't open up to her. Be honest with her. Now she wants nothing to do with me. I ruined her life."

I can't meet my mother's eyes while I speak the words. Too afraid to see the disappointment in them. Still too afraid.

Sienna would've been better off if she'd never met me. If I'd never put that mask on and sent her that message all those years ago.

"If you love her, you find her and own up to your mistakes. Be fully honest with her now."

I was. And she ran from me. "What if that's not enough?"

Ma pulls my hands from my face, forcing me to meet her

gaze. Gentle and caring, like I'm not a disappointment. Like despite everything, she's still grateful to have me for a son. "If it's real love, it's worth the risk of finding out."

"Keep it up, Valentine!" Coach shouts across the ice.

Knox snatches up the puck I blocked from the net after Damien's shot. He fakes left, then smacks the puck to my right shoulder.

I leap and make contact with a thud, sending it flying in the opposite direction.

Even though we're opponents during today's practice, Knox flashes me a proud smile. "Killing it today, Valentine!"

I haven't played this well in weeks, and it pisses me off that I wasted so much time killing myself in the gym and during practice only to perform like shit when it really mattered.

Sienna was right—I needed balance. Working out too hard was holding me back, keeping me from being my best on the ice. She knew it'd catch up to me eventually. I'd break.

My heart isn't in the game, though. Not with thoughts of Sienna circling through my mind on an endless loop.

Damien's lip curls into a sneer when he launches a shot at my net. I block it just in time. "Didn't think you were a quitter, Valentine."

"What makes you think I'm a quitter?"

He ignores the shouts of his teammates as they dart to the opposite end of the rink. "Haven't gone after your girl."

Knox's skates slice through the ice. Beneath his helmet, he flashes me a wicked grin. "Better go get her before somebody else does."

Drown in You

"Yeah, no-sisters rule doesn't apply anymore." Damien skates off before I can swing my stick at him, Knox following.

I'm no fucking quitter, and I'm definitely not quitting on Sienna. I'll tell her she was right, about everything. When I show up with flowers and chocolates and jewelry and a teddy bear and any other goddamn thing I can think of to tell her I'm sorry. To convince her to give me another chance, even if I don't deserve it. I'll earn it. I'll prove to her I'm worth it, because she's been proving that to me since we met.

After practice, I'm winning her back.

Chapter 31

Sienna

"You really didn't have to do this, Juliet." Mom grabs another box to slide into my father's hands. I can't believe we're moving his stuff back into our apartment. They already have plans to move into a house outside of Wakefield.

Juliet shrugs, grabbing a box. Impossibly, she's in a dark shirt, but I'm sure her tiny shorts offer some relief in the heat. "I had nothing better to do."

A gleam of sunshine reflecting off metal temporarily blinds me until I make out the red car whizzing past.

A red Cadillac.

Juliet flips him off. Marcus hasn't been arrested yet, but he will be.

For the first time, seeing him doesn't make my stomach plummet to my feet. I'm not scared of him anymore. I won't let him have that control over me. I'm the one who deserves justice now.

Inside, my parents tease and hug each other. Dad plants a kiss on her cheek before he follows me out the door, and it's like they haven't spent any time apart. They're right back to where they were, before everything went wrong.

I'm still not totally convinced everything won't go wrong again. But I'm holding onto hope that whatever the future holds for them, they can get through it together.

When it's just the two of us, I hand Dad a box from his car. "I talked to Deb. She's doing really well."

Even though he didn't love her the way he loves Mom, Dad still cares about Deb and he wouldn't want to hurt her. Relief softens his features. "I'm happy to hear that. I'm sorry for the mess I've made of our lives, Sienna. Especially yours. I really am."

"It's okay. You can stop apologizing now." I stack another box in his hands. "You and Mom seem really happy."

He turns back to the house and grins when Mom steps out of the door. "I'm so grateful your mother was willing to give me a second chance. I've been wallowing over losing her for ten years, and I'll be thankful every single morning for a second chance with both of you."

As soon as he heads for the house, I scramble for my phone.

Ten years. Dad spent ten years pining after Mom, and she spent ten years trying to find the love she shared with him.

I don't want to spend the next ten years pining after Luke.

My phone rings three times before a bright voice answers. "Sienna!" We haven't been friends for long, but I already miss Violet so much. "How are you? How's the move?"

"Not bad. Sweaty."

"When is your last final? We should meet up before you leave for summer break."

"Tomorrow. I'm heading back this afternoon and I was wondering if you could tell me Luke's hockey schedule."

"Practice is happening right now, actually. Do you want me to have him call you when it's over?"

"Actually, could you just make sure he doesn't leave until I can get there?"

"Um, yes!" She squeals like she's already anticipating a grand, romantic gesture. "I'll see you soon!"

Luke held back the truth for so long out of fear. With his past, he's been terrified of hurting me. He knew confessing would do exactly that. He didn't want to lose me the way he lost his dad and Chloe.

But I did the same thing. I held back the truth about what happened with Marcus. I didn't tell him about the incident or all the threatening texts for weeks.

Fear has been holding us both back. That's why I resisted him for so long. Afraid of what other people would say, what they would think if they found out about us. Afraid of what he would do to my heart if he got ahold of it.

But what I was most afraid of has already happened. Everyone knows about us; he already broke my heart.

Yet none of that compares to my fear of spending the rest of my life without him. Never getting to touch or hold him again. Never getting to hear his laugh or watch his eyes crinkle when he smiles. Never getting to hear the voice that sends a shiver down my spine.

My parents forgave each other for the hurt they caused. They overcame the fear that their relationship might end badly again and now they're happier than they've ever been. I can't let fear guide me anymore.

I race into the house and nearly run into Juliet. "Hey, Mom? Do you mind if Juliet and I head back to Diamond early?"

"No problem, sweetie!" Mom calls from her bedroom. "Drive safe!"

"Thank god," Juliet mutters as she follows me out. "They were definitely about to screw."

"Ew, don't say shit like that about my parents."

"Fine. They were about to make love."

I punch her arm. Juliet slides into the passenger seat and fixes her messy ponytail. "Why are we heading back early?"

"Because I need your help with something."

BY THE TIME we reach campus, it's already dark. Between traffic and running out of gas and a pit stop so Juliet could pee, we delayed our time by over an hour. The building that houses the rink is dim, not a single light shining from inside, and the parking lot is vacant.

My heart sinks. I missed him. I'm too late. "Shit."

"What the hell? I set up your phone to record your disgustingly adorable reunion and he already left?" Juliet points to my phone that she hooked up to the dashboard.

"That was actually sweet of you. I guess you do have at least one romantic bone in your body."

She sighs. "I can't believe I'm involved in this."

"Let's just go to their house." But the words have barely left my mouth when a giant hockey player in gray sweatpants opens the door and steps outside.

His smile makes my heart leap up to my throat.

Behind him, the door swings open again, and a girl with cropped brown hair peeks out. Violet beams and waves. "Sienna! Juliet!"

"I'll go with Violet so you can make out with your man." Juliet hits Record on my phone before she leaves.

I wait until my best friend has disappeared inside with Violet before I grab the gift, take a deep breath, and open the door.

Luke tracks every step I take toward him, keeping the gift behind my back. Eventually, he can't stand still anymore and heads right for me, footsteps echoing across the pavement.

My heart thunders against my ribcage when he stops inches from me, his hand reaching to caress my cheek. At the first brush of skin on skin, my knees turn to jelly. I want to throw myself at him. I've missed him *so* much.

"You came back." His voice is raw, splitting my heart in two.

"You're still here."

"Violet threatened me with genital mutilation if I left." Despite his glassy eyes, a small smile pulls at his lips.

Heart in my throat, I reveal the camera from behind my back. "When you were still the man behind the mask, you told me you bought a disposable camera and called me a bad influence." I can't help the smile that plays on my lips at the memory. "So, since yours got ruined, I got you another one. For all the new photos we'll take together."

Luke takes the camera from me with a grin. "Thank you. This is the best gift I've ever gotten."

"It was the best gift I've ever gotten too. Because you gave it to me."

His hand threads into my hair, urging me closer. "Everything you do is better than I deserve."

I shake my head. My turn to caress his cheek, to hold him. He leans into my touch, eyes fluttering shut like he's been to war for a decade and he's finally home. "That's not true. You're amazing, and you deserve someone who treats you that way."

He shakes his head. "I ruined your life."

"What are you talking about?"

"The sex tape—"

"That wasn't your fault. We were both there that night. We

both wanted it. Marcus is the one who filmed us and posted that video. Illegally."

Silence falls between us for a few beats. Luke examines the camera tenderly, like it's made of the rarest diamond. "What made you change your mind?"

"I thought it was a weakness to keep forgiving people who hurt me." I swallow, a lump forming in my throat. "But I realized it's a strength. I realized my parents spent the past decade in love with each other but too afraid to take the leap. Too afraid to try again. I don't want to spend that much of my life without you when we can be together now. We've both lied, we've both made mistakes, but what matters is that we learn from them. What matters is that we love each other, and nothing will ever change that. Like you said . . . we're meant to be."

He tucks the camera in his pocket and scoops me up until I'm happily in his arms again. "I really fucking missed you."

"I missed you. I couldn't think about anything else."

Luke yanks my mouth to his. His tongue sweeps past my lips, and when he moans into my mouth, I melt.

I've missed him so fucking much. Not just in the past few days—though that was a constant ache—but I missed the friend he was to me for so many years. The masked man I confided in about my worst fears, biggest insecurities, darkest secrets. He's been with me at my lowest, even if he was miles away, and he's never wavered.

When he finally lets me break the kiss, I blurt, "I love you."

"Thank fuck," he murmurs against my lips. "I love you too."

We kiss again, absolute bliss washing over me like a wave. I never want to be without him again. Just like my parents got their second chance, this is ours. And I'm not screwing it up this time.

Behind me, tires roar up the pavement. Headlights beam on us. Luke squints past me at the car that squeals to a stop.

Over my shoulder, I spot a group of guys in the dark interior of a red Cadillac.

My stomach drops.

No. *No, no, no.* It can't be him. It can't—

When the doors swing open, Stephen steps out of the passenger side and Kade from the back. Marcus from behind the wheel.

Fuck.

Marcus followed me here after spotting me in Wakefield. And this time, he brought back up.

Chapter 32

Luke

"You should've stayed out of my town, bitch. You're not welcome there anymore." Marcus saunters forward with dead eyes. Clearly the leader of this pack of nutsacks.

He's back. Daring to show his face again after the Devils restrained themselves from beating him to a pulp.

I set Sienna on her feet and nudge her behind me. If they think they're getting anywhere near her, they're out of their fucking minds.

These are the guys who attacked her back home. Who left bruises all over her body. Who sent her running into my arms.

I'll be dead before I let these assholes lay a finger on her again.

"You should've stayed out of *my* town." Sienna's normally soft soprano voice is hard, echoing back from the brick wall behind us. Even the assholes in front of us are surprised by her defiance. "I was trying to protect my friend. I'm sorry for what happened to you, Marcus. I really am. But I can't undo what's been done, and getting revenge on me won't do that either."

Silence settles around us. For a few moments, the three of them are too stunned to retort.

My chest swells with pride. That's my girl.

His mouth twists into a snarl, a pissed-off bear ready to charge. "You're trying to get me thrown behind bars. But it's not going to work. *You* should be the one behind bars."

"You literally posted revenge porn of us. You're not innocent in any of this."

Marcus takes a step forward, and I move between them, concealing Sienna behind me. "You even think about touching her and that limp will be the least of your problems. I'll rip your eyes from your fucking skull."

I wish I could've saved my pops. I wish I could've protected Chloe. Protected Violet.

I didn't.

But I won't make the same mistake with Sienna. I told her nothing would happen to her with me around, and that's a promise I'll keep until I'm in my grave.

All three of the assholes set their glares on me. "Three against one." I shrug. "Seems like a fair fight."

As soon as Marcus swings at me, I bark at Sienna to run and dodge his strike. The dude definitely fights like a fuckin' football player. Throwing his weight around like a tough guy and never making contact with anything. No one fights like hockey players.

The scrawniest guy with the greasy hair manages to scrape a knuckle across my arm, so I throw him to the ground. All the air leaves his lungs like a gasping fish before he groans.

I'd stomp him for good measure, but the other two are already swinging. I manage to dodge Marcus, but the last guy's fist connects with my jaw and *fuck*. My vision blurs for a second, eyes watering.

A terrified scream pierces the air.

Drown in You

Fuck. Sienna. She's still fucking out here.

I whirl. Marcus is heading right for her, but she's not running inside. Probably knows she wouldn't make it far before he'd get ahold of her.

Why the fuck didn't she run when I told her to?

But I know why. She couldn't bear to leave me behind.

She screams her head off, and while I'm distracted, the guy on the ground gets his revenge and sweeps my feet out from under me.

I go down. Hard.

The asshole whose fist kissed my jaw is on me in a second, raining his knuckles down like a five-year-old throwing a temper tantrum. I clock him in the side of the head but that only dazes him.

Sienna's scream is muffled as Marcus grabs her, hand covering her mouth.

My blood boils, vision going black. I'm going to fucking kill him. "Get your fucking hands off her—"

A strike to my temple makes my skull scream, brain spinning

Fuck.

He fucking has her. He's going to hurt her and I'm not going to reach her in time—

I punch the dude on top of me in the nose with the last of my strength and he finally goes down.

A loud squeal rips through the night air as the door to the athletics building bursts open.

A girl in all-black with red streaks in her hair darts out, aiming right for Marcus like a hornet. She lands a kick on his shin, and he curses, dropping Sienna to clutch at his leg.

Juliet screeches like a banshee, shoving him like he's not twice her size. "What the *fuck*, Marcus? Get out of here!"

My head swims as I climb to unsteady feet. Sienna jerks forward, striking Marcus between the legs.

He groans, hands rushing to cradle his aching balls.

Despite my pounding temple and the throbbing ache in my jaw, my back, my knuckles, I grin. That's my girl.

From the door, four of the Devils emerge. Wes, Knox, Damien, and Finn.

I've never been so happy to see them.

Wes takes one look at me and charges at Marcus.

The bastard doesn't even have time to retreat before the Devils are raining hell down on him. He goes down like a sack of rocks.

His buddy with the greasy hair doesn't bother trying to help him out. He scrambles for the Cadillac, cranking the ignition and blasting the lights in our faces.

Surrounded by the Devils punching and kicking him, all Marcus can do is hold his arms up to block their attack.

I take a shaky step forward, my lip fat and coming back bloody, but I'm doing a hell of a lot better than Marcus.

"Stop!" Sienna screams. Thank god she's smart enough not to try to intervene. "Stop! Let him go!"

Wes glances at me. When I nod, he stops his attack, and the other Devils follow suit.

In the doorway, Violet hovers wide-eyed while Juliet stands with arms crossed, fire and brimstone burning in her eyes. "You've taken this way too fucking far, Marcus."

He rises slowly, face red and puffy, before limping off and dragging his buddy off the ground who's finally come to. He tosses a glare back at Sienna. "This isn't over."

"You just assaulted my boyfriend. It's definitely fucking over for you."

I don't know what part I enjoyed hearing from her mouth more. The confident defiance or calling me her boyfriend.

As soon as the Cadillac peels out of the parking lot, Knox shouts, "Dumbass didn't get scared off the first time?"

Damien heads back to the building. "Whatever. I see a fight, I jump in."

"Worse hobbies to have." Knox shrugs, following him before grinning at Juliet. "You kicked ass."

She shrugs. "I know."

Sienna runs to me, throwing her arms around my neck and whimpering into my shoulder. My heart nearly bursts. She was so fucking worried about me. She could've gotten hurt, but she's okay. *She's okay.*

I didn't lose her again.

Wes bumps my fist and Finn nods at me before they follow our teammates inside, giving us privacy.

"Are you okay?" Sienna whispers.

I nod, pulling back to cradle her face and examine every inch. "Are you? Did he hurt you?"

I'll chase him down right now—

"I'm fine. Thank you," she murmurs through her tears. "I think we're finally going to get him now."

"What do you mean?"

She leads me by the hand back to her car and pulls her phone from the dashboard. "This was supposed to be a cute video of our reunion. But now we finally have hard evidence against Marcus."

Chapter 33

Sienna

Luke pouts in his hospital bed. "I told you I'm fine."

"And the doctors are going to make sure." I adjust his pillows for the thousandth time.

He's lucky he didn't sustain any worse injuries before the Devils showed up. *I'm* lucky. I don't know what I would've done if Marcus and Stephen and Kade had hurt him worse.

Deb brushes past a nurse in her rush to Luke's bedside. She takes one glimpse at the contusion already blooming on his jaw and gasps. "Oh my god! Are you okay? What happened?"

Luke rolls his eyes. "Relax. I'm fine. I wouldn't even be here if Sienna hadn't dragged me."

"Smart girl." Deb nods at me. "What did the doctors say?"

From the door, another gasp grabs our attention. Mom bustles in with Dad on her heels. She beelines for me, and then for Luke. "What the hell happened?"

Luke groans. "Is this how it's going to be from now on? Two moms worrying too much?"

Mom and Deb lock eyes before they both nod. "Yep."

Drown in You

Dad wraps an arm around my shoulders and murmurs, "You okay, kiddo?"

I love that no matter how old I've gotten, he still calls me kiddo. I'm so glad I forgave him. Gave him the second chance he wanted so badly. Luke too. My life is better with them both in it.

"That asshole Marcus showed up," Luke explains. "Sienna got the whole thing on her phone."

When I hand Deb my phone and she watches the video, her eyes narrow. "I'm going to get that little shit thrown behind bars for the rest of his life."

"I'm throwing away the key," Mom adds.

I love that they've developed a friendship despite all of the drama that could've easily divided them. I love how much my parents care about Luke, even when they haven't known him that long. They know how important he is to me, how much I love him, and that's enough for them.

"So have you two worked things out?" Dad asks.

The moms fall silent as they glance between us. Neither of us can fight the smiles that spread across our faces. "Yeah, we have," I tell them.

Deb bounces and claps. "Oh good!"

Mom hugs me. "I'm glad you're both okay. Let's go find these kids some food."

Once Luke finally manages to convince Deb to let him go and follow my parents out the door, I squeeze his hand. "Maybe I should put on scrubs and make your nurse fantasy come true."

He smirks. "Don't tease me."

"Who says I'm teasing?" I nod at his pocket. "Did the camera break?"

Luckily, disposable cameras are cheap. But I can't help the twinge of worry. That camera was my gift to him. The gift that was supposed to symbolize my apology, to pay homage to our relationship.

Luke slips his hand into his pocket and pulls the camera out with a smile. "Still like new."

Relief rushes through me. "Lucky."

"Yeah, I am." He squeezes my hand, gray eyes turning serious. "Thank you for forgiving me. And giving me another chance. I promise to work every day to deserve it."

Despite the little space on the bed, I cuddle up to him. He's so warm. Hard and soft at the same time. My safe place. My harbor in the storm. He pulls me close, a protective arm around my back. "Thank you for being my rock. Always."

"*Always.*"

Thanks to Deb and the video, we successfully pressed charges against Marcus, Stephen, and Kade for assault. We also finally got Marcus charged with revenge porn, and Deb's team has been able to get the video virtually wiped from the internet, though I think the invasion of privacy will always haunt me.

All five of the Devils came out of the fight almost completely unscathed. I wish they'd been there the night Marcus and his buddies attacked me in the park, but I'm so fucking grateful they were there last week.

In the reflection of the full-length mirror in our dorm, Juliet chews her lip while staring at me. I freeze, the pink lipstick hovering in front of my mouth. "Why are you staring at me like that? Is there something wrong with my dress?"

Juliet is decked out in her usual all-black, skin-tight attire like she's headed to a funeral instead of a graduation. She shakes her head, turning away from me. She can't make eye contact when she's uncomfortable. "Of course not. Pink is your color. I just . . . I'm sorry."

"For what?" I'm genuinely confused.

"For all the shit with Marcus. He could've hurt you again."

I set my lipstick down, and even though my best friend hates hugs, I wrap my arms around her. She groans, wriggling in my hold like a worm, but I don't let her go. "Stop apologizing. It's not your fault."

"It's my fault for fucking an asshole like Marcus."

I pull back to face her. "No, he's the only one to blame for this mess." The lesson I've finally learned nearly a year later. Thanks to Luke. "Besides, it's not your fault that assholes are your type."

"*Psychos* are my type, not assholes," she corrects.

I grin. "There's a difference?"

"Huge. My psycho will secretly have a soft heart, just for me."

My best friend is absolutely insane. And I love her for it. "I hope you find that someday."

"You and me both. Too bad Trey Lamont already left campus."

I snort. "Yeah, to you, he would've been a dreamboat."

Juliet grabs her purse from her bed. "I'm glad you and Valentine worked it out. You deserve someone who makes you happy." She tosses her purse over her shoulder. "Okay, enough cheesiness now. Let's go to this fucking graduation."

Chapter 34

Luke

After graduation, the Novaks guide all of us into poses with Wes in his cap and gown. A lump forms in my throat that Chloe can't be here for him on his big day. But she's watching from somewhere, cheering him on.

He'll be playing for the NHL, and Violet will be joining him on the road when she graduates after the summer semester from her accelerated program.

My chest aches a little seeing them go, knowing two of my closest friends won't be on campus with us next semester. But that doesn't mean the end of our friendship. I'm sure I'll be attending some of Wes's games and he'll come back to cheer us on, and I'll need to be in attendance for all of Violet's future book signings or she'll threaten me with genital mutilation again.

I harbored jealousy of their relationship for a long time, but now I'm nothing but happy for them. That's what happens when the girl who has your heart gives you hers.

While Juliet snaps photos of Wes and his parents with a bored expression, I sweep the crowd for Sienna. She's disap-

Drown in You

peared somewhere among the graduates and their loved ones, and my heart skips, even though the assholes who jumped her are behind bars.

A tiny pair of arms flings around my middle, knocking the wind out of me. "I'm going to miss you!"

Violet beams up at me before dropping her arms and glancing at Wes. Even though he knows he can trust us, Wes Novak's possessive streak is not to be tested.

I would know. Neither is mine.

"I'll miss you too, pipsqueak."

She sticks her tongue out at me, but she's still grinning. "Seriously though, I'm really glad you found Sienna. You seem a lot happier."

While the Novaks ask Juliet about her tattoos, Wes manages to extract himself from the photo shoot and wraps his arms around Violet from behind, dropping his chin to the top of her head. "Chloe would be happy for you too."

Chloe would be happy I'm happy, and I'm sure wherever she is now, she's rooting for us.

Violet squeezes my hand. "So would your dad."

A lump catches in my throat. "Yeah."

He'd be fucking over the moon to see me this happy with a girl I love.

"Luke!" My favorite voice in the world calls out over the crowd.

I can't help but grin. Can't take my eyes off her as she races toward me with a huge ass grin on her face, long brown hair flying behind her, and jumps into my arms.

Knox claps Damien and Finn on the shoulder. "All right, boys. Let's go find us a puck bunny."

Violet's nose scrunches. "One of these days, the three of you are going to fall for a girl and you won't even think of another."

Knox and Damien both chuckle. Even Finn flashes an amused grin. "That'll be a cold day in hell," Damien says.

Sienna turns my face to hers and the rest of the world goes quiet. Her green eyes mesmerize me exactly as they did that first time I saw her. The first time I saw her photo on social media, then again, when we finally met in person at that hotel bar. And every day since.

"I love you." She doesn't bother whispering or trying to hide it. She doesn't give a fuck about that now. As long as we have each other, nothing else matters.

"I love you too, sweetheart." She kisses me until I set her down. "I got you something."

When I hand her the photos, her face lights up. "Oh my god! Are these the photos from the camera film?"

"Yep. Although I kept the one I took of you tied to my bed."

She feigns a scowl before flipping through the photos, laughing even while the tears shimmer. The photo I took of her while she slept. A photo she snapped of Juliet in the library. Another that she took of Bud's fuzzy face. The photo she snapped of me on a whim at that hotel bar. The story of our relationship, from the moment we met.

"You're more than a pretty sight." I lift the camera she gave me to snap another of her. The same words I said to her the night we met. "Way, way fucking more."

She beams, cradling my cheek with a heartbreakingly gentle hand. "I knew this is how it would be with you."

Chapter 35

Sienna

Luke is helping me move my stuff out of my dorm. But the vibe in the room is completely different than when he helped me move in, when tension was making every muscle in my body tight.

Now there's a different sort of tension. And it involves us trying to resist jumping each other's bones on this bed for the last time. I'd happily take advantage of having the room to ourselves if we didn't have to be out of here in twenty minutes.

Just a few months ago, I was so terrified about moving to Diamond and reuniting with my estranged father and meeting my new step-family. Now, I don't want to imagine my life taking any other path.

"I don't know how I'll survive two months without you." The easy smile stays glued to Luke's face as he drapes his arms over my hips. I love how easily he smiles now. "Guess we'll have to go back to texting every day like we have for the past five years."

"Good plan. Question: When you text me, do I call you Luke or Ten? Ten is the hotter name, if I'm honest."

"Use whatever name you want. As long as you call me yours."

When Luke bends down to kiss me, my heart soars. Against his lips, I murmur, "Mine."

His smile is gone now, gray eyes intense and brimming with the kind of love and adoration for me that makes my knees weak. "And you're mine."

He shreds his shirt and picks me up, setting me on the edge of the bed, and neither of us gives a shit about how much time we have left because we have the rest of our lives. He spreads my legs, pushing my panties to the side before sinking inside me with a groan. "*Mine.*"

With every thrust, he echoes the sentiment on a growl, a groan, a plea.

Mine.

Mine.

Mine.

Until I'm unraveling, heart soaring to the sky.

"You're so fucking beautiful when you come, sweetheart."

When we're breathless, panting in each other's arms, he strokes my hair behind my ear. I draw a finger over his bare chest, writing *mine* over and over. "I imagined meeting Ten so many times. I never could've imagined this is how it would go."

Luke stiffens beneath me. "I'm sorry."

"Don't be. I'm glad it turned out this way. I'm glad I finally met you."

His arm wrapped around me tightens. "I'm glad I finally met you too. You're the best thing that ever happened to me."

"There's a lot I wanted to ask Ten when we finally met, though." I prop myself up on an elbow. "Did you actually watch *Jurassic Park* eleven times?"

He grins. "The twelfth time I watch it, I'm going to make

you watch it with me. Is your favorite ice cream actually that disgusting raspberry flavor?"

I give his shoulder a playful whack. "You mean *delicious*."

We fall silent, smiling at each other in blissful happiness. My heart is so full.

"I'm really glad it was you behind the mask. That's what I was hoping for since the moment I met you at that hotel."

"That's when I knew too."

"Knew what?"

His thumb strokes over my cheek. "That you were mine."

I can't believe I got this lucky. That the man beneath the mask was Luke Valentine.

Epilogue

Luke

W*e're back* on the ice on campus before the fall semester officially starts. But I can't focus on practice today.

Sienna will be here in a few hours. She's staying with me and Ma until the semester begins. Under the condition that we don't "fornicate" in her house.

So I'll make sure she's not home when we do. Gives Sienna the chance to scream my name anyway.

We've been texting every day again, just like old times. Except now she sends me dirty texts and pictures, and I do the same. With the mask on. She's been enjoying living with both of her parents again, so I haven't pushed her to come back earlier. She needs this time with them, especially Mike. They have years of catching up to do. I'll have the rest of my life with her.

Not sure how I went so many years without meeting her, without holding her in my arms. But I won't waste another second of the time I get with her now.

I block the puck when Finn sends it my way. Then again when Damien gains control. Bastards are relentless today. I

Drown in You

owe them a lot for protecting Sienna that night. For having my back. Even if they drive me fucking nuts, I wouldn't pick anyone else to call my teammates. My brothers.

"Thought your girl wasn't supposed to be back until later?" Damien shouts.

"She's not."

He nods at the empty bleachers.

Empty except for one person. One girl, in my jersey, cheering loud with a sign like she's at the championship game.

Did I ever tell you how I imagined cheering for you at your games? I'd be the loudest person in the bleachers. I hoped that even if your dad couldn't cheer for you, it would help, knowing someone out there is cheering for you so loud, their throat is raw after. I probably wouldn't even be able to talk, but it would be worth it if it helped you play. If it made you happy.

Coach will tear me a new one for leaving the ice during practice, but I don't give a fuck. My girl is here. *Mine.*

She grins when she spots me leaving my post in front of the net and heading for her.

Before I can cross to the wall, Knox cuts me off, finally making an appearance from the locker room, breathless and ten minutes late to practice.

"Where the fuck were you?" I ask. Stupid question. He was probably getting sucked off by some random puck bunny.

His eyes are wide. Can't remember the last time I saw calm, cool, go-with-the-flow Knox look anything close to frazzled. "You won't believe who the fuck I just saw on campus."

This piques Damien's and Finn's interest. They both come to a stop to listen.

"Who?"

Couldn't be Wes or Violet. He'd be happy to see them, not shocked. Definitely not disturbed.

Then he drops the name that makes my stomach twist.

"Trey Lamont."

Acknowledgments

To my readers, thank you for sticking with me for six books. I will always be grateful to each and every one of you for making my dream come true. I'm so lucky to do what I love every day, and it's because of all of you. Thank you from the bottom of my heart for reading my books and spreading the word about them. I hope I can write many more for you.

To my betas, Lauren, Kelsey, Kira, Erin, Bridgitt, Lianne, Miya, and Jess: thank you so much for your feedback and cheerleading.

To my cover designer, Beholden Book Covers, thank you so much for creating such stunning covers for this series. I'm absolutely *obsessed* with them.

To Zoe, thank you for allowing me to feature your gorgeous mask art on these covers.

To Alex, I love you so much. Thank you for helping me run my business, spraying the edges of my books to make them even prettier, and cooking dinner for me so I can keep writing. You love and support me like no one else, and I will never stop being grateful for the day you came into my life.

About the Author

Harmony West writes dark forbidden romance. She enjoys her love stories with a side of mystery, twists, and spice.

For updates on Harmony West's latest releases, subscribe to her newsletter at www.harmonywestbooks.com/subscribe or follow her on social media @authorharmonywest.

Made in United States
North Haven, CT
08 March 2025